Spellstruck

AF805309

ALSO BY MARTHA WATERS

And Then There Was The One

Christmas Is All Around

To Woo and to Wed

To Swoon and to Spar

To Marry and to Meddle

To Love and to Loathe

To Have and to Hoax

Spellstruck

A Novel

MARTHA WATERS

ATRIA PAPERBACK
NEW YORK AMSTERDAM/ANTWERP LONDON
TORONTO SYDNEY/MELBOURNE NEW DELHI

ATRIA
PAPERBACK
An Imprint of Simon & Schuster, LLC
1230 Avenue of the Americas
New York, NY 10020

For more than 100 years, Simon & Schuster has championed authors and the stories they create. By respecting the copyright of an author's intellectual property, you enable Simon & Schuster and the author to continue publishing exceptional books for years to come. We thank you for supporting the author's copyright by purchasing an authorized edition of this book.

No amount of this book may be reproduced or stored in any format, nor may it be uploaded to any website, database, large language model, or other repository, retrieval, or artificial intelligence system without express permission. All rights reserved. Inquiries may be directed to Simon & Schuster, 1230 Avenue of the Americas, New York, NY 10020 or permissions@simonandschuster.com.

This book is a work of fiction. Any references to historical events, real people, or real places are used fictitiously. Other names, characters, places, and events are products of the author's imagination, and any resemblance to actual events or places or persons, living or dead, is entirely coincidental.

Copyright © 2026 by Martha Waters

All rights reserved, including the right to reproduce this book or portions thereof in any form whatsoever. For information, address Atria Books Subsidiary Rights Department, 1230 Avenue of the Americas, New York, NY 10020.

The authorized representative in the EEA is Simon & Schuster Nederland B.V., Herculesplein 96, 3584 AA Utrecht, Netherlands. info@simonandschuster.nl

First Atria Paperback edition September 2026

ATRIA PAPERBACK and colophon are registered trademarks of Simon & Schuster, LLC

Simon & Schuster strongly believes in freedom of expression and stands against censorship in all its forms. For more information, visit BooksBelong.com.

For information about special discounts for bulk purchases, please contact Simon & Schuster Special Sales at 1-866-506-1949 or business@simonandschuster.com.

The Simon & Schuster Speakers Bureau can bring authors to your live event. For more information or to book an event, contact the Simon & Schuster Speakers Bureau at 1-866-248-3049 or visit our website at www.simonspeakers.com.

Interior design by Kyoko Watanabe

Manufactured in the United States of America

1 3 5 7 9 10 8 6 4 2

Library of Congress Control Number is available.

ISBN 978-1-6682-1524-1 (pbk)
ISBN 978-1-6682-1525-8 (ebook)

Scan here to get book recommendations, exclusive offers, and more delivered to your inbox.

For Sarah Hogle, most patient of friends.
(Do you think I'm funny anymore?)

Chapter One

Vesper loved autumn because she had a fatal weakness for men in scarves. It was not entirely logical, since she spent much of her time with men involved in a race to rid them of their clothing as quickly as possible. However, this weakness had led to more than one enjoyable evening in her past; so far its results had been decidedly mixed this autumn, but that was not enough to dissuade her from being fondly disposed toward the season.

October in England was admittedly rather hit-or-miss; it could be sunny and crisp and glorious, but it could also be gray and damp and miserable, and it felt so often that the latter sort of day tended to win out. Vesper found this rude; she knew that her golden bob looked particularly alluring in the autumn sunshine, and it seemed that the weather ought to oblige her.

Today, it unquestionably did not. She was in Quill & Ink, the famous magical bookshop on Marylebone High Street, hiding from the rain among the teetering wooden shelves and browsing idly when Freddie found her.

"Sister of mine."

"Toad." She didn't so much as glance up from the book she was skimming; it was by D. H. Lawrence—one of his that hadn't been banned, evidently—so she was fairly certain there was something interesting to be found within if she read far enough.

"I didn't know you could read."

She turned, blowing an errant curl out of her face. "That joke would work better if you hadn't tried it out five hundred times in the past."

Her brother shrugged, leaning casually against a shelf. His blond hair was ruffled from the same stiff breeze that had driven her indoors in the first place, and his cheeks were reddened from the cold. He was wearing a scarf, but her scarf-induced weakness decidedly did *not* extend to elder brothers.

"Don't you have a job?" she asked peevishly.

He shoved a hand into his pocket. "I don't have rehearsal for another hour." Freddie was an actor, much to the delight of their parents—who felt it reflected well on them to have "interesting children"—and to the horror of their one living grandmother. He was currently in rehearsals for a show soon to open at the Adelphi, in which he played, if Vesper had the details correct, a lovelorn clown.

"Well, don't let me keep you," Vesper said, and he smiled serenely in the way he knew irritated her.

"I heard," Freddie said, casting a casual eye about his surroundings, "that you went for drinks with Ainsley Sherwood the other night."

Vesper frowned at this; Freddie was not one to usually pay much attention to her romantic (mis)adventures.

"And?" It had, in fact, been a few cocktails at the Savoy, followed by a cab ride back to Vesper's mews flat, a rather hurried and uninspired romp in the sheets, and then a cigarette at the door as she waved Sherwood goodbye. On the whole, it hadn't been worth the bother of getting dressed up for, but she'd been feeling restless, and Sherwood had been stopping by Holloway's to flirt with her for weeks, and she supposed there were worse ways to spend an evening.

"He's a bounder. You must know this." Freddie tilted his head at her. "Surely you have better taste than that."

"Bold words indeed, from someone who, last I heard, was sleeping with a man engaged to the daughter of a duke."

A flicker of annoyance crossed his face, which was satisfying. "I don't think we *really* want to go down the road of ill-thought-out romantic entanglements, do we, Vesper?"

She sighed. "Probably not." She shook her head ruefully. "I'm not going to see Sherwood again—he was a bit lacking in stamina. The entire interlude barely took a quarter of an hour."

Freddie grimaced. "Please spare me the details."

"You raised the subject in the first place." She glanced down at the book in her hand, and then said, "Come on. I'm buying this, and then I'm going to the club. If you promise not to annoy me, you can come along."

"That is frankly a lot to ask of me," Freddie said, falling into step beside her as she made for the till.

◆

The club's name was Holloway's, and it occupied prime real estate in the heart of Marylebone just off the high street. Its

Neo-Palladian facade sported impressive columns that flanked the steps leading to its black lacquered doors. Vesper's family had owned the club for a few centuries now, meaning that when she and Freddie appeared on the front steps a few minutes later, the doors opened as they approached, and Geoffrey, the doorman, bowed them in without question.

During the day, the club was a quiet, peaceful enclave. There were luxuriously upholstered sofas and chaises, plush window seats, and intimate tables tucked into alcoves, perfect for a private conversation. The walls were painted in warm jewel tones, and a few sported wallpaper in intricate floral and woodland prints; plush Turkish rugs covered the gleaming wood floors. The large bow windows offered a glimpse of the glittering streets and headlights below, making the club's interiors look even warmer and more inviting by comparison. Waiters made their way quietly in and out of rooms, always ready to supply a pot of tea or coffee, a glass of something stronger, or a bite to eat. The establishment catered to a well-heeled, politically progressive, and fairly young set, as had been the case for most of its history, dating back to its founding by a particularly rakish great-great-et-cetera grandfather of Vesper's.

This afternoon it was crowded with patrons eager for a cozy escape from the damp gray autumn day outside; a quick glance around as Vesper and Freddie made their way through a series of connecting rooms confirmed that nothing looked amiss. She caught the eye of Sam, one of the younger waiters on staff, and smiled at him, causing him to blush furiously. She was used to having this effect on men, so she ignored it. "Sam, could you send us a pot of tea? We'll be in the office."

"And whatever cake looks nicest," Freddie added hopefully; Vesper and Freddie were each in possession of a sweet tooth. Soon they were ensconced in the back office—a large room that was a combination of a traditional office, with a desk and bookshelves, and a workroom, with a marble-topped table cluttered with any number of ingredients, vials, and sachets. Since Vesper had taken over the day-to-day running of Holloway's—and the use of illicit magic that was necessary to make the potions and spell powders that comprised a significant part of the club's business at night—she had thought often that she ought to redecorate the office, which was still painted the rich green that was her father's favorite color. The floor was covered by a thick rug in shades of emerald and navy; the intricately carved furniture was glossy oak; the bookshelves groaned beneath the weight of volumes that had been accumulated by generations of Holloways. Framed above the marble fireplace, in which a cheerful fire was already burning, was a photograph of the Holloway family at the wedding of Cecily, Vesper and Freddie's elder sister, and her husband, Simon, immediately in the wake of the Great War. Vesper loved this office, but it still did not entirely feel as though it were *hers*.

She was distracted by the prompt arrival of a tray bearing a silver tea service and a couple of plates of Madeira cake. Freddie immediately dedicated himself to this bounty, and Vesper could not resist settling herself in one of the armchairs before the desk and reaching for her own slice of cake. She was still somewhat suspicious about her brother's sudden concern regarding her love life, however, and decided to use this moment, when he was at his weakest, to try to work out what this was about.

"It was kind of you to take an interest in my evening with Sherwood," she said, all sweetness, as she speared a bite of cake.

Freddie froze with his fork halfway to his mouth and cast her a wary glance.

"In fact," she continued, "if you would like me to consult with you about all my love affairs, perhaps I could bring men to meet you, before we ever go for a drink—"

"Enough!" He set down his fork and shifted in his seat to face her fully. "I asked about Sherwood because he works for the government."

Vesper blinked. "Does he?"

Freddie nodded. "The Ministry of Transport."

She relaxed. "Oh. Well, that's nothing to do with us, then, is it?"

"No, but his father is a Forbiddance campaigner. You might consider being a bit more careful." Freddie took a generous bite of cake. "You're running a private club with an illegal side business—you ought to think twice before falling into bed with any man who happens to walk through the door."

"We don't know that he agrees with his father in politics. Plenty of men don't." Vesper and Freddie's parents were refreshingly progressive, but she was fairly certain that if they'd been born to a man like many who haunted the halls of Westminster, Freddie would have lost little time in rebelling against all his father stood for.

"I know," he conceded. "But I've heard mutterings that the Fleas are going to be conducting more raids. Just . . . be careful."

Vesper wrinkled her nose at the mention of the Fleas—or, technically, the F.L.E.A.s: Forbiddance and Licensing Enforcement Agents. In addition to issuing licenses permitting businesses to sell alcohol, they were also tasked with enforcing the government's ban on all magical substances that had been signed into law at the beginning of the decade. They spent their taxpayer-funded time investigating private clubs, looking for signs of Forbiddance violations for which they could either extract a heavy fine, or—in a rare but alarming occurrence—send in Scotland Yard to shut the club down.

The problem was, it was perfectly obvious—to the government, and everyone else—that the members' clubs that were owned by powerful magical families *must* be dealing in an illicit potion trade, but they failed to account for how much money the magical community possessed, and how easy it was to convince underpaid civil servants to accept bribes.

Vesper sniffed. "I'm always careful."

Freddie raised an eyebrow.

"All right, I'm *sometimes* careful," she amended, and was rewarded with a grin from Freddie. "Though I don't think the raids are anything to worry about—hasn't Daddy said that he's paid off his contact at the Home Office?" The unofficial Holloway motto was that there was little that couldn't be bought for the right price.

"He has," Freddie agreed, his expression thoughtful. This was an unusual enough sight that Vesper frowned.

"Freddie, what is it?"

"I've heard rumors that they're looking to make an example of someone—one of the most prestigious clubs." *Like ours* went unspoken.

Vesper sighed, frustrated. The Forbiddance laws had come

into effect during the war—"public war readiness" was given as the initial excuse, and then the laws were extended for public health reasons during the flu pandemic, since crowded clubs full of people with lowered inhibitions seemed like a perfect way to ensure germs spread quickly. Later, they became permanent, and had been a source of constant consternation for certain magical families ever since. Most of the members-only clubs—like Holloway's—that had done a roaring trade in the concoctions for hundreds of years had swiftly pivoted, keeping their public operations entirely aboveboard and relegating the purchase and consumption of potions and spell powders to secret back rooms. Everyone had carried on quite happily, though prices had gone up as a result, and many operations that had once catered to a more working-class clientele had been driven out of business. Freddie and their elder sister, Cecily, worked dedicatedly to try to turn public sentiment against the laws, but Vesper was not terribly political.

However, things might turn very nasty indeed if the government actually raided Holloway's—for one, if she were arrested, she could not imagine that the photographs would be particularly flattering.

"Have you spoken to Simon?" she asked, naming Cecily's husband, an MP who was leading the coalition attempting to overturn Forbiddance laws in Parliament.

Freddie shrugged. "Not since dinner last week—last time we spoke about it, he simply said that"—he cleared his throat and dropped his voice an octave—" 'it always pays to be cautious.' "

Vesper laughed. She was fond of Simon—the entire family was—but he was considerably more straitlaced than anyone in the Holloway clan, including his wife, and she occasionally caught him blinking around the table at family dinners, likely wondering how he'd managed to get himself chained to this bunch of lunatics (complimentary).

Vesper glanced at the clock and realized that she needed to get to work; the enchanted syrups they used to make their potions tended to lose a bit of their flavor after twelve hours or so, meaning a member of the family had to be present at the club every evening to ensure that they had enough fresh magical supplies. She crossed to the worktable and began assessing the ingredients laid out before her. "Well," she said over her shoulder, "you may inform Simon that I'll keep a wary eye out and will do my best to keep my legs closed around public servants going forward."

Freddie rolled his eyes. "I will not be having that conversation with my brother-in-law. But it wouldn't hurt for you to start taking things a bit more seriously."

Vesper smiled charmingly at him. "I *do* take things seriously. How do you think Holloway's is still running?" She turned back to the table before her. The ingredients were all prepared in advance by a trusted member of staff—the spices ground, the herbs crushed, the lemons squeezed. It was up to whichever member of the Holloway clan was present to assemble the components into the necessary configurations and speak the family's Word that would imbue them with magic. For the powders, this merely involved a mix of dry ingredients measured into a sachet and then whispered over; for potions, they mixed a series of magic-infused syrups that were later added to the soda water, champagne, and spirits that the bartenders used as each drink was ordered at the bar.

Vesper picked up a flask of hot water and carefully measured some into a large vial, then stirred in sugar, lemon juice, and muddled basil. She paused for a second; then, with her hand carefully gripping the base of the vial, she closed her eyes and spoke the family Word, quietly but precisely. There was a sensation like sparks racing down her right arm, then a tingling in her fingers, and the glass beneath her hand briefly warmed, then cooled again. And like that, it was done, and Vesper was reaching for a cork with which to seal the vial, then affixing a label identifying it as the syrup used for the Gin and Giggles, one of the club's most popular offerings.

One down; only another dozen or so to go.

She glanced back at Freddie. "You might look more impressed when I do that, you know."

He waved a hand. "I can do it too."

She raised an eyebrow.

"All right. *Sort* of," he amended.

It was true; magic was passed down along bloodlines, but for reasons no one understood, it tended to manifest more strongly in some members of a given family than others. Freddie *could* do magic if required; the Holloways' Word worked for him, just as it did for Vesper, Cecily, and their father, but the effects of him employing it were never quite as impressive as for other members of the family.

"If you're done trying to warn me about the dangers posed by underpaid government workers, then I've actual work to do here." She turned back to the worktable before her, reaching for dried lavender. Behind her, she heard Freddie making rather a production of getting to his feet.

"I should be off anyway—don't want to be late to rehearsals. I need to properly channel my character."

"Isn't it a clown?" she asked. "I wouldn't think that would take a great deal of effort—not much acting involved for you." Without even glancing behind her, she ducked, narrowly missing the napkin Freddie had lobbed at her head, and laughed as she heard him leave the room.

There was magic to be done, and a club to be run, and—most importantly—an approaching weekend's worth of plans to be made.

Brothers and their dire warnings could be safely ignored.

Chapter Two

Maxwell Ashbridge prided himself on being an efficient sort of man. He knew precisely what time to walk out his front door to catch the Underground that would see him settling down at his desk ninety seconds before his scheduled arrival time. He'd been employed by His Majesty's Civil Service for the better part of five years, first in the Passport Office, and more recently in the Forbiddance and Licensing Enforcement Agency, and regularly received glowing performance reviews. He used all the produce in his kitchen before making another trip to the greengrocer's. He returned library books on time. He got things done with a minimum of fuss, which was just the way he liked it.

It was only now, sitting in Raffles's office and listening to the brief she was cheerfully assigning him, that he wondered if perhaps he hadn't made himself a bit *too* reliable.

"I'm sorry," he said, cutting into his superior's monologue. "You want me to shut down Holloway's?"

Raffles broke off, looking annoyed at having been interrupted. He was never quite certain what to make of Effie Raffles; she was about a decade his senior, slender, and with a silvery blond bob that she kept in perfectly shackled waves. She came to work every day dressed smartly in a Chanel suit and sensible black pumps; she had tea delivered to her office in an immaculate bone china tea service twice a day; she wrote all of her correspondence on engraved stationery that she brought from home. She was whip-smart and also very well-connected; her husband was a prominent Tory MP, Michael Raffles, who stopped by the office to collect her each day at five. Max understood that they were often to be found in the evenings drinking cocktails at the Savoy or dining with some of Raffles's allies in Parliament. Michael Raffles was fervently in favor of Forbiddance—he was close friends with Jacob Finlay, a fellow MP who was the original architect of the Forbiddance legislation. Now, several years into the prohibition of magical substances, the two men and their various allies were fixated on thwarting the efforts of Simon Covington, the leader of the Alliance Party, who was attempting to create a voting bloc of Alliance, Labour, Liberal, and even a few renegade Conservative MPs to repeal the legislation.

Given all this, it was perhaps unsurprising that Raffles's wife should hold a prominent role at the F.L.E.A., where she was tasked with enforcing the laws that Raffles and Finlay had brought into existence. She certainly seemed passionate about the job—Max had never yet seen her arrive late or take a sick day. He had never worked beneath a female superior before, despite the success women had had in gaining the vote a few decades earlier, during the reign of Queen Victoria. He was certain some of the other men in the office made her job more difficult than it needed to be, and so he generally tried to avoid doing so himself—but, considering the assignment she'd just given him, he couldn't bring himself to be his usual acquiescent self.

"Yes, Holloway's," Raffles said curtly. "Am I not speaking in English?"

"We've tried to investigate Holloway's before," Max reminded her. It had been before his time at the agency, but he'd read the reports. "Agents have been unable to find any hard proof of magical substances being sold."

Of course, "unable to find" might simply mean "paid handsomely not to notice," a fact that Max knew Raffles understood as well as he did.

"I am aware," Raffles said, with a grim twist of her mouth. "But those agents didn't have the advantage that you do."

Max stilled; he'd wondered if this had been where this was going. It was nice, he supposed, of Raffles to admit it outright. "Oh?"

"I know that you and the Holloway son—what is his name—" She broke off, rummaging through a stack of papers before her.

"Freddie."

"Ah, yes. Freddie." Max was all at once certain that she'd known Freddie's name perfectly well and had simply wanted him to acknowledge it. "I know you were friends."

"At university, years ago."

"He'll be your ticket to entry, and I trust you to take things from there."

"He and I haven't kept in touch," Max said—a wild understatement—"and he'll think it decidedly odd if I appear at the doors of his club." Given the reasons he and Holloway were no longer in touch, "decidedly odd" was putting it mildly.

"Ashbridge. You came to this post highly recommended. I expect your ingenuity will allow you to work something out." Raffles leaned forward, bracing her elbows on her desk and pressing the tips of her index fingers together. "There is a general sentiment that it would be beneficial to show the public that no one is above the law, and that Forbiddance is being enforced fairly. And since we're not fortunate enough, in this department, to employ many people who spent their university years rubbing elbows with the magical elite, you seem like the perfect man for the job."

Indeed, Max thought darkly. Because most of the posh boys—men now—who'd been with him at Cambridge were probably eyeballs-deep in potions at any given moment and had no interest in ceasing the practice.

He sighed, then met Raffles's keen gaze. "Fine. I'll see what I can uncover."

"Brilliant. Off you go, then." Her eyes were already drifting back to the headache-inducing stack of paperwork on her desk as Max rose from his seat. He turned toward the door but paused, hand outstretched toward the handle, when she spoke again.

"Oh, and Ashbridge? Be sure to keep quiet about this around the department."

Max offered Raffles a nod. "Noted."

◆

The Holloways were not terribly serious about most things, but the one thing they took very seriously indeed was the weekly family dinner.

The family lived on a quiet, leafy street in Marylebone, near Regent's Park, where they'd been holding court for the past couple hundred years in considerable splendor. Marylebone had been developed north of Mayfair hundreds of years earlier by magical families seeking to create their own enclave separate from the mundane aristocrats—those lacking magical abilities. Today the neighborhood was known both for its concentration of wealthy old magical families *and* for its preponderance of somewhat clandestine magical businesses.

The Holloways had spent the past couple of centuries cashing in on the family's prized recipes for potions and spell powders, which were all that remained of Britain's rich magical heritage. Magic had once been so woven into everyday life that it would have been impossible to imagine a day without it. No one entirely understood why it had waned. One popular theory was that the farther removed Britain was from the days of King Arthur's court and Merlin and all the rest, the less magic lingered in the land. Others pointed to the days of the Tudors, and to the bloody conflict between Catholics and Protestants, as the moment that religion became more important than magic. Still others noted the dilution of magical blood in families that intermarried with mundanes, as these intermarriages were proven to slowly diminish magical abilities in a family line over time, or the dwindling variety of magic in the families that continued to marry only among each other.

What wasn't up for debate was the fact that the fading

of spellwork, which had commenced around the time of Queen Elizabeth's reign, had accelerated since the Industrial Revolution—the last true spells had been cast during the Regency (many an illegal duel had featured a bit of spellwork), and since then, all that had remained was the magical families' ability to imbue physical substances with temporary magic through the use of their family Words, passed down through the generations. The families kept their recipes for magical concoctions as closely guarded secrets, and turned a sizable profit from selling the resulting products to the mundane population and other magical families alike.

This took several forms: There were the half dozen or so private members' clubs that sold potions and spell powders that could be consumed for purposes of revelry; another few pubs, popular with a more working-class clientele, that sold beers and ales that the proprietors brewed with the use of family Words, though their magical effects tended to be a bit more muted than those of the stronger potions; there were also a couple of magical pharmacies, a gardening emporium that sold various elixirs for use on all sorts of plant life, and a select number of cooks—some employed by restaurants, others by wealthy families—who used their family Words to imbue their cuisine with an extra degree of flavor.

The fact that there was a seemingly limitless appetite for these magical substances meant that the fortunes of the magical elite had continued to grow, even as many wealthy mundane families whose prosperity relied on rural agriculture had seen their finances teeter precariously for a few generations now. The Holloways had no country estate—they were creatures of

London and always had been—and had moved into their current mansion at some point in the eighteenth century; they had not seen fit to move since. Here, Lucian and Amelia Holloway reigned over a household that was rather emptier these days, now that all three of their children lived elsewhere, but they maintained the tradition of Friday night family dinners, and none of their offspring were brave enough to miss the occasion.

For Vesper, the commute was not a long one; her parents had allowed her to move out of her childhood bedroom several years earlier, for the sake of their collective sanity, and into the flat in the mews behind the house, which had once held the stables and had since been converted to a garage for the family's motorcars. (Vesper's mother, in particular, was fond of a spin around town or out to the Surrey Hills in her Bentley on fine days.) This meant that Vesper could leave it until approximately two minutes till six before making her way down the stairs, out into the cobblestoned mews, and in through the kitchen door and up the back staircase into the main house—which was precisely where she found herself, a week after her conversation with Freddie over tea and cake.

"There you are," Cecily said, as soon as Vesper walked into the drawing room, where the rest of the family were already assembled. Vesper glanced at the clock above the mantel, confirmed that it was only thirty seconds after the hour, and then stuck her tongue out at her elder sister.

Cecily handed her a champagne coupe. "Lovely. I hope your face gets stuck that way one of these days."

"I'm beginning to think Mummy was lying about that," Vesper said with a sly glance at her mother, who was already making her way toward her, leaning down to drop a kiss on her cheek.

"Nonsense," said Amelia. "I never lie."

All three children raised a howl of protest at that; even mild-mannered Simon, sitting happily with a snifter of brandy, murmured quietly, "A bit of revisionist history, there."

"Not you too, darling Simon," Amelia said.

"I'm sorry, Amelia," Simon said, looking genuinely disappointed to have caused any offense, and rededicated his attention to his drink.

Vesper flopped inelegantly down onto the chaise her father currently occupied. "Daddy."

"Ve—hmm." Her father tapped his chin thoughtfully. "Wait. Which one are you again? I seem to have forgotten your name, it's been so long."

"It's been three days."

Her father shrugged. "And it's a very short walk from the mews to the breakfast room to join your humble parents for an occasional meal."

"Humble" was not a word that anyone could use to describe Lucian Holloway. He was tall and lithe, his hair once dark but now a handsome salt-and-pepper; his eyes were an arresting blue. He'd been a horrible cad when he was younger, Vesper knew; her parents had never made an effort to hide any of the whispers from their children. But he'd taken one look at her mother and fallen desperately in love; apparently, polite society had talked of nothing else for weeks. It would all have been quite romantic, if they hadn't been *Vesper's* parents, and if she hadn't been the one who risked walking in on them kissing in corners at inappropriate times of the day. (Vesper considered kissing to be a strictly nocturnal activity; best not to do it during the daytime and give men any rosy-hued ideas.)

"If you and Mummy could keep your hands off each other for more than five seconds, I might find the invitation more tempting," Vesper said, and her father flashed a lazy grin at her.

"Did you hear that, my love?" he called over his shoulder to his wife, who was busy opening a bottle of champagne. "Our youngest feels that we are too amorous."

"Our youngest might see her way to being a bit *less* amorous herself," Amelia called back, hands still busy with the cork. "Ainsley Sherwood, Vesper, really?"

"How do *you* know about that?" Vesper asked, then shot a look of betrayal at Freddie.

"It wasn't me!"

"Have I taught you nothing?" Amelia asked, removing the cork and pouring herself a fresh glass of champagne. "You should always keep an ear out for gossip." She reached for the small silver bowl of spell powder that sat on the drinks tray and scooped a careful half spoonful into her glass, tilting her head to watch the shimmering powder slowly descend through the liquid and dissolve. It was an appetite-enhancing powder—one of Amelia's favorite indulgences before special meals, to ensure she enjoyed the food as much as possible.

Vesper took a moody sip of her own champagne. Sometimes she wondered what it would be like to be an orphan (a wealthy one with a doting but largely absent guardian).

"Now that we're all here," Cecily said, rising to her feet and resting a hand on Simon's shoulder, "I think there's something we should discuss." Cecily, unlike her siblings, favored her father, with dark hair and the same blue eyes; they were just as appealing on the daughter as they had been on the father at her age. Cecily's charms, however, had been reserved for Simon for nearly a decade; they'd met at a wartime hospital in France where Cecily had been a nurse.

Vesper shook her head. Again: *so romantic*. Why did her family insist on being this way?

Redirecting her attention to the matter at hand, she realized that Cecily's keen gaze was fixed directly on her.

"Yes?" she asked, lowering the glass she'd been about to take a sip from.

"It's about the business," Cecily said.

"Last I checked, it hadn't caught fire, and I was just there this afternoon, so . . ."

"Ha." Cecily shook her head imperiously, the gesture a bit more impressive on her than it was on Vesper, since Cecily was allowing her hair to grow out and it now reached her shoulders. "Simon thinks that there is a real chance for his bill repealing Forbiddance to pass Parliament this session."

There was a considerable uproar in the room at this announcement.

"Labour can be won over?" Lucian asked, his expression thoughtful.

Simon nodded. "That is the hope." Simon was an MP for the Alliance Party—the party that had historically represented the interests of the magical families. "However, there is a fear that we'll lose votes if MPs from other parties grow . . . spooked."

Vesper frowned. "How so?"

Freddie, however, appeared to comprehend. "The cock-up at Plenus Venter?"

Simon nodded.

Vesper turned to her brother. "What's this?"

Freddie ran a hand through his blond hair in a gesture that usually signaled some disquiet on his part. "Last weekend someone had some sort of potion that made them ill—they became horribly dizzy as soon as they drank it, and then fainted directly into the champagne fountain."

Vesper gasped in genuine horror. "Ruining all that perfectly good champagne?"

"I don't think *that* was the primary concern regarding the incident."

"Surely whoever it was simply overindulged," Vesper said.

Freddie shook his head. "I've heard from three separate people who were there that he'd only had the one potion, and nothing to drink before that."

"Perhaps he has an allergy?" Vesper suggested. It wasn't unheard of.

"He'd been to Plenus Venter loads of times and never had an issue."

"Hmm." Vesper leaned back in her seat, taking another sip of champagne.

"Mundane MPs—particularly those who aren't terribly comfortable with magic to begin with, even if they feel Forbiddance has gone too far—won't vote for the bill if rumors start spreading that the magic on offer at the clubs is dangerous," Simon said; next to him, Cecily's brow was wrinkled, her expression troubled. "And Jacob Finlay is already trying to work the Tories up into a frenzy over this bill." Everyone present grimaced at the name; Finlay, the son of landed gentry with an old, profitable estate in Oxfordshire, was one of the most fervent anti-magic MPs, and had been key to ensuring that Forbiddance had come into law after the war. There was a vocal minority of the mundane population—particularly among the wealthy—who disliked the existence of an entirely different sort of privilege that was unattainable to them, especially after the aristocratic financial downturns of the past half century; Forbiddance was the result of this sentiment.

"You're all very hysterical lately," Vesper said, the previous week's discussion with Freddie still fresh in her mind. She turned to her parents; her father, in particular, could usually be relied upon to take his youngest daughter's side in any argument. "Daddy," she said warmly, "you don't think we actually need to be concerned, do you?"

But her father, for once, was looking very serious too. "Hopefully not," he said. "But it would behoove us all to behave sensibly, I think."

"Easier for some of us than for others," Cecily said.

"Have I not kept the club running and more or less scandal-free for the past four years?" Vesper asked, feeling a bit offended.

"You have," Amelia confirmed. "But between this and the rumors Freddie's heard about them looking to make an example of someone, it *does* become worrisome. Perhaps it would be good if someone else from the family was there with Vesper every night—"

"What!" Vesper sat up straight, nearly—horror of horrors—splashing champagne onto her lap, but righting her glass just in time. It would never do to waste perfectly good champagne (or a perfectly good Lanvin dress). Vesper didn't like to think she was easily offended, but her family's complete lack of faith in her was beginning to rub. "I understand the situation, so I don't think there's any reason I need a nanny dogging my every step."

"The club is a considerable financial asset," her father said, and Vesper narrowed her eyes at him. "If we get shut down by some overzealous civil servant, it will be extremely irritating."

"Then I promise I'll watch any potential civil servants who walk through our doors like a hawk."

"Hmm," Freddie murmured. "Watch them as closely as you did Ainsley Sherwood?"

"For the last time, I am not going to see bloody Ainsley Sherwood again." Being the youngest was maddening; was anyone listening to anything she was saying?

"My point is," Lucian said, seeming determined to steer the conversation back on track, "we'll want to keep an eye out, in case they send a Flea."

The entire room shuddered in unison.

"That reminds me," Freddie said, reaching into his back pocket and producing a wrinkled square of paper. "I've the most recent list of personnel employed as Fleas."

The identities of Fleas were meant, technically, to be a secret—but bribery was an ancient, noble art, and Freddie got his hands on a list of staff at the agency a couple of times a year.

"Anyone interesting?" Vesper asked.

Freddie gave her a thin smile. "Take a look."

Vesper took the proffered square of paper. She skimmed the

list before her; there tended to be a fair amount of turnover among the Fleas, so many of the names were unfamiliar.

Midway down the list, however, her eyes snagged on a name.

Maxwell Ashbridge.

A name she hadn't considered in years. She would've been perfectly happy to keep it that way, considering that she'd once embarrassed herself horribly in front of the man in question.

Her gaze flicked back up to Freddie's. "Is this—"

"The very one. It suits him, really, given his feelings on magic." Freddie's expression was dark.

"Who are you talking about?" Cecily queried.

"D'you remember Max Ashbridge?" Freddie asked; Vesper's gaze had returned to the list, her eyes stuck on that name.

"Your friend from Cambridge with the stick up his arse?"

"That's him. That'll be one to keep an eye out for, Vee," he added, glancing back at Vesper. She didn't think she was imagining the slight tightening of his jaw.

"I will," she said, and before she could add anything further, there was the sound of a loud yodel from the kitchens, which was their cook Mrs. Holstein's favorite way of summoning the family to mealtimes. Simon startled slightly from his spot on the sofa. "Sorry," he said sheepishly. "Simply cannot get used to being called to dinner that way."

"It's been nearly ten years, Simon, and I worry about the state of your nerves if you don't get a bit less jumpy," said Amelia, sweeping around him and Cecily to where their offspring crouched behind the sofa. Vesper hadn't even noticed her nephew's presence until this moment: George was five, and she harbored dark suspicions that he possessed some sort of latent magical ability, because she found the degree to which he managed to go unnoticed somewhat uncanny.

"George, darling, I am going to pretend not to have noticed the fact that you are now coloring on the floorboards instead of the perfectly good roll of paper I gave you, only because I had Mrs. Holstein make black forest pudding for dessert tonight, and I know it is your particular favorite, and I do hate to deprive a child of sweets before sending him home with his parents. But if you do not cease in the next three seconds, I am going to reconsider that decision."

"Sorry, Nan," George said, leaping to his feet at the promise of this treat. The Holloways did not believe in sending children to eat in the nursery, which meant that George was becoming alarmingly precocious. Vesper liked to keep a close eye on her nephew; she loved him, but was not convinced he wasn't plotting against them all. He was certainly clever enough.

"Right," Lucian said, clapping his hands together as Mrs. Holstein yodeled again, louder this time; she became very distressed if it seemed possible that her food was going to get cold before the family had the chance to offer rapturous praise. "Shall we? We can continue this discussion later—no doubt we'll work out a rotating schedule, so that one of us can be at the club with Vesper every evening until this fuss blows over, and all will be well."

The rest of the family, considering the matter settled, trailed into the dining room, chattering happily, not seeming to notice Vesper lagging behind, quietly seething.

They clearly didn't trust her. Despite the fact that she'd spent six nights a week ensuring Holloway's was running smoothly for the past few years. Despite everything she'd done to prove she wasn't flighty and irresponsible. At the end of the day, they still thought she was the same reckless girl who'd once made a series of disastrous romantic decisions—Maxwell Ashbridge being the very *least* of them—and whose judgment couldn't be trusted.

But she wasn't that girl anymore, she thought now, lifting her chin. And she was simply going to have to prove that to them.

Prove that nothing at all was going to happen to their club, so long as she was at the helm.

And—she spared a last, disgusted thought for Ainsley Sherwood—that meant, first and foremost, that she certainly wasn't going to allow her head to be turned by another man anytime soon.

Chapter Three

By the time Vesper arrived at Holloway's, it was nearly ten, and the club was busy.

By night, the place was transformed; gone was the daytime sense of peaceful escape from the world, replaced by an air of revelry. On the second floor, there was a bar and lounge where cocktails were mixed and champagne flowed freely; a live band entertained the assembled crowds, and space was cleared on the floor for dancing. The overhead lights had been dimmed, and there were candles in sconces along the walls, along with electric lamps. The entire atmosphere was one of romance and temptation.

And, if you knew who to speak to, and which password was in use that month, then a particular bookshelf in the club's library could be moved aside to allow entrance to rooms that, until a few years earlier, no one outside of the Holloway family had even known existed. The rooms—known as the backdoor bar, by the family and staff—were often the most crowded in the club; Holloway's capped entry and frequently turned would-be revelers away: Those so disappointed had to content themselves with the consumption of the legal variety of intoxicating substances that particular evening.

Tonight, Vesper made a beeline for the backdoor bar. She would never have admitted to anyone in her family that she was worried, but the concerns that Freddie and Cecily had raised today felt like heavy weights on her shoulders, and she knew that she would only be able to relax once she'd confirmed that all was running as it should.

"Vee."

Lost in her thoughts, smiling absently at people in the assembled crowds whom she recognized as she walked, Vesper hadn't even noticed that she was passing within a foot of her best friend, Hazel.

She whirled around so quickly that she nearly lost her balance; Hazel reached out with a steadying hand at her elbow. The motion mimicked twenty years of friendship in a single, tidy moment.

"Hazel!" Vesper squeezed her friend's hand. "I didn't know you were coming tonight."

Hazel grimaced. "I didn't want to, but John Delacqua wanted to take me for a drink, and Papa didn't want me to say no." She looked very pretty, in a robe de style made of pink lace; her hair was a couple of shades darker than Vesper's, and this evening her riotous curls had been tamed somewhat with a headband featuring a golden rose. Her expression was unhappy, however, and Vesper cast a worried glance at her.

She gave Hazel's hand another squeeze. "Delacqua's nice."

Delacqua came from an old, storied family that was the product of a number of mixed marriages between the magical and mundane worlds; over time, the intermarrying had diluted the family's magical abilities to virtually nothing, but they still had plenty of money and were well situated in both magical and mundane society.

"I suppose you're right, but—what's wrong?" Hazel asked, seeing that Vesper's gaze had become fixed on a point in the distance. Not a point, in fact, but a figure.

"Vesper?" Hazel asked, craning to look over her shoulder in an attempt to follow her friend's stare.

"Sorry!" Vesper said. "I just . . . er . . . need to speak to someone."

Hazel looked at her, brow wrinkling. "Who is he?"

Vesper cast a surreptitious glance around, though she knew they were unlikely to be overheard, given the noise inside the club. "Max Ashbridge."

Hazel's frown deepened. "Who?"

Vesper sighed, impatient, but she supposed, given her rather lengthy romantic history, it would be unreasonable to expect Hazel to keep track of all of the names. "Max. Ashbridge," she repeated in an undertone, enunciating each word very clearly. "He was at Cambridge with Freddie—he's the one I met at Freddie's twenty-third birthday party and . . ." She waved her hand illustratively.

Hazel's eyes widened. "Not the one you propositioned!"

"Hazel, I didn't *proposition* him, I simply . . . made my interest known." The memory was mortifying; Vesper had largely succeeded at putting it out of her mind for the past seven years.

She had been eighteen at the time, and nervous around Freddie's university friends. She'd found herself in an incriminating situation with one of them—hidden away in a coat closet, gown pushed down to her waist, the man's hands beneath her skirts—when Ashbridge had walked in, got quite an eyeful of Vesper's bare breasts, and then icily reminded the man in question of the existence of his fiancée. In *the next room.*

Ashbridge had been exceptionally decent about the whole thing, averting his eyes while Vesper had put her clothing to rights and then escorting her to a private corner where he had brought her a glass of champagne and pretended not to notice her surreptitiously dabbing at her eyes. He had been kind, in other words. At the time, she'd been certain that this meant he had some sort of romantic interest in her, and so she'd leaned in to kiss him. In the years since, Vesper had kissed a great many men, and never had one leapt backward so quickly to escape her as Ashbridge had done that night. It had been the final humiliation in what had already been an exceptionally humiliating three-quarters of an hour.

Fortunately for her, Freddie and Ashbridge had fallen out soon afterward—some sort of political quarrel, she remembered vaguely—and she could only be grateful for this fact, since it meant that she had never had to look him in the eye again.

Until now.

"Wouldn't you rather avoid him?" Hazel asked; her philosophy tended to be that discretion—or, at least, avoiding people one didn't want to speak to—was the better part of valor. Vesper was never sure whether to find this quality admirable or troubling in her friend.

"It's a bit more complicated than that, unfortunately," Vesper said, her eyes still fixed on the man across the room even as her mind returned to the list Freddie had shown her just a few hours earlier. She lowered her voice. "Ashbridge is a Flea."

Hazel's eyes widened in alarm. "Vesper, I don't think you would be suited to prison."

"I don't either," Vesper assured her. "I doubt they'd let me bring my silk pajamas. Or champagne." She looked past Hazel toward the bar, where she spotted Amir, one of their most experienced bartenders, who'd worked for the Holloway family for nearly twenty years. With a distracted wave to Hazel, Vesper made a beeline for the gleaming bar, where Amir was adding a cherry garnish to a cocktail.

"Miss Holloway," he said, nodding at her as he slid the glass across the dark, polished wood of the bar to a waiting couple.

Vesper leaned forward across the bar so that she could say in an undertone, "There's a Flea."

Amir stilled for a moment, his dark eyes catching hers; then he reached for a rag to wipe the bar. "One we can bribe?" he replied in a low murmur.

It was a fair question; part of the reason Freddie spent considerable time greasing palms to stay abreast of who was currently employed by the Forbiddance and Licensing Enforcement Agency was to get an idea of which ones were likely to show up at Holloway's, and which could be bribed with a few packets of spell powder to ignore their duties.

"I don't think so, unfortunately. Can you send word to the backdoor bar not to let anyone out for a quarter of an hour, until I can get rid of him?"

"There are already a few people from the backdoor bar out here," Amir said, with a discreet nod of his head; Vesper saw a group of men who looked to be a few years younger than her laughing uproariously. They were clutching (entirely legal) cocktails, but there was the telltale shimmer around the hairline that indicated that they'd consumed something magical in the past hour or so. The club was strict about ensuring that no magical substances were taken outside the backdoor bar, but less so about keeping the clubgoers confined to those rooms once they'd had their fill of potions and powders.

Vesper swore under her breath, then said, "Tell Anna not to let anyone else out, at least—I'm going to see if I can distract Ashbridge." Anna Llewelyn was the bartender who ran the backdoor bar so competently that if it hadn't been for the need for a family member to oversee the club and perform the necessary magic every night, Vesper would have felt entirely superfluous.

"Going to flirt with him?" Amir asked wisely.

"I'm going to *speak* to him," she corrected; admittedly, these two things tended to look quite similar when coming from her.

Amir regarded her skeptically.

"I've met this one before—I'll do it all under the guise of welcoming an old family friend."

"Hmm," said Amir, his skeptical expression not budging.

Vesper turned on her heel and began to make her way toward Ashbridge, who was still standing just through the doorway, surveying the scene around him rather like someone observing an unknown animal species at the zoo. She didn't think he'd noticed her; his attention was fixed on some point in the distance, an expression of vague distaste on his face.

"Max Ashbridge," she said, placing a hand on her hip and allowing herself a languorous perusal of his body, head to toe and back again, as his head jerked toward her. He looked largely the same as she'd remembered; there were faint lines at the corners of his eyes that she didn't remember from before, which made him look older than twenty-nine. Everything about his appearance was as neat and fastidious as she recalled; his jaw was closely shaved, his dark hair combed into ruthless submission and further quelled with pomade, and his tie carefully knotted. Even the angle at which he held his chin seemed very proper.

"Fancy seeing you here," she said, meeting his gray eyes again.

"Miss Holloway." He cleared his throat. "It's been quite a while."

Merlin, she'd forgotten his voice—low and smooth and dark, somehow. It sounded like the voice of a man she'd like to get up to no good with.

"You can call me Vesper," she said, giving a tinkling little laugh. "I don't like to be very . . . formal." She batted her eyelashes at him, trying to look appropriately seductive while still watching him carefully to see if it was working. His expression was impassive enough that it was impossible to tell if she was setting him at all off-balance.

"Unfortunately, I do," he said, offering her a thin smile, and Vesper frowned, before immediately wiping the expression from her face. She had a nearly one hundred percent success rate when it came to flirtation, and this was not the reaction she was accustomed to.

"It must've been years since you were last here," she tried

again, plastering another seductive smile on her face determinedly. "Perhaps you'll join me for a drink, and I can show you around? Unless you're meeting someone here—I suppose you must have been invited?"

The unspoken implication—that this was a private club, to which he decidedly did *not* hold a membership—was loud and clear. He obviously heard it, because he reached into his jacket pocket and produced a card, printed on thick, expensive stock embossed with a coat of arms, which he handed to her now.

Glancing down at it, she saw that it belonged to Dashiell St. Clair. He was the heir to a viscount, and one of Freddie's oldest friends from his school days. Flipping it over, Vesper recognized his hasty scrawl—*Ashbridge—meet me at my club. Holloway's, New Cavendish Street. Tell the doorman the password is "liquidity."*—as well as the signature at the bottom of the card. She bit back a swear. It wasn't as though she could deny St. Clair the right to bring a guest; his family had been members at Holloway's for generations, and he had deep pockets. Vesper was mercenary enough to not wish to risk offending one of their best customers, even though he had—she cast a suspicious glance at Ashbridge again—invited a traitor into their midst.

She looked back up at Ashbridge and saw that something close to a smile was playing at the corners of his mouth.

"All in order?"

She returned the card with ill grace. "Of course."

"Good." He tucked it back into his jacket pocket. "I was unaware you were such a thorough hostess."

"I do what I can." She smiled at him again, determined to not allow this man to best her—and determined, too, to work out what he was actually doing here. She hadn't seen St. Clair this evening, though admittedly that didn't mean that he wasn't present.

"Now," she said, her tone syrupy sweet. "How about that drink?" Anything to loosen his tongue a bit—though not, sadly, in the way that she usually enjoyed loosening men's tongues.

"You *are* attentive, aren't you?" he asked, eyeing her consideringly. "Tell me, is there any particular reason?"

Vesper narrowed her eyes at him.

He raised an inquiring brow in return.

"What is it that you do for work these days?" she asked, lifting a hand so that she might examine her nails idly, as though his response were not terribly interesting to her. "I thought I heard that you were doing something for the government."

"Yes. I worked at the Passport Office until recently."

"Lovely."

"Is it?"

"Of course." She gave him a sickly-sweet smile. "I do so admire anyone who works for the civil service. Such an honorable line of work."

"Ah, yes. I know how much the magical families care about obeying the government." His tone was dry as toast; Vesper was amused against her will.

"I don't recall you having a sense of humor."

"Was that a compliment?"

"No. I preferred you without one. Why are you here?"

A flash of a smile crossed his face. "There's the Vesper Holloway I remember. I vastly prefer you when you come out and ask for information, rather than trying to trick it out of me."

"I haven't the faintest idea what you mean," she said airily.

"Don't you?" he asked.

"If you're not with the Passport Office anymore, then where is it that you're working, did you say?"

"I didn't."

A lengthy pause.

Vesper frowned at him.

He frowned back, just for a moment, and then his gaze flicked away from her—a relief, that; it was rather piercing—and focused on something in the direction he'd been looking before she approached. She turned, trying to see what had caught his attention, and saw the same raucous group of boys she'd noted earlier, now sounding decidedly less celebratory and considerably more panicked.

Not that she could blame them, because one of their number was currently levitating somewhere near the ceiling, upside down, spinning like a top and jerking around as if controlled by the invisible strings of a marionette.

Vesper mentally raced through a litany of swears.

"Is that what's meant to be happening?" Ashbridge asked.

"Obviously not," Vesper said, the words clipped, and turned on her heel to race across the room to where the cluster of panicked university boys were debating loudly what was to be done.

Vesper attempted to interrupt, but could barely make herself heard above the din; in addition to their arguing, the surrounding clubgoers had noticed what was afoot, and a clamor of excited voices made it difficult for her to hear herself think. Overhead, the spinning boy was moaning in terror.

At last, Vesper took the expedient measure of aiming a kick to the shin of one of the arguing gaggle of boys—the loudest one—who broke off his blustering and gaped at her.

"Did you just *kick* me?"

Vesper didn't waste breath apologizing. "What on earth has your friend here gone and done?"

"He's not 'gone and done' anything," one of his friends said angrily. "He drank a Flotation Fizz half an hour ago, but he thought it was a bad batch, it wore off so quickly. And it *says* on the menu that it's for 'low-level levitation' only; it didn't say anything about him spinning like a top up round the chandelier—"

"What *else* did he take?" Vesper interrupted, not willing to waste too much of her valuable time listening to a man whinge. "Clearly it wasn't the Flotation Fizz alone."

"I didn't see him drink anything else all night," the brow-furrowing friend informed her. "He said he'd a rotten hangover after too many bottles last night, and so he was sticking to potions tonight."

This was, in Vesper's opinion, highly dubious logic—she got wicked headaches from potions of the sort that her cherished bosom friend (champagne) would never give her—but about what she'd expect for a man of this age and general background. (Posh, overeducated, underintelligent.)

But, if he were correct . . . could something have gone wrong with the Flotation Fizz? She tipped her head back and watched as the unfortunate fizz-drinker continued to rotate, gaining and losing elevation with alarmingly unpredictable jerks, as if there were an invisible string wrapped round one of his ankles. She thought that the movements might be slowing a bit, but it was difficult to tell for sure. Unfortunately, he was already looking quite green about the gills, and a moment later—

"Watch it," came Ashbridge's voice in her ear, sudden and unexpected, the warmth of his breath on her neck. His hand came around her upper arm in a firm grip, pulling her backward.

But not in time.

Because at that precise moment, the bespelled man whirling in midair saw fit to vomit directly onto Vesper's shoes.

Chapter Four

It was half past midnight on a Friday night, and Max was ensconced in a taxi with a woman whose shoes smelled of sick, and who seemed to wish she were anywhere other than in his company.

Needless to say, this was not how he'd planned to end the evening.

They were making slow progress up Marylebone High Street, which was full of cabs and pedestrians on their way home after an evening spent, presumably, flouting Forbiddance laws in any of the half dozen or so magical clubs that still operated within the neighborhood, their illicit offerings hidden behind a thin veil of law-abiding respectability. He glanced sideways at Miss Holloway, who kept her forehead pressed to the window, apparently trying rather desperately to pretend that she was alone.

Unfortunately for her, Max wasn't in the mood to humor this pretense.

By the time things had settled down at Holloway's, it had

been nearly midnight—closing time for the magical clubs. The unfortunate lad who'd had a bad batch of whatever it was had eventually returned to the floor, where he lay in a pitiful heap—not that Max could blame him. Vesper had tried to send for a doctor, but he'd recovered enough to protest, leading Max to grimly suspect that his family disapproved of magic, and that he didn't want to anger the parents who likely controlled the purse strings. In any case, he'd been bundled into a cab by his friends, and the remaining patrons of the club had gradually returned to their business as the night's unplanned entertainment had wound down.

Vesper had been going to catch a ride home with a friend of hers, Miss Thomas, who was there on the arm of John Delacqua, an acquaintance of Max's from his Cambridge days, but here Max had intervened.

"I'll see Miss Holloway home," he'd said, his tone brooking no objections, and Vesper hadn't even bothered to protest. Which was how he'd found himself here, in this taxi, with a woman who very clearly wished to be anywhere else.

He cleared his throat, and she glanced over, her green gaze flashing with irritation as she considered him for a long moment. At last, she asked, "Is this the point where you tell me that you're very sorry, but you're going to have to ask me some questions about my family's business?" Her chin was raised, and her expression was defiant. Neither of these facts made her look any less lovely; her hair was the gold of a new coin, her cheekbones sharp, her eyes large and luminous. She was beautiful. And she knew it, too; he'd watched her batting her eyelashes at every man she spoke with tonight.

She was not, however, batting her eyelashes at him at this moment.

"Do I want to know how it is you've discovered who I work for?"

She harrumphed, crossing her arms over her chest. "Please. Fleas all have a certain look about them."

"F.L.E.A.s, if you don't mind," he said.

Vesper rolled her eyes. "I seem to recall you being a terrible prude about potions even when you were at university. Then you show up unexpectedly at my club, on the same day I've received news that the government might be looking to make an example of someone . . . it hardly takes a staggering intellect to put things together."

Perhaps not, but this still proved that she was cleverer than she looked.

He weighed his options for a moment, wondering how frank to be with her. He sensed that continuing to deny his profession would not do him any favors, and so he decided to lay his cards on the table. He turned in his seat so that he could face her more fully; glancing toward the front seat, where the driver was humming tunelessly, he lowered his voice. "The impression I received from my superior was that you're more or less correct, and there's an interest in sending a message. Holloway's would not have been my personal choice of club to target, but I was instructed to visit."

"And you never disobey instructions, of course."

"Not all of us come from families with the resources and clout to get us out of trouble, you know," he shot back.

She blinked, her brow wrinkling for a moment. "Fair

enough, I suppose. In that case, I don't suppose there's any way we can make it worth your while to turn a blind eye?" She gave him a coy smile. Max had expected this; people with money were extremely predictable.

"After what I witnessed tonight?" He raised a skeptical brow. The chap had seemed none the worse for wear by the time he'd left, but Max did not think it was a ringing endorsement for the Marylebone members' clubs if people were dangling from the ceilings for unexplained reasons. Once he wrote up his report, Raffles would doubtless call in the authorities in short order.

"Hmm," she said, watching him carefully. "And I expect you're already aware that that's the second such incident in recent days?"

Max stilled. "What do you mean?"

"I mean, I've heard whispers of another similar mishap, just last weekend—at an establishment that purveys similar wares."

Max ignored the linguistic gymnastics employed; he knew perfectly well what she meant. "You mean that two separate clubs have managed to make a hash of whatever bespelled cocktails you're shoving down people's throats?"

"Oh, yes." Her voice was positively dripping with sarcasm. "We're kidnapping innocent, law-abiding citizens off the street and plying them with our sinful wares."

"All right," he allowed. "I might have exaggerated."

"Someone last weekend was made quite ill from a potion they'd apparently consumed regularly prior to that evening. I didn't think too much of it when I first heard about it, but now . . ."

"You think something underhanded is behind it?"

"We've never had anything like this happen at Holloway's before," she said grimly. "And coming on the heels of that other accident, it does make one wonder."

He drummed his fingers against the leather of the seat, considering her words. He was a bit surprised he'd not heard a whisper of the previous incident, but these clubs were insular—their survival depended on it—and if it had just been the one instance, he supposed it must've been easy enough to keep quiet. But combined with tonight's events . . . the thought excited him. If there *was* something rotten afoot in the magical world, and he could expose it . . .

Wasn't that precisely what he'd joined the F.L.E.A. for?

He noticed Vesper's expression turn calculating. The idea of a calculating Holloway was a bit unnerving; they were naturally inclined that way, but when they put their minds and energies toward it, the effects of the extra effort could be downright alarming.

"Why do you look like that?" he asked warily.

She smiled, an expression that shouldn't have made him feel even warier—but it did. "It *seems* like the sort of thing that might be a bit of a headache to investigate on your own—especially if you don't want anyone to know what you're up to."

"I'd hardly waltz into a club and announce who I work for," he pointed out, more amused than offended that she seemed to have so little confidence in his professional abilities.

"And you don't think they'd—*we'd*—work out who you were?" It was her turn to sound amused. "It's not as though you fooled me tonight. But what *if* I were able to . . . lend you a hand?"

"Is that meant to sound like a proposition?"

She laughed, a sound of genuine, infectious delight. "No. You've already indicated that you're immune to my many charms."

Somehow, in incredulous tones, was unspoken but understood.

"How do you propose to help me, then?"

"Access." She raised an index finger to silence him when he opened his mouth. "Think about it. If we were able to work out that you're a Flea—"

"F.L.E.A."

"—then surely other club owners with more than two brain cells to rub together will do the same. And if you want to investigate this discreetly, you can't just swan into these clubs—they're private. You'll need to go as someone's guest."

"And that someone is . . . you?" he asked, skeptical.

"Precisely. There's an understanding among all the families that own clubs—we're all welcome to visit. As sort of honorary members, if you will."

"Of course you are," he muttered. It was like his introduction to Harrow all over again, when he'd realized that despite the scholarship that had got him there, despite the fact that he knew himself to be more than capable, he was already miles behind. He didn't have the right accent or know the right people.

Of course, there was someone who could have helped with that—could have helped with his school fees, too, if Max had let him—but that was a door best kept tightly shut.

Swallowing his initial distaste, he tried to consider the offer fairly. It was a tolerable plan—she'd save him a considerable amount of effort if she could help him waltz into the various magical clubs without any sneaking about or clever planning on his part, and her presence at his side would likely dispel any curiosity his sudden appearance at a number of Marylebone clubs might provoke, should anyone take notice of him.

"It's not a terrible idea," he admitted. "If I can count on you to be discreet, that is."

Her eyes widened. "Oh, goodness, I didn't know you wanted me to be *discreet.*" She clapped a dramatic hand to her breast. "Why, I was planning to walk in, tap a knife on a champagne glass to get everyone's attention, and then ask, in the loudest, most carrying tones, if anyone on the premises had a bit of magical mischief planned for the evening and, if so, if they'd be so good as to sit down with us to discuss their plans in great detail. But if you think there's a better way to do it . . . ?"

Max waited patiently until she had finished—no point interrupting a woman who'd worked herself up into a proper temper—and then said, "Point taken. I apologize."

"You—what?" Her brow wrinkled.

"I. Apologize," he said, clearly enunciating each syllable. "Not familiar with the expression?"

"Not coming from the less-fair sex," she said, and Max pinched the bridge of his nose. He could already tell this was going to be exhausting, and they'd not even started yet.

"Why do you want to help me?" he asked, and she froze in the process of shifting slightly in her seat, lifting her skirts to facilitate the motion. He caught a brief flash of smooth, creamy thigh, and resolutely decided not to notice this.

"Well," she said, giving him a shrewd look, which, perversely, he found that he preferred to the charming, seductive smiles, "I was thinking we might come to some sort of arrangement."

"Arrangement," he repeated.

"Agreement," she amended.

"Ah." He ought to have expected it—and, furthermore, he couldn't even call it that unreasonable a demand. The country ran on the backs of little agreements like these, after all. "What did you have in mind?"

"Perhaps you can promise that you'll tell whoever at the Flea sent you to Holloway's that you could find no evidence of wrongdoing whatsoever, and that we appear to be operating an entirely law-abiding business?"

"I think we can work something out," he said wearily, and she visibly brightened. He did not add that it was something of a relief; the thought of shutting down Holloway's, of repaying the kindness of Freddie Holloway and his family in such a way, had not sat right with him from the moment he'd walked out of Raffles's office. He felt a bit like a French aristocrat avoiding the guillotine.

Vesper clapped her hands together, delighted, as the taxi turned onto Devonshire Street and crawled to a stop before her parents' house—an imposing stone building with bow windows. Max had visited a couple of times, on trips home from Cambridge years earlier, when he and Freddie had been close. His parents' house could have fit inside the Holloway mansion three times over. Vesper rummaged in her handbag for a few coins, which she now pressed into his hand—enough to cover the taxi ride home, and the remainder of the journey for Max as well. He opened his mouth to protest, but she was speaking before he could. "Come to mine for dinner tomorrow—or today, technically, I suppose. Shall we say half seven? I'm in the mews flat just behind my parents' house—the one with the green door. I hope you're not allergic to cats!"

And, with that, she flung herself from the cab, turning to give him a brief, breezy wave as the cab drove away.

Leaving Max with plenty to occupy his thoughts for the rest of the drive back to Hampstead.

Chapter Five

Vesper had many virtues—presumably; most people did, after all—but being an early riser was not one of them.

"Ugh," she said later that morning as she opened her eyes to autumn sunlight streaming in through a crack in the curtains. She squinted at the clock on her bedside table—half eight, an hour that she would happily never greet consciously again in her life—and turned back to scowl at the reason she was awake right now:

Her cat, Sheep.

"Meow?" Sheep asked from her favorite perch: directly atop Vesper's chest, her fluffy white face approximately three inches from Vesper's.

"Urgh," Vesper said.

"Meow," Sheep replied, sounding offended. She leaned close enough to lick Vesper's nose, twice.

"Sheep, for Merlin's sake," Vesper said, reaching up to bodily toss the cat—all eight pounds of her—off the bed. Sheep landed on her feet, naturally, and leveled a wounded gaze at Vesper, allowing approximately one second of silence to elapse before commencing a rousing chorus of indignant meows.

"I'm up, I'm up," Vesper said, flinging back the eiderdown and shivering in the cool air of her bedroom. She'd worn her coziest flannel pajamas to bed the night before, not having any company that she cared to impress, and was glad of it this morning. She pulled back the curtains enough to glimpse a sliver of perfect, autumnal blue sky, and then—no longer able to ignore Sheep's mournful laments—padded to the kitchen, where she opened a tin of tuna for her ladyship.

Vesper set the kettle to boil on the hob and spooned tea leaves into her favorite yellow teapot that Cecily had brought home as a gift from her honeymoon in Italy. She considered the shelves above the hob, and reached for a tea tin that was labeled ASSAM but which, upon being opened, was revealed to contain a shimmering, faintly green powder. Vesper carefully spooned half a teaspoon into her pot, where it would dissolve into her tea, and replaced the tin on the shelf. Mackleworth's Headache Powder; there were any number of mundane headache remedies, of course, but none of them worked so well as Mackleworth's, which had been made with the Mackleworth family's carefully guarded Word for over two hundred years, and Vesper certainly wasn't going to stop using it just because it was technically illegal.

Once the water had boiled, Vesper took herself and her tea tray into the sitting room, eyeing the fireplace. Four hundred years ago, she—or someone in her family, at least—would have been able to light that fire with a single Word. Vesper thought, sometimes, about what it would have been like to have so much more power readily available—but, on the other hand, she was rather fond of automobiles, gramophones, and indoor plumbing, and so wasn't certain she'd wish to trade the many technological comforts of her life solely for the sake of a bit more magic in return. So, instead, she contented herself with crossing the room to toss a handful of Speedy Sparks Powder onto the logs in the grate, which obligingly burst into cheerful flames. It was still considerably more efficient than trying to coax a fire to life without magical assistance, even if it lacked the flair of spoken-word spells.

Stirring a healthy amount of both milk and sugar into her tea—Vesper was not one to skimp on little luxuries—she stared down at the morning papers, flicking through them hastily to see if there was any word of the previous night's events at Holloway's. After several minutes, she sagged back onto the settee, breathing a sigh of relief—the dailies did not seem to have picked up the story.

But still—if this was twice now, in a week, that someone had suffered a bad reaction to a potion or spell powder at a magical club, surely it was only a matter of time before the papers took notice. Which meant that, for the time being, helping Max bloody Ashbridge with his little investigation was a matter of self-preservation in multiple ways.

Vesper sighed, shaking her head as she sipped her tea. Sheep, having finished her breakfast, trotted into the room as if she owned the place and fixed Vesper with an inquisitive look.

"Meow?" she asked, tilting her head to the side.

"I don't know, old pal," Vesper said, reaching down to scoop the cat into her arms; she was fairly light, as most of her bulk was fluff, rather than body mass. "But I'm going to find out."

◆

Vesper might have known her reprieve from interrogation would only last so long—and the fact that she made it until eleven fifteen that morning was, in truth, nothing short of a minor miracle.

"Hello, darling," her mother said, causing Vesper to jump about a foot in the air as she poked a cautious head out her front door and prepared to set off, vague thoughts about a walk in Regent's Park and then popping round to see if Hazel was available for lunch swirling in her head. Her mother, however, had clearly anticipated that some such evasive maneuver was likely, because she was waiting, fully dressed, complete with a stylish pink cloche and a matching cape, directly outside Vesper's door.

"How long have you been standing there?" Vesper demanded, clutching her chest and waiting for her heart rate to return to normal.

"Only five minutes or so," her mother said brightly.

"Then how—oh," Vesper said, realizing at once what her mother had done. "Not that bloody prediction potion again."

"Yes, darling, that bloody prediction potion," Amelia agreed. The potion in question was made with a specific Word that Amelia had inherited from her own magical family, and allowed her to know whenever her children were about to leave or return to the house.

"I was just about to go for a walk in the park," Vesper said, in a desperate attempt at escape.

"I'm sure you were," her mother said, unfazed. "Why don't I join you, and while we walk, you can explain to me what exactly happened at the club last night."

Vesper sighed; she'd been hoping to stop by her parents' for cocktails that evening and present the tale of the previous night's events in a calm, rational manner, one that would reassure them that there was no cause for concern. The moment her mother had trapped her outside her front door, however, she'd known that this plan was no longer going to be possible. She wondered gloomily who had betrayed her: Amir? Any of the other half dozen staff members who had been present? Or did gossip simply travel that fast?

Vesper and her mother set off in the direction of the park. It was the sort of day that October was meant for, crisp and sunny and smelling faintly of woodsmoke. Vesper found herself possessed by the wild desire to gather conkers or pick apples, as if she were some sort of wholesome countryside lass and not someone who only owned one pair of shoes suitable for walking great distances.

"There was an incident last night," Vesper said, having delayed as long as was plausible by making a great show of cooing over every dog they passed on the street. "A gentleman had an unusual reaction to a Flotation Fizz."

"I see," Amelia said, her tone giving away nothing of her thoughts. They had reached the edge of the park, and began to meander down the Broad Walk. "And is he all right?"

"He is," Vesper said quickly. "The effects wore off quite rapidly."

She glanced sideways at her mother in time to see Amelia's

brow furrow slightly in thought; it was a gesture she tended to avoid if she could help it, out of vanity. The line-eliminating elixir she drank with her breakfast each morning—procured at considerable cost from the Grimme-Noxes, whose skills had always lain in the line of small, appearance-modifying spells and who in addition to their club ran a lucrative pharmacy as well—only lasted for a few hours, after all.

"If it was another one of these idiots with an allergy—"

"He said he'd never reacted badly to potions before," Vesper said, considering her words carefully. She didn't want to outright lie to her mother—that had a history of ending badly for her—but nor did she want to encourage even more meddling at Holloway's, not when she had a plan in place to get to the bottom of the matter. "But as it happens, there was someone present last night who wants to . . . look into it. So I'm going to help him."

An arched brow. "Oh? And who was that?"

"Maxwell Ashbridge."

"Ashbridge," her mother repeated, as if trying to place the name. A moment later, she cottoned. "Not Freddie's friend from Cambridge?"

"Yes," Vesper admitted.

"Is he not the one that your brother noted on his little *list* at dinner last night?"

"Mummy—"

"Oh, Vesper, for heaven's sake!" Amelia flung her hands into the air, startling a nearby pigeon, which hopped away in alarm. "When we were just discussing the fact that we need to be particularly careful."

"*I* wasn't the one who invited him to the club," Vesper said, nettled. "You might tell Freddie to speak to Dashiell St. Clair about the company he keeps."

Amelia sighed, shaking her head. "Wasn't he always horribly prudish about magic, too? That'll make him more difficult to bribe."

"Yes," Vesper said, the word clipped.

There were any number of reasons that the magical families had run into trouble and disapproval from the mundane world over the years—there were the aristocrats who had always found the magical families threatening; the royal family, too, had never been thrilled by the existence of a subset of society with powers the crown could not harness for themselves; there were the superstitious and the religious who believed that all so-called witchcraft was the work of the devil. Vesper didn't much care which camp Ashbridge himself fell into.

"It doesn't matter," Vesper said. "He's agreed not to shut down the club if I help him investigate the source of the bad potion, though."

"Help him how?"

Vesper shrugged. "Take him to a few of the other magical clubs—ones he'd have difficulty getting into on his own."

Amelia stopped in her tracks. "Vesper Holloway, you do not mean to tell me that you're helping him conduct *raids*."

"No!" Vesper protested. "He's not going to raid any of them—we're just trying to see if we can work out who's responsible for tampering with the magic. It's not as if the government's going to continue turning a blind eye if people are repeatedly falling ill when they visit one of the clubs. And *we* certainly don't want word to spread—it would be very bad for business."

"It will *also* be very bad for business if all the clubs in Marylebone are shut down by the Fleas. *And* if we find ourselves blacklisted among our colleagues because you became a government informant."

This, while a touch melodramatic, did give Vesper pause. An unpleasant chill crept through her, because she realized that her mother was right—her idea, which had seemed so brilliant at half past midnight, when she was shaken up from the evening's events and scrambling desperately to work out how to keep Ashbridge off her back, did have a rather obvious flaw to it.

A moment later, however, she brightened. "Ashbridge is coming to dinner tonight," she assured her mother. "I'll speak to him about all of this—see if I can't work some sort of promise out of him." While Ashbridge seemed to be alarmingly immune to her charms, that must simply indicate that she'd not been trying hard enough. She would *force* him to see things from her perspective, somehow. She was Vesper Holloway—she always got what she wanted.

Well, *almost* always.

Amelia still looked skeptical. "Darling, I'm not certain this is wise—"

"Well, I've no other choice. He saw someone quite plainly under the influence of a magical substance within the walls of Holloway's last night, and if we don't want him to shut us down, I'd better keep myself in his good graces. Unless you'd rather I rang him up and said that oh, never mind, I won't be helping him after all, and would he please consider *not* informing his superiors about the illegal trade we conduct on a nightly basis?"

Amelia sighed, but she was a practical enough creature to realize when a battle was lost—at least for the moment.

"Perhaps you ought to consider going to bed with him," she said, very casually, as if she were suggesting that Vesper invite Ashbridge over for tea.

"Mother!"

"What?" Amelia raised her hands. "If you seem lovestruck, then no one will think it odd to see you waltzing about with him. And he might prove *very* convincible afterward, you know—men so often do."

"I think that option will be my last resort," Vesper said diplomatically, not wanting to admit the fact that, unfortunately, Ashbridge had made it quite clear in the past that he had no interest at all in going to bed with her. "And I expect merely being seen with him will be enough to allow people to draw their own conclusions about what we're doing together."

"I suppose so," her mother agreed, sounding somewhat glum at being deprived of the entertainment of her youngest child whoring herself out for the sake of a clandestine investigation. "Your romantic history is a bit checkered, after all. I never thought that would be a good thing!"

And then, with a tinkling sort of laugh, she led Vesper on a brisk circuit of the park, during which Vesper wondered if her mother had just, in a backhanded sort of way, called her a loose woman, and whether she ought to be offended if she had.

Chapter Six

Max despised being late.

His father had been late, every time he'd ever spent an afternoon with Max during his childhood. His mum had always told him not to fret—that his father would be there in due time, that he'd likely got caught up with some sort of urgent business—but to Max, every time, it was a reminder that he was not important enough to be on time for.

"You can't possibly expect a woman to be ready when she says she will," Caro had scolded him more than once during their year together. He made it a general policy to not spend much time thinking about the woman he'd once thought he would marry, but she did have a way of occasionally creeping into his mind, unbidden. He wondered belatedly if Vesper Holloway were the same sort of woman as he stood at precisely half seven outside the green door in a narrow, cobblestoned mews that she had instructed him to call at.

The door opened, and she appeared, wearing a simple cream-colored dress and a thick blue cardigan that looked as though it had been in use for a number of seasons. It was quite a contrast to the glamorous Vesper Holloway that he'd seen at the club the night before.

"Hello," she said cheerfully, and glanced at the bakery loaf in his hands. "Don't trust me to feed you?" He chewed on the inside of his cheek for a moment, trying to work out a polite response to that, but she laughed and spared him. "Don't worry, our cook makes enough for about twelve—though, given how much my brother eats, that's barely sufficient when he comes round—and is constantly plying me with leftovers. I think she worries about me starving out here."

"Well," he said, following her into the flat, "you don't strike me as someone who would have spent much time in the kitchen."

"You have an awful lot of opinions about me for someone who doesn't know me." Vesper led him into the kitchen, which was filled with copper pots and expensive-looking crockery. A lemon was half-sliced on a butcher's block. "Sorry," she said over her shoulder, reaching for a knife and making quick work of the rest of it. "I wasn't expecting you yet."

"You did say seven thirty, didn't you?"

"People usually aren't quite so punctual."

"Fashionably late?" he asked. "I can't say I am very fashionable."

"Why does that not surprise me," she murmured. "Would you like a drink?"

"Depends on what's in it."

"If you're worried I'm going to slip you some sort of love potion and have my wicked way with you, you can relax. The Holloways' magic has never been good at that sort of recipe."

Max was busy trying *not* to allow a single image associated with the idea of wicked ways and Vesper to creep into his mind, and did not manage anything resembling a reply before she added, her tone brisk, "I was thinking perhaps a sidecar, but if you're more of a gin man—or whisky—or there's champagne, of course . . ."

"Of course," he muttered, at last recovering enough to speak. She narrowed her eyes at him, as if trying to work out whether he was teasing. "A sidecar is fine," he said, and after another moment's scrutiny, she nodded, scooped the lemon slices onto a plate, and led him through a doorway and into what turned out to be a small, cozy sitting room.

One that appeared to be inhabited by a ball of cotton wool.

"Meow?" the cotton wool said, revealing itself to be a mammal, rather than a bit of fluff.

"Who's this?" he asked, crouching next to the ottoman atop which the bit of fluff was elegantly reclining.

"That's Sheep," Vesper said, crossing to the gold-and-glass cart that housed any number of bottles of spirits, as well as several small amber bottles with handwritten labels on them. She glanced quickly over her shoulder at Max and tucked those out of sight behind the ice bucket, seeming to think he hadn't noticed. "She's spoiled rotten, so don't let her trick you into scratching her—she receives plenty of affection as it is."

"You have a cat named Sheep," he said, as Sheep enthusiastically thrust the top of her head into his hand.

"Yes," Vesper said, as though this should have been obvious. "Look at her. She looks like—"

"A brand-new feather duster that hasn't had the opportunity to be used yet," he suggested, and she frowned at him.

"Ah," he said, with great regret. "I forgot. You've no notion of what that is. You see, there is a substance called dust that accumulates on furniture—"

She laughed, turning back to the bar cart.

"She's a lovely cat," he said, by way of a peace offering. Women, he understood vaguely, appreciated compliments about their familiars.

"Thank you," she said, shaking her mixer with some vigor. He hadn't seen her behind the bar at her club, but the motion spoke of experience. He became conscious of the fact that they were alone in her flat, a fire lit in the grate, cocktails about to be consumed. It felt a bit intimate, and he cast his eyes around the room in an attempt to distract himself from any thoughts along those lines. It gave the impression of a tiny, perfect jewel box, every detail having been chosen with care: the dusky rose color of the walls; the blue willow vase on the mantel filled with a fat bouquet of dahlias; the enormous, gold-framed advertisement for a famous singer who had once appeared at Holloway's, before the war; an étagère filled with books, the spines worn and cracked; and a gramophone. The entire room seemed wonderfully, perfectly Vesper, despite the fact that he wouldn't have thought he knew her well enough to make any such assessment.

At the bar cart, Vesper divided the cocktail between two glasses and reached for a slice of lemon, then turned, handing him his drink. "Thank you for coming tonight." She raised her glass in a toast.

"Cheers." He took a sip; it was a rather nice cocktail. Under different circumstances, it would have made an excellent beginning to a promising evening.

But he was here to discuss business.

Vesper gestured to the dark blue silk sofa, and they took seats at opposite ends, keeping as much cushion space as possible between them.

"So," he said, setting his glass down decisively on the trunk she seemed to use as a coffee table and shifting slightly in his seat so that he could look at her more directly. Sheep took this as an invitation and immediately hopped onto his lap.

Vesper fixed her cat with a reproving stare.

Sheep lifted her back leg and licked herself in a delicate location, which was essentially the feline equivalent of the cut direct of the previous century's ballrooms.

"Cats have no loyalty," Vesper said, sounding so annoyed that Max nearly grinned, before he caught himself. He was there for business, not for smiling at pretty women.

"Did you have an idea of what our first night out together should be?"

"Well," she said slowly, and his focus sharpened on her, something in her tone sounding an alarm bell. "I was hoping to speak to you about that."

"What do you mean?"

She took a sip from her glass. "The fact is, Ashbridge, I'd like something in the way of . . . assurances. From you."

Christ almighty, hadn't they already covered this terrain

last night? "I told you, I'll lie about Holloway's and ensure that you're able to stay open."

"No—I know—but I need . . . something more."

"Such as?" he asked, biting back his impatience with some difficulty.

"I don't want you to use any information you gain to shut down the other clubs."

He stared at her, incredulous. "You do realize that's my *job*, don't you?"

"Yes, but—well, I can't be the person who helps you gain entry to a club, only for you to then pass on whatever you see there to Scotland Yard."

"What do you expect from me, precisely? Shall I give you my word that, for the duration of our work together, I'll not pass on any information I gather to anyone else at the F.L.E.A.?"

"I was rather hoping you'd agree to take a Promising Potion," she said matter-of-factly.

He blinked. "A what?"

"It's quite clever, actually—one of the other families brews it. You take the potion, and then anything you say in the quarter hour after consuming it can only be uttered if you're speaking the complete truth, and you mean it wholeheartedly. A lot of magical couples drink it during their weddings, before saying their vows."

"No."

She frowned. "What?" This clearly had not been the reply she was expecting.

He leaned forward. "I am not drinking a potion."

"But if you truly mean what you say—"

"I *do* mean what I say. But I don't use magic. Ever."

"You'd be the first Flea I've ever met who didn't," she muttered, irritation lacing her voice.

"F.L.E.A. And I can't speak to what anyone else is getting up to, but I promised myself a long time ago I'd never use magic, and I don't intend to change now."

She threw her hands up. "And you just expect me to take your *word* for it?" She gave a sharp shake of her head. "No. If you betray me, our business and reputation in the magical world could be destroyed. I want you to give me something that could be equally damaging to *you*."

He stared at her. "You want me to tell you a secret to use as blackmail?"

She smiled sweetly. "Hopefully I won't have to use it, if your word's as good as you say it is. Or are you such an upstanding citizen that you can't possibly think of *anything* that you'd be embarrassed to have known about you?"

He hesitated, even though he knew precisely what he could tell her—the piece of information that could destroy his career, if it were known. "There's something," he said at last.

Her smile turned smug. "I thought there might be." She rose to her feet, and crossed to a rolltop desk tucked into one corner; there were a number of novels with somewhat lurid titles stacked atop it in haphazard piles. She rummaged in a drawer, and returned a moment later with a piece of heavy stationery, embossed with the words FROM THE DESK OF VESPER HOLLOWAY, complete with a fanciful illustration of a golden bumblebee. "Write it here."

He accepted the paper and the fountain pen she handed

him, and then, after considering for several seconds, scrawled a single sentence. He felt her eyes on him as he wrote, but he didn't look at her, instead looking at the words he'd just written, which stared up at him in stark black ink. He hesitated for another long moment, and then handed the paper to her, his heart pounding heavily in his chest.

She met his eyes, and held them for a second. And then, without glancing down at the piece of paper she held, she folded it in half, slid the document into an envelope decorated with another embossed golden bumblebee, and sealed it. "I'll be keeping this, of course."

"Of course," he agreed, watching as she tucked the envelope carefully inside the rolltop desk and locked it again.

She turned back to him, leaning one hip against the desk. "I must have lost my mind, to trust you—"

"I'm feeling exactly the same," he replied. "Since we both seem to have temporarily gone mad, we might as well agree to trust each other, and get on with it."

She clinked her glass gently against his in some sort of unspoken sealing of their contract, took a sip, then sat down next to him once more, her manner suddenly businesslike. "I was thinking we'd start with Mauve's," she said, and he frowned, searching his mind for any knowledge of that particular club. He drew a blank.

"Which one is that?"

"It's on—" She broke off, suddenly looking a bit canny. "You'll see."

This did not instill great confidence in him. "Why won't you tell me?"

"Because you're a bloody Flea."

"All right," he said, because he suspected that his lack of a reaction would irk her, and he was rewarded with a flash of disappointment in her gaze. "When shall we go? Tonight?"

She shook her head. "No. I'm meant to be at Holloway's in a couple of hours, and—well, I don't want to take an evening away from the club at present."

"Surely someone else in your family can keep an eye on things," he said.

"Oh, they certainly could," she agreed, "but I'd rather be there myself. Perhaps we might go on Sunday evening instead?"

He frowned. "Is it open on Sundays?"

"Yes. Private members' clubs are exempt from your ludicrous licensing rules." This was true; while Britain had not followed the lead of America in making alcohol entirely illegal, there were still strict licensing laws that limited the hours during which alcohol could be sold. These laws, however, did not apply to private clubs that held licenses; they were instead allowed to operate according to their own bylaws. As Max understood it, however, they had some sort of agreement with the illicit nightclubs that sold spirits late at night, out of licensing hours—the magical clubs closed up shop earlier than the nightclubs, so that their patrons would move on elsewhere to consume their out-of-hours alcohol, having imbibed their fill of magical cocktails first.

"Don't suppose anyone minds about the Sunday hours anyway—I can't imagine you're much of a churchgoing set."

She let out a hoot of laughter.

"It's nice to know that you are so concerned about our immortal souls, but no. However, you'll be pleased to learn that I did protect your virtue in one regard."

"How's that?"

"My mother suggested I go to bed with you," she said serenely. "But you needn't worry I'm about to start flinging myself at you—I told her no."

Max choked on his drink.

"There's no need to be so virginal about it, Ashbridge."

Sheep, meanwhile—offended by the amount of coughing-and-spluttering-and-general-movement from the man who had been so conveniently serving as her seat—hopped off his lap and settled onto the sofa next to Vesper instead.

"Dare I ask why your mother thought we should go to bed together?" he asked, recovering somewhat.

"I confessed our plan to her—"

"Brilliant. Just what we need. More Holloways involved."

"—and she thought that if we were romantically intertwined, it might add a frisson of realism to our covert activities. However, I convinced her that merely the appearance of us bopping about together will likely send people's minds in that direction anyway, and we needn't get our genitals involved."

She smiled at him, reclining against the back of the couch and draping one arm lazily along its top. Next to her, Sheep rolled over once again, her fluffy fur brushing against Vesper's leg where the skirts of her dress had ridden up. It was a simple garment with a drop waist and pleated skirts that hit just below her knees, but now there was quite a lot of thigh on display.

He kept his gaze fixed carefully northward. No thighs. Nothing below the . . . waist? No, chest? No, chin. Safest to keep things above the chin.

Above the mouth, actually. She was merely a pair of green eyes and a nose that was currently being wrinkled at him in a skeptical sort of way.

He reached for his voice and tried not to think about the word "genitals" being uttered in that matter-of-fact-way. "This is the plan, then? We're to go to Mauve's tomorrow evening and start our investigation, no genitals will be involved, and people are free to assume whatever they like."

"Correct on all fronts," she said, looking a bit downcast, as though he'd spoiled her fun.

"Brilliant," he said, downing the rest of his drink. "Now, how about that dinner?"

With that, the business portion of the evening concluded, and several minutes later he found himself seated at Vesper's kitchen table, eating a delicious beef stew under Sheep's watchful eye. ("She's hoping for crumbs," Vesper said, with a jaundiced look at her cat, who gave an innocent-sounding chirp by way of reply.)

The stew was warm, and the kitchen was cozy, and Vesper spent several minutes relaying the (frankly ridiculous) plot of the novel she was currently reading, as if she and Max were old friends, and Max realized, to his astonishment, that it all felt vaguely . . . companionable. This was not an emotion he'd ever expected to feel around a member of the Holloway family again.

And one that would prove to be remarkably short-lived, because, not fifteen seconds after this thought crossed his mind, there was the sound of a door opening, and a still-familiar voice hollering, "Vesper!"

Five seconds later, Freddie Holloway poked his head into the kitchen.

His gaze immediately landed on Max. Narrowed.

And then, without preamble, he said, "What the fuck are you doing here?"

Chapter Seven

Vesper supposed she should have expected something like this.

"Freddie, sit down," she said, brandishing a crust of bread at the lone empty chair at the table she and Ashbridge currently occupied.

"I'll pass," her brother replied, his tone clipped. He was dressed for the evening—in a full suit and tails—and his blond hair was artfully disheveled in a way she recognized would have taken him at least a quarter hour before the mirror.

"Go on," she coaxed. "There's bread and butter."

"Well, perhaps . . ."

He was seated and had Vesper's pot of expensive salted butter before him on the table in a trice. "Now," he said threateningly—though the effect was somewhat diminished by the crust of heavily buttered bread in his hand—"what's this about?" He split a menacing look between Vesper and Ashbridge, who was looking inscrutable. And handsome, in his wool jacket and tie, his carefully shaved jaw a bit tight—his only tell.

Not that his handsomeness had anything to do with the proceedings, but Vesper, as a connoisseur, couldn't help but notice.

"We had a small incident at the club last night," Vesper began, and Freddie waved an impatient hand.

"I know—what do you think I wanted to speak to you about?"

"Well, Ashbridge was there."

Freddie turned to Ashbridge. "Was he?"

Ashbridge cleared his throat. "I was." He met Freddie's gaze.

"For a simple evening's pleasure, no doubt?" Freddie asked, his voice lightly laced with venom. "You being so fond of cutting loose."

Vesper had to hand it to Ashbridge: He must be a hell of a card player. His expression—sharp-eyed, stern-mouthed—didn't waver. Instead, he merely said, "Something like that."

"It's the second incident of a contaminated potion in a week," Vesper reminded her brother. "Which seems like a bit of a coincidence, don't you think? So Ashbridge and I have decided to visit some of the other Marylebone clubs and see if we can uncover who's behind this."

Freddie looked at her, incredulous. "You're going to take *him* to clubs in"—he lowered his voice to a dramatic stage whisper—"*Marylebone*?"

"It's always seemed like a very nice neighborhood," Ashbridge offered blandly, and Vesper was sorely tempted to laugh. She could practically see the steam coming out of Freddie's ears.

"Are you trying to get us all arrested?" Freddie asked, ignoring Ashbridge entirely. "Vesper, I know good judgment isn't your strong suit, but this is mad, even for you."

"Ashbridge isn't going to arrest anyone," Vesper snapped, her patience growing thin. "We have an . . . agreement. He's here to investigate the contaminated potions, and will not be sending in Scotland Yard to raid any of the clubs in question."

"I can't believe Mother didn't try to talk you out of this. Perhaps Dad—"

"Is there a reason," Ashbridge asked, "that you can't treat your sister like an adult?"

Vesper and Freddie blinked in unison, and turned to him. "What business is it of yours?" Freddie asked.

"Merely a question." Ashbridge sounded cool and unbothered, but his gaze was fixed on Freddie with a keenness that Vesper could tell was irking her brother.

"Right." Freddie turned back to Vesper as if this interruption had not occurred. "I see you're going to be stubborn about this, so I won't waste my time further, as I've somewhere to be."

"Who's the unlucky gentleman?" Vesper asked, then darted a quick glance at Ashbridge; he looked unfazed, so he either had an even better poker face than she'd thought, or—more likely—was already perfectly well aware that Freddie preferred men. The two of them had been quite close, after all. The laws outlawing sodomy had been repealed decades earlier—magical society had never been very prudish about what went on in the privacy of the bedchamber, and these attitudes had eventually worn off on the mundanes as well—but these relationships were still a bit frowned on by a certain subset of mundane society.

"None of your concern," Freddie said, with a significant look at Ashbridge, and Vesper nodded. That meant it was a political assignment, rather than a romantic one. Freddie was active with an underground group that worked on several fronts—distributing pamphlets, giving public speeches, and trying to educate the general populace on the uses of magic and the harm of Forbiddance, while *also* infiltrating more conservative spaces in an attempt to keep tabs on what the anti-magic cohort in Parliament and employed by the government was up to. In another moment, he was on his feet, nicking a last slice of bread from the platter—where Ashbridge had carefully sliced the loaf—before vanishing with a last nod for Vesper, and not so much as a glance in farewell for Ashbridge.

A few seconds later, they heard the front door slam behind him.

Vesper turned an inquiring look to Ashbridge, who had rededicated himself to his stew with an expression of intent concentration. His fingers were oddly elegant where they gripped his spoon, she noticed—somehow at odds with the rest of him, so broad-shouldered and sturdy-looking.

"I don't suppose that you'd like to make nice with Freddie, just to make this a bit easier on us all?"

"If Freddie wasn't such a meddling idiot, it *would* be easier," came his terse reply. He set his spoon down in his empty bowl, then pushed his chair back and carried the dish to the sink.

"Are you . . . doing the dishes?" she asked, astonished, as he turned on the tap and reached for the scouring brush.

"I know this might shock you," he said over his shoulder, "but they do not, in fact, wash themselves."

"You are the most mystifying man."

"I'm so glad—anything to keep Vesper Holloway on her toes." She couldn't be certain, with his back to her once more, but she thought he might be smiling. "I was thinking, by the way, that I ought to come to work with you tonight."

"Whatever for?"

"We didn't get a chance to question the staff last night."

This was true; it had been rather chaotic, and everyone had been quite focused on ensuring that none of the club's patrons were unduly distressed (and, more importantly, that no one did anything stupid, like summon the police).

She brightened, spotting an opportunity. "If I tell my parents that you're coming with me to the club, they're less likely to insist that I need a nursemaid."

Ashbridge glanced at her with a frown as he set his bowl on the drying rack. "A nursemaid?"

Vesper waved a hand. "They're worried about—" She broke off, realizing, belatedly, to whom she was speaking. "They don't want to take any chances with the club."

He looked back over his shoulder at her again for a long moment, clearly trying to work out what it was that she wasn't saying. She kept her lips firmly pressed together, however, and at last, he merely said, "You seem to have things well in hand, from what I saw last night."

Her brows rose in surprise. "Thank you. My family don't *quite* seem to see it that way, though."

"Well. Perhaps they ought to come tonight, so they can see what I did."

"They'll be there often enough—they don't want me alone

at Holloway's until . . . well, until things feel a bit less . . . uncertain."

He turned to face her, propping a hip against the counter. In the close confines of her kitchen, he seemed particularly tall. "I don't know what it is that you think you know—what tip-off you've received—but if you're concerned that someone is going to . . ." He trailed off with a frown, clearly choosing his words carefully. "To make an example of you, in some way," he continued at last, "then I'll remind you of what I promised you. I don't go back on my word."

"I know," she said. She had, after all, asked him not to tell Freddie anything about what had happened on that humiliating night years earlier, and he hadn't spoken a word. She was trusting him rather a lot, at the moment—and yet, she somehow didn't think she was wrong to do so. She held his gaze for a second, and *almost* thought that she could read something in it. Just as quickly, however, it shuttered.

Instead, he reached for a tea towel, and nodded at the dishes still on the table. "Bring those here. If we're going to play detective, let's at least finish the dishes first."

◆

When they arrived at Holloway's, the Saturday night revelry at the club was already in full swing.

Vesper had changed clothes before they'd left her flat, vanishing into her bedroom and reemerging in a black evening gown with a plunging neckline, a string of pearls, and a ridiculous headdress with feathers.

"Do you have a swan corpse hidden in your bedroom?" he asked as he reached for his coat.

"Coming from you, that's downright flattery."

Now, they were at Holloway's at half past nine, the club heaving with patrons—more than a few whom Max recognized from his university days, and at least one whom he knew from the Home Office. Nice to see that the grand tradition of government hypocrisy was alive and well.

Vesper linked her arm through his as soon as they'd left their coats with the cloakroom attendant. "Now, pretend that you enjoy my company," she said out of the corner of her mouth, and Max obligingly plastered a neutral expression on his face. Vesper gave a dramatic sigh.

They made their way through the crowds, and Max watched as Vesper greeted what felt like every person she passed. Cheeks were kissed. Compliments were exchanged. At least one blatant attempt at seduction was fended off (aided, perhaps, by the glower that had crept across Max's face before he could stop himself). It was all surprisingly interesting to witness; he had never possessed the sort of easy charm that seemed to come naturally to all members of the Holloway family, and he found himself admiring the skill involved in putting everyone at ease.

A brass band was playing on the stage in the bar, and the dance floor was packed with couples, cocktails in hand. Plenty more clubgoers were grouped around the small tables that lined the edges of the room. The scene was not dissimilar to those of many of the mundane nightclubs that Max had visited, except for the greater sense of luxury here—the glasses were crystal;

the tables of the glossiest, finest wood; the chandelier overhead glittering, the jewels on the clubgoers sparkling in its light. Many nightclubs felt a bit seedy, Max thought; Holloway's, despite its trade in illicit goods, felt anything but.

It felt glamorous, and Max could understand its infectious appeal.

Vesper, her arm still linked with his, led him through the packed room, waving at the man and woman behind the bar, who nodded in greeting at her but otherwise carried on with the business of making drinks; the man had a cocktail shaker in hand, while the woman was sliding a delicate curl of orange peel onto the rim of a glass. Vesper headed for the edge of the room, where, through an arched doorway obscured by a gauzy curtain, a small alcove contained a bookcase. This nook was guarded by an attendant, attired in an immaculate coat and tails; upon seeing Vesper, he stepped aside with a nod. Vesper reached out with a sure hand, removed a book from the shelf, and—with a faint *click*—the case creaked open, revealing a doorway that Max had to hunch to pass through.

The space that he emerged into was low-ceilinged and intimate. The lighting was dimmer here; instead of a glittering chandelier, there were floor lamps with rosy shades tucked into corners and candles flickering in golden holders on the tables. The walls were papered in a beautiful navy-and-silver pattern, the ceiling decorated with intricate molding. An antique mirror in a silver frame hung on one wall, reflecting the room's inhabitants; a marble fireplace occupied an enormous expanse of the wall opposite the bar, flames crackling cheerfully on this chilly autumn night. The music from the other room was easily audible here—Max gazed along the walls and ceiling, searching for the vent that would allow it to pass through so clearly—but there was no dancing. Instead, the clubgoers were far more likely to be engaged with themselves and their friends and the effects of whatever it was they had consumed.

There was one table whose occupants had clearly had the Flotation Fizzes—the very potion that had gone so disastrously wrong the night before. Instead of spinning alarmingly near the ceiling like that unfortunate fellow, however, this group merely hovered a foot or two off the ground, laughing uproariously and clinking glasses of champagne. At another table, there was a delighted exclamation as, before Max's eyes, a woman finished the dregs of a drink and then was immediately engulfed in a puff of smoke, which cleared to reveal an entirely different dress to the one she'd been wearing seconds before.

"What the hell," he muttered, and Vesper glanced at him, grinning. "It's the New-Fashioned—gives you a new outfit. Only temporarily, though—you drink a second one before you leave the club, which will restore your original clothing."

"What happens if you don't drink the second one before leaving?"

"The moment you set foot outside the club, your magical outfit vanishes, leaving you in your knickers," she said, and laughed in delight at whatever expression crossed his face. "Come on," she urged, tugging him toward the bar, where a woman in a black silk dress with ruby-red lips was handing a packet of spell powder to a customer.

"Hello—oh, it's you," the woman said, her practiced smile slipping from her lips when she recognized Vesper. Her gaze slid to Max; she blinked, then looked back at Vesper questioningly.

"Anna Llewelyn, meet Max Ashbridge," Vesper said, and Max leaned forward to reach across the bar to shake Miss Llewelyn's hand. She was about his age, or perhaps a bit older, he thought; she had dark curly hair and dark eyes, and the lilt in her voice made him wonder if she came from one of the magical villages in Wales. He'd never visited them, but knew from all he'd read and heard that their remote location in the mountains meant that they were largely carrying on as though Forbiddance didn't exist.

"Anna, were you the one to serve the chap last night?" Vesper asked. "The one who—er—"

"The whirling dervish?" Miss Llewelyn asked, a mischievous grin breaking across her face. "Indeed I was."

"Could we speak to you for a moment, then?" Vesper asked. She tilted her head toward the other end of the bar, where another bartender was uncorking a bottle of champagne. "Aiden can manage on his own for a spell, I think."

"All right." Miss Llewelyn's gaze was nakedly curious now. Vesper led them behind the bar and through a small doorway set among the shelves of spirits and mysterious bottles. They emerged into a narrow hallway painted a rich blue, the walls lined with framed newspaper articles. Leaning closer, Max realized that they contained coverage of the club from over the years—largely from *The Spark*, but some from *The Times* and *The Evening Standard* as well.

Vesper brought them to some sort of sitting room, presumably for use by the club's staff, which was filled with well-loved furniture and an enormous carpet in an intricate blue-and-brown pattern. There was a fireplace, though the fire within had been allowed to go out; Vesper crossed to the mantel, retrieved a bit of powder from a battered silver pot, and, with a surreptitious glance over her shoulder at Max, tossed it in the grate. Immediately, flames whooshed to life.

Precisely how many small bits of magic, he wondered suddenly, were the Marylebone families still using?

She turned back to them, looking pleased with herself as she tucked an unruly curl behind one ear. Miss Llewelyn wasted no time in sinking down onto one of the tartan sofas that faced the fireplace. After a moment's hesitation, Max joined her. She eyed him with considerable interest; Max couldn't work out if she suspected, somehow, that he was an F.L.E.A.—or at least somehow not sympathetic to the magical cause—or if it was solely his presence here with Vesper that was causing such scrutiny.

Vesper perched on the edge of an armchair; the fire that had roared to life in the grate behind her now gilded the bare skin of her arms, the curve of her cheek. She met Miss Llewelyn's gaze. "We're trying to work out what went wrong last night, so we can ensure it never happens again. Do you recall anything about the chap who ordered the Fizz?"

Miss Llewelyn looked back at Vesper, chewing her lower lip thoughtfully. "There was a group of boys who all wanted Flotation Fizzes—five or six of them, at least. And it's an easy enough potion to make—just gin, lemon, champagne, and a bit of the lemon-flavored syrup, isn't it? I could make it in my sleep. I made them all at once and handed them off to the boys. I can't understand how something could have gone wrong with the magic itself, if none of the others were ill."

Vesper was frowning now. "You're certain you made the whole batch at the same time?"

Miss Llewelyn nodded. "They were all standing there—one of them offered to buy me a potion so I could join them. Somehow, I mustered the willpower to decline," she added with an eloquent eye roll.

Vesper's frown deepened. "And you handed them all to the boys themselves?"

Miss Llewelyn paused, clearly deep in thought. "A couple of the boys—and one of them I handed to a girl they were with."

"A girl?" Max asked, straightening in his seat. "What girl?"

Miss Llewelyn shrugged. "Blond. Slender. She had beautiful blue eyes, and the loveliest long eyelashes—she was very pretty, and clearly one of those women who knows it. She'd already had a potion or two—I noticed the shimmer." She gestured at her hairline. "Actually, come to think of it, I'm not certain she *was* with them—the boys, I mean. She sort of materialized as soon as I began handing out the potions, and the two boys who had come to collect them couldn't carry them all, so she took one to deliver to someone."

"The one whose potion was contaminated?" Vesper asked.

"I don't know. I wasn't looking at their faces that carefully. They all sort of blended together—young, posh, English, you know?"

Max, after years at Harrow and then, after the war, Cambridge, *did* know.

"How long were they in the backdoor bar, after drinking their potions?" Max asked.

"About three-quarters of an hour, I suppose; the Flotation

Fizz is pretty fast-acting, only takes about five minutes or so for it to kick in, but then it only lasts for about a half hour—unless," she added cannily, "you buy another." She leaned forward confidingly. "Vesper's *very* good at convincing men that they ought to just buy a second potion to have on hand when the first one wears off."

"Why does that not surprise me," Max murmured, and Vesper laughed. It was a loud, delighted sound—entirely different from the coy, tinkling, flirtatious laugh she'd given him the night before at the club, when she'd been trying to work out why he was there.

"I lost sight of them at some point," Miss Llewelyn continued, "so they must've gone out to the main bar once they stopped floating. Or once they *thought* they had."

"And what about the woman who was with them?" Vesper asked.

"I didn't see her again," Miss Llewelyn said. "I didn't think about it, given all the chaos."

Vesper turned her head sharply in Max's direction, and he met her gaze with a grim twist of the mouth.

If someone *had* somehow tampered with the potion—slipped something into it, or performed some magic of their own—then this woman sounded like an excellent candidate. The problem now, of course, was that they had no bloody clue who she was, or how to find her.

Chapter Eight

The following evening found Max standing at a corner on Marylebone High Street, hunching his shoulders against a nip in the air and wondering somewhat warily what the evening held in store. He was, after all, a representative of His Majesty's government, headed into a hotbed of illegal magical activity with only Vesper Holloway to act as his guide.

There was a tap on his arm, interrupting these somewhat dark thoughts. "There you are!"

He turned, and Vesper was standing before him on the street corner, her blond hair gleaming in the light of the streetlamps and the passing motorcars. She wore a red velvet cape and a matching hat.

"You're fifteen minutes late," he informed her, and instead of apologizing, she smiled.

"I *knew* you would be one of those sorts of men," she said, and then, without another word, reached out to link her arm through his before setting off down the street. Despite the fact that it was a Sunday, Marylebone was bustling, light and music and laughter pouring out of open doors all around them, motorcars inching past on the crowded streets. A decade or two earlier, there would have been people spilling onto the pavement from the various restaurants and clubs, clutching packets of spell powder in their hands or visibly under the temporary effects of some spell or other. Now, however, they were more circumspect, and the merriment that surrounded them showed no blatant signs of being magical in origin, for all of Max's suspicions.

"Here we are," Vesper said, coming to a halt so abruptly that Max's shoulder jostled hers as their linked arms forced him to stop as well. She was standing in front of what at first glance appeared to be a brick wall, but she took a step forward, tugging Max along with her, and he realized a moment later that it was merely a very well-cast spell; before him was a nondescript wooden door, and above it an illuminated sign reading MAUVE'S in letters that sparkled in a way he felt certain had to be magical in origin.

He arched a brow, willing himself not to be impressed. "Spellwork?"

"Spells—good ones, powerful ones, *proper* ones, like we used to be able to cast—don't wear off for centuries," Vesper confirmed. He noticed a slight note of wistfulness in her voice; the fact was, for all his irritation about the magical families blatantly flouting Forbiddance laws right beneath the government's nose, the magical world was still a shadow of what it once had been. Their potions and powders and elixirs were impressive, but nothing compared to the ability to cast spells by hand, to the powerful magic that had once been commonplace in this country.

"Is there a way to . . . tell?" he asked, a bit uncertain. "If something's been bespelled, I mean."

She nodded. "You know the sheen around the hairline when magic is consumed?"

"Yes. Always seemed like a bit of a weakness with magic, actually."

She frowned. "How so?"

"Well. It makes it pretty obvious that someone's eaten or drunk something, doesn't it?"

"Yes," she said patiently. "Almost like a guardrail."

It was his turn to frown. "A guardrail," he repeated.

"Think about it—it makes it safer. If someone's been bespelled to change their appearance, you'll know it—or at least you'll know that they've done *something.* It's not very specific, of course, and it doesn't tell you what sort of powder or potion they've consumed, but you know that something magical is occurring. So if you're in a circumstance where you're feeling suspicious, it can alert you that magic's being used, even if you don't know what sort."

"I," he began, and then fell silent, considering. He'd always thought of magic as a sneaky, underhanded sort of thing—a way of cheating the natural order, so to speak.

"It's helpful for women, too," Vesper added, almost as an afterthought. "Why do you think we like checking our appearances so much? If you're out for a drink with someone for the first time, you can pop to the toilet and make sure he hasn't slipped anything into your drink when you weren't looking—

unless you're already drinking something magical, of course." She shrugged. "It's not foolproof, obviously, but it feels . . . honest, I suppose. If you're going to use magic, it feels like there *should* be a sign of it somewhere, don't you think?"

It was a view of magic that Max had never considered before, one that he didn't quite know how to reconcile with his feelings on the matter. And now clearly wasn't the moment to work it out.

"Anyway," Vesper continued, waving her hand as if to dismiss the conversation, "there *are* signs sometimes, if a physical item has been enchanted. If it's painted, there's usually a bit of a glittery sheen at the end of a brushstroke, for example. With a wall like this, it's trickier to tell, but sometimes, if you catch it out of the corner of your eye, you might notice the faintest layer of shimmer." She turned to look up at him with a single raised eyebrow. "Now, if you're done asking questions, are you ready to actually go in?" It felt like a dare somehow. He tucked her arm more firmly against his side and reached out to seize the brass doorknob and tug the door open.

"After you," he said and, with a slight incline of his head, ushered her inside.

Mauve's was . . . feminine, with its blush-pink walls and delicate chaise longues and spindly-legged tables. Chandeliers hung from the ceiling, and the resulting light was soft, rosy. Romantic. There were waiters—male and female alike, all attired in rather dashing black coats and bow ties—quietly making their way around the room, bearing trays of burnished silver, piled with cocktail glasses, goblets, and pearlescent envelopes, each sealed with a distinctive bright pink wax heart, that Max suspected contained spell powders.

"Well, Ashbridge, what do you think?" Vesper asked, from where she had drawn to a halt a few feet ahead.

"It's very . . . pink," he offered, and she laughed. She wasted no time in shedding her coat, and Max closed his eyes for a brief moment at the sight of her, shoulders bare but for a few feathers, shimmering in a gold sequined frock that ended in another festoon of feathers just above her knees. She handed her coat off to a cloakroom attendant, Max following suit, and then turned back to face him.

"Shall we find somewhere to sit first?" she suggested. "I'd like to take a look around, see if there's anyone I recognize here tonight before we do anything else."

"Do you know the owners?" he asked.

"Yes, of course," she said. "Everyone knows Genevieve Colton."

He frowned, the name worrying at the edge of his mind.

"Her husband was Horatius Colton," Vesper prompted. "Who owned *The Spark*?"

Ah, yes. A newspaper baron who'd died decades prior; he'd owned the storied magical newspaper beloved by the Marylebone families, which was more or less the bane of Max's existence, obsessed as it was with reporting on the mistakes and mishaps of various employees of the F.L.E.A., Scotland Yard, and any politicians who supported Forbiddance.

"Genevieve's quite colorful," Vesper informed him, lowering her voice as if worried that the lady in question might pop out from behind a chaise longue at the sound of her own name. "Ever since she was widowed, she's had a never-ending string of affairs with actresses and lady artists—the club used to be called

Colton's, but she renamed it after a lover who died in a tragic mushroom-foraging accident."

"I've always said fungi are dangerous."

Vesper blinked at him. "Don't tell me you've got a sense of humor buried in there somewhere, Ashbridge."

"Only very deeply."

"Genevieve's friends with my grandmother—a terrifying woman," she said with a shudder. "Grandmama," she clarified, seeing Max's inquisitive look. "Not Genevieve."

"I can only imagine," he murmured, and Vesper narrowed her eyes at him. "However," he added, before she could make up her mind whether or not to take offense, "if you know her, perhaps you might convince her to open up a bit? Could you ask her if there's been a blonde lurking around the club lately, or if she's ever left her workroom unattended while mixing spell powders? Perhaps you could . . ." He trailed off, realizing that Vesper was regarding him with an expression of disbelief.

"What is it?" he asked, reaching up uncomfortably to straighten his tie.

"You cannot be serious," she stated quite firmly, as though to will this to be true.

"About which part?"

"All of it." He had the impression that had they not been in a crowded nightclub she would have thrown her hands up in exasperation. "Is this your idea of a stealthy undercover operation? You may as well slap on that badge of yours and climb up onstage and announce to the entire club what you're doing."

"And I suppose you've a better idea?"

"We've only been here two minutes, so let's perhaps give the illusion that we're out and about having a good time before we start interrogating the staff like . . . well, like . . ."

"Like F.L.E.A.s?"

"Precisely. Let's find a table."

She hooked her hand around his wrist and proceeded to lead him deeper into the club, which was busy enough but not entirely packed. Based on the number of people they'd passed on the street while walking here, he'd expected more of a crowd.

He mentioned this to Vesper, and she smiled at him. "They keep a list."

"A list?"

"Of living people who've been given the address. Every time Genevieve tells the address to someone, she enters it into this enormous ledger she has in her office. It's enchanted to never allow more than a set number of names in the ledger at once; when someone dies, or moves away, or simply falls out of favor, the name is removed, making room for a new one."

"Falls out of favor?" he repeated. "But even if they fell out of favor, wouldn't they still remember the address? How do the staff ensure they don't come back?"

"The door won't appear for them. The magic of the door and the ledger are linked—some spellwork the family did when the club was founded in the days of the Georgians, when our magic was more powerful."

Max wasn't certain whether to be impressed or horrified that magic this ancient could still exist in the heart of London, in the present day. He contemplated this as they made their way around the tables and armchairs and settees that littered the space. At one table they passed, he saw a man tap the contents of a paper packet into the drink before him, using his finger to give the mixture a quick stir. They'd moved on before he could see what the effects of the spell powder would be.

"This will do," Vesper said at last.

She'd led him to a table set into a darkened corner so that two sides were parallel to the walls. She and Max took these seats, and as Max leaned back slightly, feeling the comforting protection of the wall just inches behind him, he felt a tiny bit of the tension in his shoulders release.

Vesper was more observant than he'd expected, because she cast him a long sideways glance and said, "Now, will you relax a bit?"

"I'm not—*not* relaxed."

"Your shoulders are practically at your ears."

"That's just how I sit."

"No one sits like that. Shall I go fetch you a drink? I can't remember the last time I saw someone in such desperate need of one."

"What about the bits of magical frippery you're so fond of? Not going to encourage me to take a relaxing potion instead?"

"Knowing you, you'd spend so much time feeling guilty about it that you wouldn't even enjoy it," she said, which he was very much afraid was actually the truth.

Willing his shoulders to loosen just a bit, he decided that a change in subject was necessary. "Do you come here often?" he asked. He imagined that her responsibilities at Holloway's kept her evenings occupied.

"Sometimes," she said, with a lazy, one-shouldered shrug that had the effect of drawing his attention to the shoulder in question, to the smooth skin on display. Her hair was so short that it did nothing to hide the small birthmark in the shape of a crescent moon sitting just above her clavicle, and he found his gaze fixed on the spot.

"Is there something on my dress?" she asked, the sound of her voice sufficient to draw his eyes back to her face. She was glancing down at the bodice of her dress, a faint frown on her forehead, her short golden curls falling into her face as she searched futilely for a stain.

"I was woolgathering. You were saying?"

"I—oh, yes. I do come here sometimes, when I have a night off from the club. I like that the staff here don't suffer fools gladly."

"Meaning . . . ?"

"Meaning," she said, "that if a man gets overly friendly with a lady—or another man, I suppose—who doesn't welcome his attentions, they waste no time in booting him out and ensuring the doors to the club are barred to him for the rest of his life. We do the same at Holloway's," she added. "After a while, you learn which places take things like this seriously and which ones don't. Grenoble's for example—I'd avoid it. The younger son frequents the place, and he's a cad."

Max offered a regretful sigh. "If only I hadn't promised not to shut any clubs down while conducting this investigation . . ."

Vesper grinned. "Don't tempt me." Next to them, there was a sudden clatter of breaking glass, and Max startled slightly. A quick glance confirmed that someone had merely dropped a champagne coupe, but it was too late: Vesper was giving him an exasperated look. "Ashbridge, you're downright twitchy. Illegal activity doesn't agree with you."

"I think it is very telling that you consider that to be an insult," he informed her, and she laughed.

"Go and fetch us some drinks," she said. "A gin fizz for me, please. You might want to consider something stronger for yourself, if you're going to survive the evening with your nerves intact." She looked at him expectantly, as if she thought he would immediately trot to do her bidding. He sat, very pointedly *not* moving, and she threw up her hands in exasperation. "We're telling a *story*, Ashbridge." Registering whatever expression had now taken up residence on his face—utter mystification, if he had to hazard a guess—she sighed, then elaborated. "Tonight, we need people to see us together, so it won't seem so strange when we start appearing all over town in each other's company."

"If the point is to see and be seen, then why are we sitting in a corner?"

"*Because*," Vesper said through gritted teeth, "we don't want it to *seem* like we're trying to be seen."

"Is this how your brain works all the time?" It sounded exhausting.

"More or less."

"It's impressive."

"Thank you," she said, smiling in a satisfied sort of way. "No one else seems to notice that. So, you will go to the bar, order a round of drinks, and people will notice you—not having seen you here before—and wonder who you are, and who you're with. When they realize that you're delivering that gin fizz to *me*, they'll take notice."

"They'll take notice . . . simply because it's you?"

"Yes," Vesper said, not a hint of modesty in her voice. She

brushed an invisible fleck of dust off her shoulder. "If anyone *does* recognize you, we'll look like old family friends, perhaps rekindling a romance, and people won't think anything else about it, meaning we can poke around to our hearts' content."

"And you just expect that people will be too stupid to notice that we're making our way to every club in the neighborhood, and trying to discreetly interview the staff?" he asked a bit skeptically.

"Ashbridge, you twit. I'd have thought in your line of work, you'd have learned something very important already."

"And what's that?"

She leaned closer, a mischievous grin flitting across her face. In that moment, he didn't wonder in the slightest at the fact that apparently half the men in London were in thrall to her. He'd follow that grin anywhere.

"People are *frightfully* stupid."

And Max—in spite of his better judgment, and the fact that he knew perfectly well that there was nothing about this woman that he should trust . . .

He laughed.

◆

All in all, Vesper thought, the evening was off to a promising start.

She and Ashbridge were rubbing along together well enough, and he was proving quite amenable to sitting still and listening to her sensibly, which was really all that she required of him.

"Thank you," she said, accepting the gin fizz he handed her several minutes later when he returned to the table. He had a tumbler of some sort of amber liquid in his other hand—and wasn't that just the *most* predictable? Of course he was the sort of man who drank stodgy amber spirits. "What took you so long? You were ages."

"Just . . . conversation," Ashbridge said, his cheeks going slightly pink. Absolutely fascinating. She peered round his shoulder toward the bar, and she spotted Genevieve Colton herself mixing a drink. She must've been in her seventies by now, but she was smiling flirtatiously at a man at the bar who couldn't have been older than Vesper; the man was gazing at her, rapt.

"Ah," Vesper said wisely, turning back to Ashbridge. "You received the full Genevieve Colton experience, then."

"She asked if I had a penchant for older women."

"What did you tell her?"

"That I'd never had the pleasure, but that I wasn't opposed to the idea."

"Ashbridge," Vesper said, torn between being impressed and alarmed, "be careful. She'll have you in a bedroom, flat on your back, putting your mouth to work in about three seconds if you don't watch yourself."

"Well, she asked who the gin fizz was for, and I nodded in your direction, and she seemed to think I already had my work cut out for me."

Vesper was unsure whether to be offended or flattered, so instead she merely took a fortifying sip; Ashbridge was still looking somewhat flustered by the experience, though Vesper supposed she couldn't blame him.

"Have a drink, and try to look as though you're enamored

with me," she instructed, "and not as though you were recently propositioned by a septuagenarian." For once, he proved obedient, though his version of "enamored" was, predictably, rather less effusive than Vesper might have hoped. "Can't you try to look a bit more like you find me nearly impossible to resist?"

"I'm *trying*," he said through clenched teeth. "I am not naturally very . . ."

"Lustful?" Vesper suggested, merely for the entertainment of watching him look as though he were about to have apoplexy.

"Demonstrative."

She sighed. "I suppose that isn't surprising." Onstage, the band wound down a rousing number and struck up a softer, slower song. "Why don't we dance, then?" she said, leaning forward a bit so that she did not have to speak too loudly for Ashbridge to hear her.

He looked back over his shoulder; there were several couples swaying on the open dance floor before the stage, where a girl about Vesper's age with dark skin sang in a low, throaty voice, accompanied by another woman—short-haired and wearing men's attire—on the piano.

"All right," he said, pushing his chair back and coming to his feet without a single word of protest. Vesper was a bit surprised—she wasn't sure why, but she'd expected him to object. Instead, he extended a hand toward her, tugged her to her feet, and led her to the dance floor without another word.

Once there, Ashbridge turned, drawing Vesper nearer until she was within the circle of his arms, one of his hands still holding hers, the other coming to rest at her hip. His height was particularly pronounced at such close range; she had to tilt her head back to look him in the eye. She rested a hand on one of his broad shoulders, and looked away briefly when his eyes—darker in the low light of the club—met hers, the eye contact feeling too intimate, here in his arms with his hand burning through the silk at her hip. This close, she could see how immaculately put-together he was: the carefully combed hair, the cleanly shaved jaw, the perfectly knotted tie. Vesper wondered suddenly, wildly, without warning, what he was like in bed. She could not picture this man coming undone.

"You're a good dancer," she said, because she needed to distract herself from that line of thought in a hurry. Ashbridge was surefooted as he twirled them around the room, his hand on her hip gently steering without really giving the impression of doing so. Vesper had danced with enough unskilled partners to recognize—and appreciate—a good dancer when she found him.

"My mother taught me," he said with a lopsided smile, the quirk of the lips all at once making him look boyish and far too charming. "She's a ballet dancer. Or *was*, I suppose. She danced in music halls before I was born." His mouth pressed into a thin, grim line. "It's where she met my father."

Vesper, having come from a happy (albeit infuriating) family, had never herself had cause to utter the word "father" with the amount of disdain Ashbridge had infused it with.

"I take it you're not close," she said, and he looked at her, considering, for a moment before he spoke again.

"He was a posh twat who seduced her with false promises, and then refused to marry her when she realized she was pregnant, so. No. I wouldn't say we're close." He shook his head, as if shaking off the memory of the unfortunate man who'd sired him. “Fortunately, my stepfather came into the picture—he’d been a family friend for years, and offered to marry Mum when the situation came to light.” His mouth quirked a bit. “Turns out he’d been in love with her for ages. And, over time, she fell in love with him, too. He’s the only father I’ve ever needed.”

“Is Ashbridge his name?” Vesper asked.

He nodded. “He’s never made me feel as if I wasn’t his son, even when my siblings came along.”

Vesper sighed, feeling a bit gooey. “That’s awfully romantic.”

Ashbridge grimaced. “Please don’t. They’re my parents.”

“Parents can be romantic, too,” Vesper said, then shook her head. “Believe me, I should know.”

“I do recall your parents being rather . . .” He trailed off, appearing to search for a polite word.

“Nauseating?” she suggested.

“Enamored,” he replied diplomatically.

She wrinkled her nose at him.

“Have you ever seen your mother dance?” she asked, as a way to avoid thinking about the time she’d walked into the dining room to find her mother seated on the table, her father standing between her spread legs. She’d taken a daily forgetfulness potion for weeks afterward, before accepting the fact that, once the potion wore off, the memories inevitably returned. It would be her (traumatizing) cross to bear, apparently.

He nodded. “She opened a ballet school, and one year, her pupils convinced her to close a recital by dancing herself. And I just remember thinking . . .”

“Yes?” she asked after a moment.

“It made me wonder how my father could bear it—giving

her up." There was something so soft, so warm in his tone as he spoke of his mother that, for a moment, he didn't sound at all like the Ashbridge that Vesper thought she knew. She wondered what it would be like to be loved by him; he struck her as the sort to be extremely loyal.

"It was his loss, clearly," she said, and he gave a quick nod. He was no longer quite meeting her gaze—it could not have been any clearer that he didn't wish to discuss this any further.

"I'm glad you have those memories," she added lightly. "And you can tell her that she did a good job with you—I've not had my toes trodden on a single time."

"She'd disown me if she thought I was taking pretty girls out dancing and stepping on their feet."

"She'll be able to sleep at night," Vesper said, grinning at him. Her mind tripped over the word "pretty," which was ridiculous—it wasn't as though she were unaccustomed to men telling her she was pretty. She cast a glance around them; the light of the chandelier made it easy to see the other couples dancing nearby, but nearly impossible to see much beyond them into the shadows.

"Do you think people are watching us?" she asked, leaning forward so that her words fell quietly into his ear. He ducked his head, and she resisted the impulse to inhale, to breathe him in.

She felt the brush of his hair against her forehead as he glanced sideways. "Maybe," he said, his breath warm on her cheek. "It's hard to tell in this light."

She nodded, then dropped his hand to reach up and curve her arm around his neck instead. "Don't worry," she said. "I'm not going to kiss you."

Without missing a beat, he asked, "Why, precisely, would that worry me?"

And all at once, Vesper was at a loss for words.

She *hated* being at a loss for words.

And she particularly hated that it was Max Ashbridge, of all people, who had put her in such a state.

Ashbridge, however, didn't seem to be expecting any sort of a response from her. Instead, he curved his arm around her waist, pulling her closer to him, his hand warm through the fabric of her dress. He didn't look her in the eye, but instead gazed past her, his eyes seeming to scan the room beyond the dance floor.

"Have you noticed anything suspicious?" she asked.

"A hooded figure in a corner furtively filling packets with mysterious substances?" he asked in an undertone, an edge of wry amusement to his voice.

"I was thinking more along the lines of a blonde swiping someone's drink."

"I doubt we'll be so lucky on our first attempt."

"And," Vesper added in the interests of fairness, "we don't *know* this mysterious blonde is responsible—we're basing this entire theory on Anna's memories of a few seconds in a chaotic night."

"At the moment, it's the only lead we've got. I can't exactly show up on—what was the name of the fellow who had the tainted potion?"

"Everett Carlisle—Amir, one of our bartenders, has been asking around. He was a guest of a member but has visited the club a few times before."

"Well, I can't exactly show up on Carlisle's doorstep announcing myself as an F.L.E.A. and asking questions—not if we hope to keep this quiet."

"But how long *can* we expect to be able to keep word of this from spreading—if it keeps happening, I mean?" Vesper asked. "Incidents of rogue magic aren't easy to cover up, you know."

"It's a bit easier when you have the government on your side," he said, a slow, smug smile curving his lips.

"Don't look so pleased with yourself. And if you're expecting me to fall over myself fawning at how wonderful it is that the Fleas can help us—"

"F.L.E.A.s. And don't worry, I *have* met you before, you understand."

She opened her mouth to reply, then shut it again. That should have been an insult—or, if not precisely an insult, then not entirely a compliment, either. But there was something about the way he said it—something knowing and teasing, something that implied that he knew who she was and liked her the better for it—that made her feel warm inside.

So, instead of retorting, she merely said, "Will you speak to your superior at work tomorrow?"

He nodded. "Perhaps I can stop by your flat and tell you what I've learned before I head home in the evening?"

She shook her head. "I'm at Holloway's tomorrow evening starting at five—why don't you come see me there instead? And could you try to ensure that you don't look like you're about to whip out a Flea badge at a moment's notice, this time?"

"You're incredibly irritating when you want to be, aren't you?"

Somehow he made this sound like a compliment, too. Instead of replying, Vesper allowed her gaze to wander around the room; no one seemed to be paying them any mind, and she couldn't see anything out of the ordinary. There were tables full of revelers, though the crowd was, as Ashbridge had noted, not overwhelming, and the audience skewed slightly female. There were at least three tables occupied by ladies who were exchanging rather seductive glances—or, in one case, an open-mouthed kiss—secure in the knowledge that no one present this evening would be bothered by the sight.

Vesper was fond of Mauve's for this reason. When it had been Colton's, the magic on offer had lain in the way of hallucinatory effects—the sort of magic that Vesper, personally, didn't like much. After her husband's death, however, Genevieve had started making the potions and powders using her own family Word—hers was an old family whose magic was nearly gone, and she was the last of its line. The menu items on offer now were gentler, solely focused on erasing unpleasant memories, lifting moods, creating feelings of well-being and trust. It was, honestly, quite lovely. It was the sort of place where people might come for an evening to escape, without worrying about the consequences.

"You look happy," Ashbridge said, and Vesper glanced up at him, startled, wondering what he'd read in her expression.

"I like Mauve's. It always feels so cozy and safe."

His brow wrinkled a bit. "As safe as one can feel while breaking the law?"

Vesper rolled her eyes. "It's only been illegal for a few years."

"No," he corrected. "During the war, too." This was true;

licensing laws had been tightened during the war, and magic had been caught in that net—it was what had led to the government eventually making the changes permanent, with the Forbiddance and Licensing Act of 1920. The thinking at the time had been that an intoxicated and bespelled population was not good for war readiness.

"We thought that was temporary, though," she reminded him. "And before that, these clubs had existed for generations—my grandmother brought me to Mauve's once when I was a child."

"Charming. Indoctrinate them young, is that the philosophy?"

Her grip on his shoulders tightened. "It's not *indoctrination*, Ashbridge—it's our way of life. You wouldn't understand."

"Isn't that always the line? None of us mundanes would understand—we're not *sophisticated* enough to grasp the complexities of the magical world."

"No," Vesper said shortly. "It's that you've not even tried—you decided you disliked magic before you ever knew anything about it."

"For good reason," he informed her, his jaw tight. In the dim light of the room, his gray eyes looked troubled. It struck her once again, the rankling sensation of irritation still coursing through her, what a risk she was taking, inviting a man inside this magical club who could so easily shut it down, ruin everything that was special about this place, this world—*her* world.

However, as she turned in his arms in the soft light, looking at his handsome, frowning face, she decided—in a fit of will that was completely untethered to logic—that she simply wouldn't allow it. She would not allow this man, representing a government that she despised, to ruin everything that she held dear.

She loved magic.

And by the time she was finished with Max Ashbridge, she vowed to herself in that moment, she was going to make him love it, too.

Chapter Nine

The next day found Max nursing a headache, and some resentment.

He'd only had the one whisky while he was out with Vesper, but once he'd made it back to North London and climbed the stairs to his small top-floor flat on a quiet lane in Hampstead village, he'd found himself feeling frustrated, nerves jangling. He'd poured himself another whisky from the decanter he kept on the mantel in his sitting room, drained it too quickly, then poured another. Sleep had been too long in finding him, leaving him bleary-eyed this morning, which had felt particularly Monday-ish as he'd moved about his small kitchen, boiling water for tea and frying an egg.

By the time he made it to the office, after a sweaty journey on a couple of crowded Underground trains, his headache (literal) had faded, which was convenient timing, as his headache (metaphorical) was about to commence.

"You've done what now?" asked Raffles, lowering the letter

she'd been reading when he entered her office at her shouted summons.

Max cleared his throat. "Made a judgment call, ma'am."

Raffles's eyebrows inched toward her hairline. "And that 'judgment call,' as you so quaintly put it, involves you getting yourself tangled up with a family that is operating an illegal magical club right under our noses, all for some little cloak-and-dagger caper?"

Max resisted the urge to wince. The advantage of his visit to Holloway's—and of his ensuing agreement with Vesper—taking place on a Friday night was that it had given him a solid two days to work out how he was going to explain his little off-script jaunt to his superior. Said advantage wouldn't actually help that much, however, if he didn't use the extra time to come up with some sort of explanation that would keep Raffles's eyebrows safely in their normal, slightly lowered position. Better a frowning Raffles than an incredulous one.

"It was a good opportunity, and I decided to take it," he said, striving for the sort of light tone that would imply that he'd done nothing at all wrong and didn't care one whit about Effie Raffles's opinion on the matter.

"Hmm," Raffles said by way of reply, not *precisely* displaying the wild enthusiasm that Max might have hoped for. "And it's the Holloway daughter who's helping you in this endeavor? Did she . . ." Raffles trailed off delicately; Max's hackles instantly rose. "Promise you anything? In exchange for this assistance?"

"No." His voice was short, bordering on curt. Raffles's eyebrows inched even higher

"Vesper Holloway has a bit of a reputation."

"Miss Holloway's reputation has nothing to do with any of this," he said. "I have a history with the family, and they're able to give me access to the magical clubs that I'd be unable to obtain easily without the Holloways' help. If this had happened at any other club, I'd still want to investigate who's behind this—and I wouldn't have been lucky enough to know someone at the club able to help me look into it."

"But," she pointed out, eyebrows still alarmingly elevated, "you'd have perhaps considered sending in Scotland Yard to shut things down, wouldn't you?"

He swore internally. This was, of course, the weak part of his plan, when it came to explaining it to Raffles. She'd asked him to look into the club, find evidence of magic, and then arrange a raid; he'd accomplished both of the former agenda items, but had now given Vesper his word that he wouldn't do the last. And if he did, she had a rather large piece of career-damaging information about him tucked away in an envelope in her flat.

"I thought it would be best not to let it be known that the agency is looking into matters," he explained. "If this is some sort of organized attempt to tamper with magic, then this could grow quite dangerous, and if we shut down one of the first clubs to be hit, they'll realize that we're investigating and might act more cautiously."

Raffles nodded slowly, her eyebrows mercifully lowering somewhat. "That's a good point." She pressed her index fingers together for a moment with her elbows braced on her desk. "I suppose there's no harm in you investigating this if we're able to produce a splashy story about several magical clubs operating dangerously. However," she added, her gaze flicking to the door to her office, currently shut tight against the noise and curious eyes of the rest of the department. "This is a rather . . . unconventional arrangement. Considering how highly recommended you came when I hired you, I feel confident that I can trust you to see this through, but I'd prefer you keep it quiet. It's a bit of a delicate time for the F.L.E.A."

"Oh?" Max kept his voice carefully neutral. He had no doubt that Raffles was privy to a great deal of political chatter, given her husband's role as an MP—and close ally of Jacob Finlay—but Max tried to keep out of any discussion of politics while at the office. While he knew that he saw eye to eye with Raffles and Finlay on the subject of Forbiddance, his own politics otherwise had little in common with theirs (his views were more aligned with the newly ascendant Labour Party, not that he planned to ever mention this to the woman sitting before him).

"We're concerned that Covington might be growing closer to having the votes for his bill repealing Forbiddance. Michael spent the weekend having meetings, and he's worried."

Max realized, after a beat, that "Michael" referred to Raffles's husband. All at once, he felt uneasy. The F.L.E.A. was tasked with enforcing laws as they existed—not with politicking. This felt, at the very least, like treading on dangerous ground.

"That's none of our concern though," he said, meeting Raffles's inscrutable gaze. She was one of those mildly terrifying posh women who never gave away what their true thoughts were. "As we're not politicians, nor are we working for the Conservative Party."

"Of course not," Raffles agreed, smiling at him, which was

almost more alarming than a frown would have been. "I am merely noting that if word of this investigation spills out, Scotland Yard will get involved, and we'll come under a fair bit of scrutiny. It would be far better if we could simply present this to them as a fait accompli."

Despite his unease, Max couldn't argue with this particular line of reasoning; it would make his job considerably easier if he and Vesper were allowed to continue as they were, without anyone else getting involved. "Understood," he said, and rose to his feet. "If there's nothing else . . . ?"

"No, that's all. But Ashbridge—I meant what I said about watching yourself around the Holloway girl. I've met her father on more than one occasion, and if the daughter inherited even a fraction of his charm, you'll be in a dangerous way before you even realize it."

"I think I can manage. I've never had much of a weakness for blondes."

Which was true, he thought to himself as he strode out of Raffles's office, even if it didn't go any way toward explaining why he could not get the image of Vesper's golden hair gleaming beneath the light of a chandelier the previous evening out of his mind.

◆

He arrived at Holloway's at half seven—he'd lingered at the office long after most of his colleagues had departed for an after-work pint at the pub. The Monday night crowd at the club was rather subdued; as he glanced into various rooms en route to the bar, he noted that the patrons were largely gathered in pairs or small groups of three or four, nursing drinks and engaged in quiet conversation. A couple was deeply immersed in a game of chess at a table near the fireplace in one of the lounges; he spotted more than one person reading a book. It was all rather cozy, and did not precisely look like a hotbed of vice and illegality.

He found Vesper tucked into a nook in one corner of the main bar, deep in conversation with the friend of hers he'd seen the other night—Hazel Thomas. They sat with their heads bent together, each clutching a champagne coupe loosely in hand. Delacqua, who had been escorting Miss Thomas the other evening, was nowhere in sight. Shame, that; Max had always liked Delacqua, who came from a nauseatingly posh family of both the magical and non-magical variety but who had always been unfailingly kind to Max whenever their paths had crossed at Cambridge.

Neither lady noticed his approach, and he cleared his throat.

Vesper glanced up, a blinding smile firmly in place until she registered who he was, and her facial muscles seemed to relax in unison. "Oh, it's you." Max chose not to devote much mental energy to deciding whether or not her tone was disappointed. "You're later than I was expecting for a man who seems to be so fanatical about timeliness."

He inclined his head in apology, refusing to take the bait. "I'm sorry—I got caught up with work and left the office later than I'd planned." He nodded politely at Vesper's friend. "Miss Thomas."

"Mr. Ashbridge." Miss Thomas smiled at him, seeming more

receptive to his presence than Vesper had at any point in their (re)acquaintance thus far.

"Can I get you another round?" he asked, nodding at their nearly empty champagne coupes.

"No, thank you—I can't stay. My father will fuss if I'm out too late. I just wanted to . . . pass something along." Miss Thomas looked a bit uneasy, worrying at the beaded sleeve of her dress, and Vesper hooked a thumb and forefinger around her friend's wrist. It was the sort of small gesture born of familiarity that spoke of a long friendship.

"What's wrong?" Vesper asked.

Miss Thomas glanced up and met her friend's eyes. "Delacqua and I went to Plenus Venter last night."

The name niggled at Max's memory. "Isn't that the club—"

"That had a mishap with a potion just like ours," Vesper finished for him.

"I didn't drink anything magical while I was there—the whole thing is making me a bit nervous," Miss Thomas continued. "But Horatia Montgomery was there, and her uncle and aunt are the owners. When she saw I wasn't drinking, she told me I needn't worry—that they'd got rid of the staff member responsible for what went wrong, so it wouldn't happen again."

Vesper glanced at Max, a frown wrinkling her usually smooth brow. "How did they work out who it was?"

Miss Thomas shook her head. "I don't know—she didn't seem to have heard about what happened here on Friday, and I didn't want to spread gossip."

"I expect we ought to pay them a visit," Max said.

"Indeed." Vesper's brow was still furrowed, and she was clearly deep in thought. She looked entirely different to the smiling, flirtatious Vesper Holloway who had greeted him when he'd first walked into this club three nights earlier.

Miss Thomas rose. "I'd better go." She smiled at Max. "Nice to see you, Ashbridge." She divided a curious sort of glance between Max and Vesper, one that made Max feel seen in a way that he didn't think he liked.

Not that there was anything *to* see, of course.

"I'll pop round to collect you for lunch tomorrow at one," Vesper said, and watched her friend walk away with a slightly worried look on her face.

"What's wrong?" Max asked, taking the seat that Miss Thomas had vacated. He had not considered, when sitting, that he was both taller and broader than Miss Thomas by a fair margin, and the space felt decidedly cozy as a result. Vesper was wearing an evening dress of golden satin, a gold bumblebee clip in her hair, and as he turned to look at her as he settled into the seat next to her, something in his throat ached. She was beautiful even when looking a bit sad.

"Nothing," she said, in response to his question, and he let it lie; they weren't close enough for him to prod her about whatever troubles plagued her. They were none of his concern.

"Did you want a drink?" she asked, more briskly now, draining her own glass, and he shook his head.

"Overdid it last night."

An eyebrow lifted. "You had one drink."

"I indulged a bit more when I got home. Couldn't sleep."

The eyebrow inched higher. "I see."

"Too annoyed," he added, just to needle her, and he was rewarded with the sight of an eye roll, which gave him the strangest urge to smile.

He resisted the urge.

He was good at resisting urges.

"I spoke to Raffles," he said, prompting a deepening of the pucker in her brow, and clarified, "Effie Raffles—head of the F.L.E.A."

"Right. I believe she's married to . . . someone my brother-in-law dislikes."

"Who is your brother-in-law?" he asked; he knew that Freddie and Vesper's elder sister had married years earlier, but he couldn't recall the details of the match.

"Simon Covington. He's an MP."

Max stilled. "Simon Covington is your brother-in-law," he repeated, his mind on his conversation with Raffles earlier that day. Surely Raffles must have been aware of this; he wondered uneasily if her initial order that he target Holloway's in particular had anything to do with the family's connection to Covington. The thought did not sit well with him.

"Yes. What's wrong?" Vesper was giving him a strange look.

"I just hadn't made the connection. Then yes, your brother-in-law *would* dislike Raffles's husband. He's a Tory MP—one of the leading advocates of Forbiddance. Allied closely with Jacob Finlay."

Vesper's nose wrinkled at the name. "Nice company you keep, Ashbridge."

"I've nothing to do with Raffles's husband—or Finlay. I've never met either."

"You merely enforce the ridiculous law they forced through Parliament."

"I don't think any forcing was required—they had the votes."

"By a *very* narrow margin," Vesper said. "It only passed because of that *Daily Mail* article about a virtuous young woman being led into a life of vice and sin by her addiction to spell powder. Don't you recall?"

Max frowned, casting his mind back. He'd been at Cambridge at the time of the bill's passage—he'd delayed university until after he'd returned home from the war—and hadn't followed the politics of it all very closely. "Vaguely," he said. The story rang a bell, but Max, frankly, had been more focused on how bloody infuriated his father would be by Forbiddance than anything else.

"It wasn't true," Vesper said. "To start with, you *can't* get addicted to spell powder—it's not like strong drink. *The Spark*—Cecily's paper, you know—tracked the woman down a couple of months later. She'd been paid by someone to go to the *Mail* with the story. But by then, it was too late—and she wouldn't go on the record for the exposé, anyway."

Max frowned at her. "I've never heard anything about this."

"Well, Ashbridge, it's *almost* as if there are people in this country with very deep pockets who want to ensure that you wouldn't." Sarcasm positively dripped from her voice, but oddly, Max didn't find it off-putting. He liked Vesper like this—annoyed, curt, sharp—more than he liked the smiling and flirting version of her that she presented most of the time.

"Just as there are people in this country with very deep pockets hell-bent on flouting the law and ensuring that they don't have to sacrifice a single bit of the privilege their ability to perform a bit of hocus-pocus gives them."

"Hocus-pocus," Vesper muttered, shaking her head, but there was a smile creeping across her face; a dimple appeared in one cheek. He did not think someone with a face like hers should be allowed dimples; it was unsporting.

Rather than focus on her dimples or be dragged further into an intractable debate on magic, privilege, and the British class system, Max attempted to return to business. "The point of all this is, I spoke to Raffles and explained our plan. She wasn't thrilled—seems to think I went a bit off-script with this—but she's letting us proceed, so long as I keep quiet about it. I expect she thinks we might make a hash of things and doesn't want it to reflect poorly on her."

"Well, then, we shall simply have to crack on with it and prove her wrong." Vesper sounded very matter-of-fact. Max had not known that he was attracted to matter-of-fact women until this precise moment. She lapsed into a thoughtful silence, her gaze fixed idly on a table across the room, where a trio of couples were clinking glasses. Max's eyes narrowed as he spotted a faint sheen along the hairline of one of the men in the group.

"Which potion did they drink?" he asked, and Vesper glanced at him, startled. He jerked his chin in the direction of the table. "I can see the spell residue on one of them—you aren't terribly careful about keeping them in your hidden bar, are you?"

"Plausible deniability." She gave him an angelic smile. "It's none of our concern if someone comes to Holloway's having partaken of something illegal prior to arriving here, so long as *we* are not the ones providing any illegal substances."

He gave her a speaking look. Her smile widened, before her gaze flicked back to the party in question. She tapped her chin. "Not having served them myself, I can't be certain, but if I were to hazard a guess, I'd say they've had a Gin and Giggles."

"Ah. I expect it does what it says on the tin?"

"More or less. Our magic tends to be a bit . . . frivolous. Our potions are meant to be fun, and not much else."

"Isn't that the point of all magic these days?"

"Different families' Words are suited to different types of magic—they used to be more flexible, centuries ago, but as magical ability faded, the results of employing the Words seemed to narrow. So, for example, the Montgomerys, who own Plenus Venter, are almost entirely focused on food- and appetite-related magic; a member of a different branch of the family sells cooking-enhancing potions and powders. The potions at Grenoble's all result in reducing inhibitions in some fashion. The Grimoire is good at appearance-altering powders—they run a pharmacy selling magical beauty products, too. And ours are just . . . good for a laugh. The Gin and Giggles makes everything you hear approximately twice as funny. It's one of our most popular offerings." Her expression turned sly. "You should try some."

"No, thank you."

"Afraid you might actually enjoy yourself for a couple of hours?"

"Afraid that I'd be a crushing hypocrite, actually."

"Plenty of those among the Fleas—and the police, too," Vesper said, then clammed up in a hurry, looking as though she was afraid she'd said too much. It wasn't news to Max, though. He was perfectly well aware that there were a good number of people working in Forbiddance enforcement in some fashion who were gleefully flouting the rules themselves.

"You're rather noble, aren't you?" Vesper asked now, regarding him as if he were some sort of puzzle that she wanted to work out.

"I don't think I'd describe it that way."

"Of course not. Noble people wouldn't."

"I'm a government employee, Vesper, not a knight."

"But you actually believe in the work you're doing, Ashbridge. I call that noble."

"That sounded perilously close to a compliment."

She gave a careless shrug. "Even Fleas merit compliments occasionally, I suppose."

"F.L.E.A.s."

"So you keep insisting," she said, dimpling at him, and he found himself powerless to resist the urge to smile back at her.

"You ought to try that more often," she added. "Your face looks rather nice when it's not doing an impression of a storm cloud." She glanced over his shoulder, and her expression turned apprehensive. "Ah."

He turned and found her brother striding toward them.

Freddie's face darkened at the sight of Max, and he came to a halt before their table. "You didn't mention you'd have company," he informed his sister.

"Because I knew you'd behave just like this," Vesper replied. "Pull up a chair and stop looming over us, please."

Freddie complied with much grumbling, and Vesper turned to him expectantly. “Well?”

“I found him at home yesterday morning at an ungodly hour,” Freddie said, and Max frowned.

“Sorry, what’s this?”

“I had Freddie pay Everett Carlisle a visit,” Vesper said, sounding pleased with herself.

“Didn’t feel like mentioning that plan to me?”

“I assumed you’d get a bit hysterical about it all, so I decided to simply skip to the bit where Freddie obtained some useful information.”

“Carlisle is in his last year at Oxford and stays with his parents when he’s in town. They have a house in Mayfair. Some distant relative is a mundane aristocrat. The usual sort.” Freddie waved a dismissive hand.

“Whose guest was he?” Vesper asked.

Freddie pressed his lips together into a grim line. “Edward Grenoble.”

“Urgh,” Vesper said, wrinkling her nose. “I didn’t even notice Grenoble that evening.”

“Apparently he broke off from the group quite early—found someone to occupy his time, if you know what I mean.” Freddie waggled his eyebrows suggestively.

“Thank you, Frederick, I think even George would know what you mean.”

“Merlin, let us hope not,” Freddie said, going pale.

“Who’s George?” Max asked.

Vesper and Freddie shuddered in unison, which made the resemblance between them appear particularly pronounced.

"Our nephew," Vesper explained. "He's five. A little young for innuendo, but he's alarmingly precocious."

"Ah," Max agreed. "I see." Vesper watched him expectantly for a moment, and he added, a bit warily, "What?"

"Well, if Edward Grenoble was here last night, then *clearly* we ought to visit him, too."

"What—you think Grenoble poisoned his own friend? To what end?"

"Competitive advantage?" Vesper suggested. "Nothing's happened at Grenoble's yet."

"This is a bit half baked," Max said.

"Did you have a better idea?"

He sighed. "No." He rubbed a hand over his face, considering. "All right. So we'll visit Plenus Venter, and then Grenoble's." He thought longingly of the quiet, orderly weeknight evenings he usually passed at home, listening to the wireless or reading a book, or at the pub with his best mate, Will. "Shall we start with Plenus Venter on Wednesday? I've plans tomorrow evening."

"A whole night spent without Max Ashbridge darkening my doorstep like some sort of grumpy gargoyle, *however* will I survive?"

Freddie grinned at that, and Max surveyed the pair of them darkly as he rose to his feet. "Is being annoying some sort of Holloway family trait?"

"Coming from you, Ashbridge, I'm going to call that a compliment," Vesper informed him. He gave her an exasperated look and nodded in farewell, but the sound of her laugh followed him as he made his way to the door, clear and bright like autumn sunshine.

Chapter Ten

With a full two days before her next evening with Ashbridge, Vesper decided to attempt to put the matter of the contaminated potions out of her mind.

This would have been easier to manage if her family had not been behaving like utter lunatics.

On Monday evening, no sooner had Ashbridge and Freddie left than Simon had appeared at the club, pretending he was there merely for a drink and a hand of cards with some of his friends from university and a couple of fellow politicians. This would have been more convincing had he not begun yawning around nine o'clock and looking longingly at the exit. Vesper had never seen someone so happy to hear the clock chime midnight as Simon was that evening.

The next night, however, things were even worse, because in Simon's place was her father. He was greeted like a king returning from exile by all and sundry, and spent most of the evening holding court at one of the choicest tables in the library by the fire, receiving one well-wisher after another, keeping the waiters and the kitchen staff busy long past the point that the kitchens usually stopped serving food, and generally charming the knickers off everyone he encountered.

He was, in other words, being his usual Lucian Holloway self.

"You know, I really think I have this under control," Vesper said around eleven, dropping into the seat next to him, miraculously vacant for a few seconds.

"I've not the slightest doubt," her father said, nursing the glass of red wine that he'd been sipping for the past couple of hours. His gaze was alert, and she wondered if the other occupants of the room realized how closely they were being watched. Likely not—part of the power of Lucian Holloway was his ability to give the impression, most of the time, of being a lazy, charming cad, while actually keeping a sharp eye on everything that happened around him.

"No potions tonight?" Her father was particularly fond of a First Word—which guaranteed a witty reply to every query—though he'd become a less-frequent imbiber with age.

"I needed a clear mind."

"But nothing's gone wrong, as you can see," she said, gesturing around her. It was a Tuesday evening, and as a result, the club was fairly sedate; the telltale sliding sound of the bookcase admitting clubgoers to the backdoor bar had only been heard occasionally.

"And I'm delighted to see it," he said, not budging from his seat. His gaze on her was keen. "Your mother told me that you asked her to cover the club in your place tomorrow. More plans with Ashbridge?"

Vesper mentally cursed, even though she'd known there was no chance that Amelia wouldn't have shared this information with Lucian. "Yes. We're going to Plenus Venter, and then to Grenoble's on Thursday."

Her father's expression darkened at the second name. "Don't try too hard, there. If the Fleas want to shut down that one—"

"It will be bad for all of us, and you well know it," she said, even though she shared his particular distaste for the club in question. The Holloways and the Grenobles had never been bosom friends—there was bad blood dating back to the Georgian era, allegedly over some sort of romantic entanglement that had resulted in a duel and a missing thumb—and Vesper's unfortunate inability to make intelligent decisions about her love life was merely the latest iteration of a decades-long feud.

"Hmm." Her father sounded unconvinced. "Well, Ashbridge looks like he could throw a punch if necessary."

"There will be no punches thrown, thank you," Vesper said, a bit nettled. "And if there were the need, I'm perfectly capable of throwing them myself."

Her father's expression softened a bit. "I know you are."

"Do you?" Vesper asked.

Lucian frowned. "What do you mean?"

"Everyone in the family seems to think I can't do much for myself these days."

"This is a serious matter, and we don't want you to get in over your head."

"I'm not," she protested. "But I have kept this club running for the past four years, I've performed all the magic we need, and nothing has gone wrong on my watch until last Friday."

"Vesper." Her father turned to face her fully, his expression very serious. "Your tenure at the club has, in truth, gone far better than your mother and I expected. I don't mind telling you that we had no notion of how this would go, allowing you the day-to-day running of Holloway's, particularly since, at the time, you were . . . not quite yourself."

This was a diplomatic way of putting it. She'd been twenty-one, and had spent the three years prior allowing her head to be turned by every handsome face that had come her way. As the beautiful youngest daughter of the storied Holloway family, she'd had no shortage of men interested in taking her to dinner, to drinks, and yet she'd made a string of terrible decisions in a row. It had started with the engaged man at Freddie's twenty-third birthday party whom Ashbridge had so humiliatingly rescued her from, but that had only been the beginning. There had been the man a dozen years her senior who'd wooed her in a whirlwind romance featuring bouquets of roses, candlelit dinners, and heady nights at a series of posh hotels, implying but never quite promising a rosy future between them—because, it transpired, he had a wife and baby at home. Then there had been the pair of brothers who had got into a public brawl on Marylebone High Street when they realized that Vesper had been seeing both of them, trying to make up her mind about which she preferred. (It had been particularly annoying because she had just decided, too. Unfortunately, the man in question had informed her—while pressing a handkerchief to his heavily bleeding nose—that their courtship was at an end.) The final blow, however, had been the young mundane aristocrat, the fourth son of a viscount with a town house on St. James's Square and a romantic, possibly haunted country estate on a Cornish cliff. He was the first man Vesper had thought she could happily marry; he was pursuing an advanced degree at Oxford and was only in London periodically, kind and serious and yet he still, still seemed to like her, just the way she was.

Until he didn't anymore. Until he'd fallen in love with someone else—some meek aristocratic daughter of an old family friend whom he'd not seen in years. The worst of it was that he'd been so decent about it; he'd called things off with Vesper immediately, had taken her on a walk through Regent's Park and spoken so beautifully of not wanting to hurt her, told her all the things he admired about her. Told her he wished to be friends, of all things. Vesper had said all the right things, and kissed him on the cheek, and then had gone home and cried for two days.

It was at this point that her parents had decided that she needed a distraction—and Holloway's had been just that. She threw herself into the running of the club, finding that the work suited her, that she liked having something she was responsible for, for the first time in her life.

She'd also promised herself that she would not fall in love again—would not even allow herself to grow particularly attached to a man. That she would be the one to leave in the mornings, rather than the one who was left. It had proved an easy enough vow to keep.

"However," her father continued, drawing her out of her maudlin thoughts, "the stakes at the moment are incredibly high. If Simon can get this bill through Parliament, it could be only a matter of months until we can operate openly again. We can't risk something else going wrong—not when we're so close to a victory."

"I know," she said, grinding her teeth. "What do you think Ashbridge and I are playing detective for, a lark?"

He dropped a kiss on her head. "I know that you're doing your bit. Just humor me, and let me ensure that you're not in over your head—and that means that you'll have someone else with you at the club, until things settle down."

It seemed futile to argue the point further, but Vesper could not help but wonder, as she fell asleep that night, if anyone in her family took her even the slightest bit seriously.

◆

"Let me be certain I understand this," Max's mate Will Chamberlain said late Tuesday evening as he and Max lingered over whiskies, a fire burning low in the grate in Will's sitting room. Will's flat was on a quiet street in Bloomsbury, a stone's throw from the British Museum and not too lengthy a walk from the luxurious town houses in Marylebone where the old magical families resided in considerable splendor. It felt, however, a world away. "You, of all people, are visiting magical clubs with *Vesper Holloway*?"

"Correct," Max said curtly, already regretting confiding in his friend.

Will grinned. "Vera is going to be *furious* she missed this," he said, naming his wife, who was out to dinner with a friend and not expected back until late. "I wonder if she knows Miss Holloway."

"She might," Max admitted; Vera was from a posh old

once-magical family, and was extremely well-connected as a result. She didn't move as frequently in that world as she had prior to her marriage—her family did not approve of Will, given that he was a member of the (to quote Vera's mother) "muck-raking press"—but she had an enormous number of friends. Max had always, frankly, found Vera mildly terrifying, but she undoubtedly made his friend happy, which was good enough for Max. He and Will had been friends since the war; though their paths had diverged after they'd returned from France, with Max heading to Cambridge while Will took up employment on Fleet Street, they'd rekindled their friendship once Max moved to town after finishing university, and Max now counted Will as his closest friend.

"Well," Will said philosophically, "this at least sounds more interesting than whatever it is you're doing the rest of the time—reviewing licenses. Issuing fines. *Paperwork.*" He gave a dramatic shudder; given that he was a crack reporter for *The Times* who'd managed several spectacular scoops in the past few years, Max could well imagine that "paperwork" would indeed sound rather dull by comparison.

But that was fine. Dull was fine. Max didn't need excitement at work; he simply needed . . .

To prove a point? said a sly voice in his head.

As if reading his thoughts, Will shook his head. "Weren't you happier before, stamping passports?"

"That job didn't come with the potential advantages of this one."

"Annoying your father, you mean?"

"Making it crystal clear that I won't be having anything to

do with his rosy-eyed vision for my future, yes," Max agreed, his jaw tightening automatically at the mention of the man who'd sired him—a man whose existence he liked to forget as much as possible.

"Surely there are better ways to do it than—"

"There aren't, actually," Max said, the words coming out more sharply than he intended. He pinched the bridge of his nose. "Sorry. I just—"

"I know." Will's gaze on him was warm. "He gets your hackles up—and I don't blame you. He's a wanker."

"To say the least. However," Max added, realizing Will's position might make him useful, "you might do me a favor. Would you let me know if you hear anything unusual about any of the magical clubs?"

"Unusual how?"

"We're trying to track down the source of a couple of . . . accidents. At the clubs. Word doesn't seem to have spread too much just yet, but I'd be curious to learn about anything you overhear."

"All right," Will said, sounding curious. "Is it related to the vote on Forbiddance repeal in Parliament? I've heard a lot of chatter about that from magical and mundane people alike in the past week. Sympathies seem to be swinging toward Covington—particularly after that story in *The Spark* a couple of weeks ago, about the woman whose husband drank himself to death after he turned to the bottle, since he could no longer use potions."

"Christ." Max blinked. "That's grim."

"It was. Good reporting, though." Will grinned, and leaned

forward in his seat. "It was Cecily Covington who wrote it, actually." He allowed a dramatic pause, then added, "Vesper Holloway's sister."

Max gave Will a speaking sort of look, which only caused Will's grin to widen. "You know," Will said, "I really think I'm going to enjoy this."

Chapter Eleven

Vesper took her usual care with her appearance on Wednesday evening. This might be a night out for strictly professional reasons, but there was no reason she shouldn't look as delectable as always—not that she cared if Ashbridge noticed, of course.

The flimsiness of this insistence—even if it had only been to herself—was revealed by the rush of pleasure she felt when Ashbridge's eyes immediately dropped to her chest when he met her outside her door for the short walk to Plenus Venter. She had selected one of her most cleavage-forward dresses that evening (difficult, given the current fashions, but Vesper had always been one to persevere in the face of hardship, et cetera), and if even moral, upstanding Max Ashbridge couldn't help but notice, then she knew that the ensemble was as fetching as she'd thought when she surveyed herself in her bedroom mirror.

"Ashbridge."

"Vesper." He kept his eyes carefully north of her chin. "Shall we?"

She looked at him expectantly, and he looked back at her blankly. "Ashbridge. We're meant to at least *imply* that there might be something romantic between us. Perhaps you might try to look vaguely pleased to be in my company?"

"Oh." He cleared his throat. "Sorry. It's, er, been a while since I've taken a woman out for an evening."

Vesper willed herself, unsuccessfully, not to find this intriguing. "Oh?" Worrying she sounded a bit *too* interested in the topic, she added, a bit airily, "Too busy rounding up dastardly practitioners of magic to find your way into anyone's bed?"

He very nearly tripped over his own feet, which was gratifying. "Stop that."

She blinked, all innocence. "Stop what?"

"Stop being deliberately shocking to try to put me off-balance." He frowned down at her. His dark brows were lowered, his eyes a bit shadowed in the glow of a streetlamp. Vesper didn't like that he so easily recognized her tactics; she thought herself more cunning than that.

"Now." He extended his arm, which she took. "Let's get to work."

"You do know how to woo a woman, Ashbridge."

"Trust me, Vesper." He glanced down at her as they made their way across the cobblestoned mews. "If I were wooing you, you'd know it."

This time, it was Vesper's turn to trip.

The streets of Marylebone were still fairly busy on a Wednesday night, and she passed a half dozen people she knew, smiling in passing but avoiding getting drawn into chitchat. She and Ashbridge were on a mission, after all.

For his part, Ashbridge looked increasingly uncomfortable with each person who grinned at Vesper in recognition. At one point, she leaned up to murmur in his ear, "You might try to look a *bit* less alarmed each time someone says hello to me."

He exhaled slowly. "I don't like being the subject of gossip."

"You're being awfully virginal about all of this."

Ashbridge looked even grimmer. She followed the line of his gaze, but didn't see anything out of the ordinary—merely an older gentleman whose face she couldn't quite see arm in arm with a woman who was considerably too young for him, walking in the same direction they were.

"If you could *try* to look like you're remotely enjoying my company, I'd appreciate it."

Ashbridge blinked, as if he'd forgotten her presence momentarily. Vesper found that she did not enjoy this feeling, which was rather novel to her. "Sorry," he said, and then pulled her closer to his side.

Once they had sailed through the front doors of Plenus Venter, waved in with the merest glance at one of Vesper's engraved cards, they paused to assess matters. It had been a while since she'd been here, though in the years before she'd taken over the running of Holloway's she'd been a frequent visitor. Compared to the various other clubs, which were so obviously for evening pursuits, Plenus Venter, with its focus on comestibles, boasted interiors that reminded Vesper more of the dining rooms at a posh hotel than anything else.

The ground floor opened into a high-ceilinged foyer, with a tiled floor, gold-framed mirrors, and a number of potted palms. Private dining rooms branched off on either side—in one, there was a long communal table before an enormous marble fireplace; in another, small round tables for two were scattered around a room whose walls were painted a cheerful yellow; yet another held a series of low-slung sofas and settees, all done in rich jewel tones, ruby and emerald and amethyst, accompanied by an eclectic assortment of coffee tables and spindly-legged end tables, all currently bearing cocktails and bowls of various snacks.

"The bars are upstairs," Vesper informed Ashbridge. "It's table service down here, but I think we're better off trying to speak to one of the bartenders directly."

"Lead the way," he said, and followed her up the steps.

Upstairs, the entirety of one wall was occupied by the bar, made of glossy mahogany with shiny brass fittings; an enormous mottled mirror hung on the wall behind it. The dance floor was relatively small, as the rest of the room was taken up with round high-top tables in glossy dark wood.

"How do they keep the potions a secret if the bar isn't hidden?" Ashbridge asked in an undertone, watching as a redheaded bartender mixed an old-fashioned.

"They're meant to be enjoyed before eating, so a lot of people order them at their tables, and they're sent out from the bar just before their first course arrives. There's a particular turn of phrase you're meant to use, to tell the waitstaff that you want the potions menu rather than the regular drinks menu."

"What turn of phrase?" Ashbridge asked, looking curious.

Vesper hesitated. This merely made him focus his attention on her with greater intent. "What?"

"Don't make fun," she said, and he now looked more eager than she had thought him constitutionally capable of appearing.

"You have to tell me, or I'm not going to be able to sleep tonight."

She exhaled through her nose. "Fine. It's . . . um . . . it's 'Hello, old thing. Lovely evening for a tipple, what ho! I don't suppose I could trouble you for a peek at the drinks menu?' And then, when they're handed over the regular menu, they add, 'Sorry, old thing, but I'd fancy something a bit more toothsome,' and then the server produces the potions menu."

Ashbridge was gazing at her in astonishment. "Every time someone orders a potion, they have to remember that precise sequence of words?"

"Yes," Vesper said, raising her chin. "It weeds out anyone too stupid to memorize it, as well as being jolly entertaining to watch people recite."

Ashbridge shook his head. "I will never understand magic."

"That," Vesper informed him, "is just the way we'd like it to remain." With that, she led the way to the bar, where they slid onto velvet-topped stools that were sturdier than their spindly legs made them look. She considered the redhead behind the bar; she was about Vesper's age, very pretty, and, at the moment, not overly busy; the fact that it was a Wednesday night meant that they'd timed their visit well, if they hoped to get a word with the staff.

"What can I get you?" the bartender asked, making her way

over toward Vesper and Ashbridge. She glanced at Vesper, and did a double take. "Miss Holloway, isn't it?"

Vesper gave her a bright smile. "It is. A glass of champagne for me, and . . ." She looked inquiringly at Ashbridge.

"What do you recommend?" he asked, leaning forward to brace an elbow on the bar and gazing at the bartender as if she were the most interesting thing he'd seen all evening.

Vesper blinked.

The bartender blinked—and then blushed. (The curse of redheads everywhere.)

"We do a nice Bee's Knees," the bartender offered.

Vesper could not imagine Max Ashbridge, of all people, drinking a Bee's Knees, but without missing a beat, he smiled at the bartender and said, "That sounds lovely. Thank you . . . what was your name?"

"Maggie."

"Thank you, Maggie."

His smile widened; Maggie appeared temporarily blinded, not that Vesper could blame her, poor girl.

The second Maggie had walked a short distance down the bar to fetch gin and champagne, Vesper turned to Ashbridge.

"Excuse me, have you seen Max Ashbridge around here anywhere? I thought I was sitting next to him, but he seems to have been replaced by a far friendlier doppelgänger. It's all very mysterious."

Ashbridge's smile vanished; Vesper found this strangely reassuring. "I'm being polite. A course of action that is generally considered wise, if one is hoping to obtain information?"

"This isn't *polite*. You're always polite—except to me," Vesper added slyly, and enjoyed the irate look Ashbridge shot in her direction.

"You only think I'm not polite to you because you're used to men falling over their own two feet the second they catch a look at your face—or . . . other assets." He determinedly did *not* look at her chest, but Vesper was delighted nonetheless.

"Do you have a fever? You're behaving very oddly."

"Perhaps I've come down with whatever temporary, insanity-inducing malady your mere presence seems to inspire," he muttered.

Vesper laughed and he glanced sideways at her, the corner of his mouth twitching slightly. At that moment, Maggie the bartender returned, the necessary spirits in hand, and proceeded to very efficiently produce a coupe of champagne and a delicious-looking Bee's Knees that Vesper regretted not having ordered herself.

"Cheers," Max said as Maggie handed him the glass and he took a sip. "That's lovely, thank you—one of the best cocktails I've ever tried. You must've worked here quite a while, to be so skilled . . . ?"

He trailed off delicately, not quite asking a question, just leaving room for information that Maggie, clearly still reeling from the rare experience of having received a Max Ashbridge smile, hastened to provide.

"Three years this month. I worked in the kitchen before that, but I'd always hoped to make it out to the bar eventually."

"I've had the food here before," Vesper offered, and Maggie glanced at her, slightly startled, as if having forgotten that she existed. "It's very nice—everyone in the kitchen does a lovely job."

"Thank you." Maggie did not bloom beneath this praise the way she had when Ashbridge spoke, and Vesper nearly frowned. This wasn't how it was supposed to work—*she* was meant to be the charming one, and he was meant to be the stern government official whose grim countenance was only occasionally lightened by his unwilling amusement at her cheeky irrepressible charm.

"If you've worked here awhile, the, er, unfortunate incident a couple of weeks ago must have come as quite a shock." Ashbridge's voice was a soothing, empathetic murmur.

Maggie sighed, leaning forward with her elbows braced on the bar. Ashbridge inclined his head toward her. Vesper sipped moodily at her champagne.

"Nothing like that's ever happened here before." Maggie's voice was low and worried. "And Gus—one of the other bartenders—lost his place over it, but I don't . . . well, I don't think it's right." She looked at Vesper, suddenly wary, and Vesper offered her a reassuring smile.

"I don't, either," she told her. "And the whole thing is making me a bit nervous, honestly—we had something similar happen at Holloway's, and I can't imagine your bartender—Gus, was it?—could have been responsible for *that*."

Maggie relaxed a bit at these words. "There you go! I knew it couldn't have been him—but the Montgomerys were awfully upset about it, and didn't see how it could have been anyone else, so . . ." She gave a helpless shrug.

"Did they think he did something to the potion?" Ashbridge allowed a note of confusion to creep into his voice. "I hope they don't think he intentionally tried to hurt anyone."

"No, nothing like that," Maggie said. "He's been at the bar for a decade, everyone knows Gus—he wouldn't hurt a fly. But they think he was distracted—there was this handsome chap that evening, you see, and . . . well, Gus has an eye for handsome chaps. They think he must've accidentally given the fellow a double batch or something, because he wasn't paying attention—they think he was too busy flirting. But I *know* Gus," she continued, her voice suddenly vehement. "He might flirt with a handsome lad or pretty girl he sees, but he'd never make a mistake like that—he always paid such careful attention to what he was doing. He told me that he didn't even start talking to the fellow until after he'd already added the syrup, anyway—the chap was with a large group, and came over to take the final drink from Gus, so Gus wasn't even mixing the potion at that point. It doesn't make sense."

Down at the opposite end of the bar, someone hailed Maggie, and she glanced over and raised a finger, asking for a second more. She turned back to Ashbridge and Vesper. "I want whoever did this to be caught—I just really don't think it's Gus. I'm not trying to make trouble, but—"

"We know you aren't," Vesper assured her, and smiled at her again. Maggie relaxed a bit at the sight, though Vesper reflected, a bit grumpily, that she *still* didn't think her smile had been as effective as Ashbridge's had been. This was an astonishing development that she didn't care for one bit.

"I don't blame you for being upset," Ashbridge agreed now, before adding, "and I hope Gus finds another place soon."

"That's just it, though," Maggie said, twisting a stopper into the top of the champagne bottle. "It's almost impossible to be hired by any of the clubs if you've previously worked for another. He'll have to go work for the mundane clubs—or leave London entirely."

With a grim shake of the head, she was off to make a round of champagne cocktails for the gaggle of ladies at the opposite end of the bar; Vesper sipped at her champagne, avoiding Ashbridge's gaze as he turned in his seat to face her fully.

"Why," he asked, after a few seconds in which he looked at Vesper and she looked just past his shoulder, "is it impossible for this Gus to be hired by any of the other clubs?"

She sighed. "It's not *impossible.* Just . . . unlikely." Ashbridge looked unimpressed by this non-explanation, so she continued, "The families are very protective of their secrets, and so once someone has worked at one of the magical clubs, they find it very difficult to be hired by any of the others. It's why most of the staff at the clubs have been there for years."

"And that doesn't strike you as a bit . . . exploitative?"

"I hardly think—"

"You've made it so that if someone leaves their job, they know they'll have a hard time finding another one. Meaning there's little incentive to offer them good pay, or to treat them well, because you hold all the power."

This was taking things too far. "I'll have you know that we give eight percent pay rises every year as a matter of course, as well as additional bonuses for good work."

"Then your employees are fortunate. I suppose it never occurred to you that some of the other families might not be doing the same?"

Truthfully, Vesper had never thought about it before. She

had what she considered to be very good relationships with the staff at Holloway's; many of them had worked for the club since she was a girl. She knew that they were paid a fair wage, and that the family did not enforce any unreasonable rules or expectations of their conduct. However, it had never occurred to her to wonder if, despite all that, some of them might wish to seek a job elsewhere—or whether they even felt they *could*.

She glanced up at Ashbridge and some of her consternation must have shown on her face, because his mouth twitched.

"Don't look smug," she grumbled, draining her glass of champagne. "Smug men are unattractive."

"And I'm meant to be fretting about what Vesper Holloway finds attractive, am I?" he asked; rather than landing harshly, the words felt almost teasing. Vesper wouldn't have thought Ashbridge had it in him to tease anyone.

She met his eyes and held them.

He opened his mouth—

And then Maggie was back, whisking away Vesper's empty glass, looking starry-eyed once more beneath the brightness of the smile Ashbridge leveled at her.

A thought occurred to Vesper, and she leaned forward. "Maggie—you didn't happen to get a look at the man who distracted Gus that night, did you?"

Maggie nodded. "He had dark hair, dark eyes. Maybe about your age." She nodded at Ashbridge. "He was handsome, I suppose, but not in a very *memorable* way, d'you know what I mean? He looked like a lot of other handsome men."

"Did you speak to him? Hear his accent, anything?" Vesper pressed.

Maggie shook her head. "It was noisy, and Gus was serving him, so I barely paid him any notice. Only caught a glimpse of him as he walked away—I saw him hand the drink to the fellow that ended up being sick, but I only saw his face in profile. I teased Gus about him a bit, told him I thought he preferred blonds. He told me the next time he saw a blond with eyelashes that long, he'd return to his usual preferences."

Maggie was gone again, hailed by a man several stools down, and Vesper sighed. "This hasn't been very helpful."

"I don't know," Ashbridge said thoughtfully. "We now know that in both instances, someone was handed a drink by someone else. That provides a person with a perfect opportunity to do something with the potion, after it's left the bartender's hands but before it's consumed."

"True," Vesper acknowledged. "I was hoping I might recognize the man if she described him, but 'handsome with dark hair' is not exactly a limiting description. Look at you, after all." She gestured at Ashbridge's general person.

He gave her a strange look.

"What?"

"You just gave me a compliment," he said, brow creasing. "Are you feeling well? Should I take you to the doctor?"

"I'm leaving," Vesper said, reaching for the beaded clutch she'd brought with her and retrieving a few coins, which she tossed onto the bar—more than enough to cover both her drink and Ashbridge's.

She slid off the stool, and glanced at him.

"What?" he asked, taking a last sip of his Bee's Knees before rising to join her.

"I thought you'd be one of those men who take umbrage at the notion of a woman paying for his drink."

"I'm on the clock, Holloway. Saves me the bother of submitting an expense claim at work to be reimbursed." He flashed a smile at her—quick and devastating—and then took her arm and led her to the cloakroom.

It was only once they were on the street again, huddled in their coats against the increasing chill of the October night, that they resumed their conversation. "Well," Ashbridge said, sticking his hands in his pockets, "I suppose this won't make for a very interesting report for Raffles."

"Are you reporting everything we do to her?" Vesper asked, feeling a bit uneasy. She supposed this possibility should have occurred to her before now; for all that Ashbridge was proving more entertaining to spend evenings with than she'd anticipated, he was still a Flea, and it would be wise not to forget that fact.

He glanced down at her. "No." He hesitated then, and Vesper let the silence stretch out between them, curious to see how he would fill it. "I don't think she needs to know . . . every detail of our work."

Vesper considered him for a long moment—the stern brow, the serious gray gaze. Nothing about this man indicated that he would be willing to bend even the smallest of rules—and, somehow, she thought that visiting illicit clubs without the full knowledge or blessing of his employer counted as a moderately large rule, actually.

So why?

Why was he risking this? What was he about?

She realized, with a creeping sense of frustration, that she did not entirely *understand* Max Ashbridge. It had been quite a while since she'd met a man she didn't consider to be the most easily solved puzzle.

"Well, I'm glad to hear it. Shall we go to Grenoble's tomorrow, then? Perhaps find something for you to report back to this Raffles woman?"

She felt Ashbridge's gaze on her face, and glanced sideways, their eyes meeting for a brief second before he looked away. "Until tomorrow, then."

She told herself, as she walked home after watching Ashbridge hop onboard a northbound bus, that she wasn't looking forward to it.

But that, too, would have been a lie.

Chapter Twelve

"What's wrong?" Hazel asked on Thursday afternoon, as she and Vesper were having lunch at the Cauldron on Marylebone High Street.

"Why do you think something's wrong?"

"You've got that worried V forming between your eyebrows. You're usually too vain about your forehead to allow it."

"Merely thinking about Ashbridge."

Hazel gasped. "I *knew* it."

"Hazel. Merlin. Not like *that*."

"Oh." Hazel sagged. "I thought this was turning into a romance, and I was quite excited."

"Don't you have enough romance in your own life?" Vesper asked. "You and Delacqua have seemed cozy lately."

Hazel sighed, looking a bit morose. She was spared answering by the arrival of the sandwiches and soup they'd ordered, but once this had been sorted and their waiter had retreated, Vesper leaned forward.

"Why did you look like that, when I mentioned Delacqua?"

Hazel toyed with a teaspoon. "I like John an awful lot," she said, looking even more glum now. "He's so kind—I love talking to him, and spending time with him. But I just—I just don't know if I want to kiss him. And eventually, if he realizes that, he'll be off to find someone who does. And my father is *so* worried about me finding someone to marry, so I'll have to start this process all over again with someone else, and—"

"Has Delacqua been pressuring you to kiss him?" Vesper asked, prepared to sweep into a righteous fury on behalf of her friend.

"No, of course not. He's lovely."

"And you enjoy spending time with him?" Vesper pressed.

"Very much. We have such nice conversations—he's so *interesting*, I really like talking to him."

"Then why worry about it? Don't kiss him until you want to."

"But that's just it, what if I *never* want him to? I'll have wasted all his time."

Vesper huffed in exasperation. "Hazel, he's a man. Unlike us, there's no clock set to chime on his twenty-fifth, or thirtieth, or whichever birthday is arbitrarily decided to be the point at which he's too old to marry. He's a rich, handsome bachelor. He'll be fine. And he clearly enjoys spending time with you, so—let him. And don't kiss him if you don't want to."

Hazel's expression shifted into something desperately fond as she looked across the table at Vesper. "Thanks, Vee." She squeezed her hand, and then returned to her sandwich.

Vesper reached for her own, and, just before taking a bite,

asked curiously, “Do you think you might want to kiss women instead?”

Hazel choked. Vesper supposed, when asking a question like that, it would be wise in the future to consider whether the person she was interrogating might be at risk of a blocked airway before proceeding.

“You might warn me the next time you’re going to ask a question like that,” Hazel said, once she’d recovered enough to speak.

“That occurred to me after the fact,” Vesper agreed, contrite.

“But to answer the question,” Hazel said, blushing again, “I—the thought *had* crossed my mind, so I, er . . .” She looked around furtively.

“Stop that. You’re going to make the waitstaff think we’re planning a bank heist.”

“I don’t want to be overheard!”

“You look *so guilty.* We’re talking about sex, Hazel, not murder.”

“We’re talking about *kissing*, you libertine, let’s please not bring nudity into this.”

“*I* have personally found that a bit of nudity really makes kissing more interesting, and especially—”

“*My point is*, I, um, considered that option, and so I procured some, er, literature, featuring only women, that I thought might provide clarity, but I found it to be unfortunately . . . unstimulating. Compared to similar literature involving, um, men and women.”

It took Vesper a second to parse the linguistic gymnastics

being deployed, but she eventually cottoned on. "Hazel Thomas. You bought dirty books!"

"Shh!" Hazel said, despite the fact that Vesper had spoken barely above a whisper.

"Where did you get them?" asked Vesper, a seasoned connoisseur. "Quill & Ink?"

Hazel nodded. Quill & Ink was a famous bookshop in Marylebone, owned for a century by the Hawthornes, an old magical family whose specialty had always lain in the written word—rumor had it, they made spell powders that increased focus and aided brainstorming, and even one that caused inspiration to strike, though Vesper had heard from more than one rueful author that the quality of the ideas produced by the spell powder tended to be rather hit-or-miss. They also ran a roaring, albeit discreet, trade in erotic literature. Vesper had always found this impressively bold, considering that the backroom operations were flouting both Forbiddance *and* obscenity laws.

"Hazel." Vesper grinned at her friend. "I've never been prouder of you."

"That's because you're a degenerate," Hazel said, still blushing.

"Not anymore," Vesper informed her. "I've taken a vow of celibacy. Holloway's is my sole focus—well, Holloway's, and playing detective with Ashbridge."

"A real barrier to that vow of celibacy," Hazel said slyly.

Vesper offered her a repressive look. "We were talking about *your* love life, not mine. Which has nothing to do with Ashbridge anyway—"

"Except for the fact that he's seen your bare chest."

"*Years* ago. I expect he barely remembers."

Hazel shot a considering look at the anatomy in question. "I don't think that's the sort of chest that a man soon forgets."

"Thank you, I've never been so flattered. But Ashbridge and I aren't like that."

"Yet."

"Ever. He's . . ." Vesper waved a hand.

"Handsome?"

"No. Well . . ." Vesper reconsidered. "Yes, obviously. But that's not interesting to me."

"For the first time in your life?"

Vesper tossed a lump of sugar at her. "Ashbridge and I are colleagues. This has nothing to do with love—"

"Or lust?"

"Or *anything*," said Vesper, businesslike now. "We were at Plenus Venter together last night, and there wasn't the slightest whiff of romance about it."

"Well, that's not surprising, given all the blood," Hazel said, very matter-of-factly.

Vesper blinked. "Excuse me?"

Hazel frowned. "Didn't you hear? There was another accident at Plenus Venter last night, just before closing time; I heard about it when I ran into Edith Kent on the way to meet you."

"But! But! We were *there*." Vesper was feeling extremely put out; what point was there in conducting an investigation if they were going to miss something interesting?

"Not late enough, I suppose," Hazel said. "Someone drank a potion and then had a nosebleed that lasted *half an hour*. That's an alarming amount of blood." Hazel considered the soup before her, then seemed to decide that she was hungry enough to not be put off by the topic of conversation.

Vesper, meanwhile, was turning this information over in her mind. While she was infuriated to have missed this—and was frantically casting her mind back over the memory of every face she'd seen the night before—this was, in one sense, useful information: Plenus Venter had now been hit twice. Whoever was behind this was not opposed to repeated strikes on the same club, which meant that Holloway's would not necessarily be spared further mischief.

All the more reason, Vesper thought grimly, taking a bite of her sandwich, that she and Ashbridge needed to get to the bottom of this, sooner rather than later.

◆

"I've watched at least a half dozen men walk into this place in the five minutes I've been waiting for you who are already pissed, so this bodes well." This was Ashbridge's greeting to her that evening outside Grenoble's; his brow was lowered, and he looked to be in a bit of a mood. Not that she could blame him—Hazel's report from Plenus Venter had left Vesper feeling on edge as well.

"It's a rather different environment to Mauve's, you'll see," she admitted, eyeing the exterior of Grenoble's with some distaste. It was situated on Welbeck Street, an imposing building with columns and a gaudy gold front door. There was a steady stream of well-heeled patrons making their way through its doors.

She reached out and twined an arm through Ashbridge's.

"Try to look enamored, will you?" she murmured, as he

leaned down to catch her words. "I think people will think it a bit odd that I'm here, otherwise."

She hadn't worried about this as much at Mauve's or Plenus Venter, but given her family's history with the Grenobles—Lucian Holloway's fisticuffs with Anthony Grenoble had become the stuff of society legend—her presence here was likely to raise a few eyebrows.

"Did you care to elaborate on what, precisely, your history with the Grenobles is?" he murmured back, his breath warm against her temple.

"Merely a catastrophic romantic mistake, born of youthful folly and too much champagne. Oh, and my father punched the current owner once. Shall we?" she asked brightly, and led a gaping Ashbridge into the club.

She had a courtesy membership at Grenoble's and was waved through the door by a bored-looking attendant, wearing rather less clothing than the chilly evening seemed to demand. Vesper suspected she'd taken some sort of warming potion—or just had a fair amount to drink.

Once inside, she and Ashbridge shed their coats and took in their surroundings. There was a sitting room off to one side, featuring an awful lot of red velvet and darkened corners; a quick glance inside confirmed that there was at least one couple on a settee kissing so enthusiastically that Vesper spared a thought for the virtue of the furniture. Another doorway led to a dining room, full of crystal and golden goblets and an almost aggressively bright chandelier. A dish on one table was dramatically aflame. Another room featured gilt-framed paintings of women in various stages of undress—this room, unsurprisingly, was crowded with men knocking back drinks and laughing uproariously. Vesper sighed; even she, a great fan of the sensual arts, could not find this particular space appealing. It was so . . . obvious.

She and Ashbridge headed for the back of the club, where the bar and dance floor were located. Each of the magical clubs had worked out how to sneakily flout Forbiddance in different ways. Holloway's had its secret bar, and Plenus Venter its elaborately and specifically worded request for the magical menu, while Grenoble's operated entirely out of one bar, with a password needed to receive the menu of magical offerings. The password changed weekly, and members were advised of it through a glossy embossed card that appeared in their postbox every Friday morning at seven, with instructions to destroy it immediately upon reading. This had always seemed a risky system to Vesper—so many opportunities for a bit of cardstock to go astray, after all—yet the Grenoble family was wealthy and powerful enough that so far the system had operated without issue.

"Bathtub hunting," Vesper informed the bartender, who had a glimmering sheen around his hairline. The passwords were always nonsensical combinations like this, phrases that couldn't be accidentally spoken by someone not in the know. A printed menu was slid across the bar toward her, and Vesper scrutinized it, considering. Ashbridge leaned in to read over her shoulder, and she could faintly smell his cologne, something smoky and complex. Unlike many men, he hadn't doused himself in it, and she could catch only the occasional whiff if she turned her head the right way.

She wrinkled her nose as she looked over the menu; Grenoble's potions had never been her favorite. She'd always found them to have a strange aftertaste—a product of whatever Word the family used to make the magic take hold—and was not particularly fond of the effects, either. Their specialty lay in the lowering of inhibitions, usually to more or less harmless effect—the Kick Back, for example, gave the drinker a sudden overpowering confidence in their own dancing abilities that lasted for several hours. However, there were a couple of items on the menu that made her decidedly wary—the Pucker Up induced three-quarters of an hour of wanting to kiss anyone in sight. Thinking it would draw too much attention to them if they both opted for alcoholic rather than magical drinks, however, she ordered a Warm and Fuzzy, the drink that, if she recalled correctly, came closest to mimicking the bonhomie and rose-colored glasses that actual spirits often provided. It was popular among clubgoers who tended to grow melancholy rather than cheerful when drinking alcohol.

Having claimed their drinks, they made their way toward a table tucked away in a corner that would allow for some semblance of a private conversation. Once seated, Vesper sipped slowly at her potion, and wished she'd ordered a cocktail to go along with it. Out of the corner of her eye, she watched Ashbridge; he had ordered a whisky soda, which he was now nursing as he surveyed the room.

"Stop looking so alert," she muttered.

He cut an exasperated glance at her. "I'm *paying attention.*"

"Do it in a less obvious way, or no one will believe you're here simply to enjoy yourself. Have you seen me?" She gestured at this evening's dress, a fetching concoction of white silk and a few carefully placed feathers.

"Yes. Very swanlike."

"*Swanlike*. Do you know who designed this?"

"I'm going to do you the enormous favor of saving you the energy of explaining, because I assure you the name would mean nothing to me."

Vesper leaned forward to poke him in the chest. "I can't decide if it's fortunate, or a complete waste that you're handsome."

Ashbridge went slightly pink and busied himself with his drink.

"What I meant to say is, I am obviously a delicious creature and no one is going to believe you're not up to something suspicious if you don't appear to be attempting to take liberties."

"Oh?" Ashbridge raised a skeptical brow. The gesture should have been annoying—*was* annoying—but that didn't stop it from also somehow being extremely attractive. Vesper was not scientifically minded, but she really thought that considerable energy should be spent studying the whims of the human body, which were ever mystifying and frequently maddening.

Under his gaze, Vesper attempted not to fidget—not normally something she struggled with. She attempted a languorous expression. He frowned. "Something wrong? Your face went all—" He broke off, and twisted his face into an expression that, dear Merlin, Vesper *deeply* hoped bore no resemblance to the one that had been on her own.

"You're a terrible mimic," she said, willing the words to be true. "I'm attempting to set the mood, if you will."

"I won't. We're business partners."

"Ha! Not three days ago you were calling me incredibly irritating."

"Well, I'm softening in my old age."

Vesper batted her eyelashes flirtatiously. "How unfortunate for you."

"Stop that."

"But I don't want to," she said, pouting, before taking pity on him and taking a sip of her drink. "I can't be the first woman who's ever tried to flirt with you," she added after a moment.

"Flirting is one thing. You're deliberately trying to provoke me, just to see what sort of reaction you'll get."

When he put it like that, Vesper did not like how childish it made her sound. "I'm not trying to *provoke* you," she objected. "You simply seem so unmoved by me that—" She broke off suddenly, a thought occurring to her. "You're not . . . involved with someone, are you?" She didn't know why this possibility hadn't crossed her mind before; Ashbridge was handsome, intelligent, and seemingly unimpressed by her many charms. It would make perfect sense.

"No," he said, the word a bit curt. He took a sip of his whisky soda, then lowered the glass, grimacing slightly. "I—there was someone, a few years ago. I thought we'd eventually marry, but she . . . well, she didn't think that I loved her enough for that."

"And did you?" Vesper asked, curious.

He met her eyes. "No," he said simply. "She did me a favor, really—took me a while to realize it, of course. But I suppose it made me a bit wary. If I could have been so mistaken, thinking I was in love when it was mere fondness . . ."

"Better to mistake fondness for love, than to *actually* fall in love with a man who had a wife at home," Vesper said ruefully.

His gaze darkened. "You're not . . . still in love with him, are you?"

Vesper managed a laugh. "No. It was years ago, when I was young and an idiot—more of an idiot than I am now, I mean," she added, smiling.

He didn't smile back. "You're not an idiot," he said quietly. "You're extremely clever, actually, even if it seems like you don't want anyone to notice."

Vesper blinked, never having thought of it in precisely those terms. The thing was, she had realized of late that she *did* want someone to notice—her family, in particular. But she'd spent so long being flirtatious, flighty Vesper Holloway that it seemed rather difficult to change course now.

"Is this man—the bounder, I mean—is he the reason you're not—er—" He broke off suddenly, looking a bit sheepish.

"Were you about to ask me if he's the reason I'm not married?" Vesper asked, amused. "How Victorian of you, Ashbridge."

He tugged at his collar. "Sorry. I meant, more, that you don't seem to be looking for anything . . . serious."

Her smile faded. "No," she said quietly. "He was the first heartbreak, but it was the last one that really hurt—a thoroughly decent man whom I loved quite desperately, and who simply realized he was in love with someone else."

"He was a fool, then," Ashbridge said, meeting her eyes. And Vesper—who realized, all at once, that it had been years since she'd spoken of this with anyone, even her family, or Hazel—

suddenly felt uncomfortably exposed. This time, she was the one to look away, Ashbridge's steady gaze suddenly more than she could bear. She took a long sip of her drink. Feeling his eyes on her as she drank, she lowered the highball glass a bit. "You know, it's a little unnerving when you do that," she said, her voice tart.

"Well, I personally find it a little unnerving when a woman I'm theoretically supposed to be keeping from harm is drinking something that seems carefully designed to make it more difficult to do that."

"You are a wet blanket, aren't you, Ashbridge?" She was trying to annoy him, in the hopes that it might distract him from everything that she'd just revealed about herself, but his gaze on her was knowing, as if he saw right through her.

"Forgive me for wanting to make sure you get home in one piece," he said dryly.

"In case you weren't aware, I do run my family's club and manage to make it home in one piece most evenings, last I checked. And, furthermore, I'm not a complete idiot, and am aware of why we're here. I deliberately selected the drink that I thought would have the least effect on me. Almost as if I were being *cautious* and hoping that I might accomplish something this evening other than having a row with you." Her tone was sharper than the situation warranted, and she took another sip, avoiding his eyes once again. This was what came of sharing her feelings, she thought: She was behaving like a complete ninny.

Ashbridge's expression was difficult to read. After several seconds' silence, during which he regarded her steadily while she made rather a show of being absolutely absorbed by the jazz band occupying the stage in one corner, he said quietly, "You're right. I'm sorry."

"You—what?"

"I'm sorry," he repeated, patient. "You're right. I was—well, I wasn't treating you like an equal partner in this investigation, which I know is what we agreed you would be."

"A man is apologizing to me. I never thought this day would come."

"Well," Ashbridge said then, looking irate, "I think we've already established that you've been spending too much time with men who don't deserve any of yours."

It was Vesper's turn to fall silent for a moment, because she had no reply to that—because she suspected it was the truth.

Before she could work out how to steer the conversation into less emotionally fraught territory, however, she caught sight of movement out of the corner of her eye, and a face that she unfortunately recognized all too well. He was heading in their direction, though she didn't think he'd spotted her just yet, which meant that she had seconds to act—to calm herself down, to school her expression into something light and cheerful. She realized, however, in the same moment that she didn't think she could do it quickly enough; she felt raw and unprotected, and it was important, just now, that her face showed none of that. And so, she did the only thing she could think of in that instant, and slowly tilted her head up toward Ashbridge, keeping the movement as slow and languid as she could manage.

"Ashbridge," she murmured. "Can you trust me for a moment?"

A frown creased his brow. "What do you mean?" he asked, matching her undertone.

"Just—I'm sorry about this," she said, then reached her hand up, cupped his neck, and drew his face down to hers.

It was hardly the first time Vesper had kissed a man with the goal of gaining another man's attention; it was an old, well-worn trick in her playbook, men being the predictable creatures that they were. It was, however, the first time that the man being kissed had gone as completely, entirely still as Ashbridge did the moment her lips met his. In an instant, Vesper was years younger, only eighteen, kissing Ashbridge because it had never occurred to her that a man might simply want to *speak* to her, to show her kindness, without expecting anything else. And now, in a sudden rush of embarrassing memories, she wondered if she were about to be pushed away again—

But then, after a second, it was as if his brain caught up to the situation, and he relaxed against her, his mouth softening to return her kiss. She pressed closer to him, sliding her hand into the short hair at the nape of his neck, holding him close. His mouth was warm as it moved against hers; his arm dropped to her waist, then her hip, pulling her against him so that her breasts were flattened against his chest and she could feel the pulse of his heart racing in time with her own. He turned his head, and their noses bumped; with his free hand, he reached down to cup her jaw, angling her face slightly so that he could deepen the kiss.

Vesper's body felt as if it had come alive; all she knew was the warmth of his mouth, the woodsy, smoky scent of his skin, the firm pressure of his fingers at her jaw. The faintest, fleeting slip of his tongue against hers.

And then, as if from a great distance, there was a voice—one that Vesper knew, dimly, but it took her a full two seconds to register it, to remember why she was there, why she was kissing *Ashbridge* in the first place . . .

"Vesper Holloway, I did not expect to see *you* here tonight."

Slowly, she drew back, gazing up at Ashbridge. His cheeks were a bit flushed, and his eyes were unreadable as they met hers. She blinked, and slowly shifted in her seat, turning on her brightest smile, which she now directed at Edward Grenoble.

"Edward!" she said, shaking her head slightly as if to clear it, which wasn't entirely an act. "It's been ages!" She allowed him to kiss her hand in a manner that made her want to shudder. A hand kiss was the most innocuous of gestures, but leave it to Grenoble to turn it into something that felt slimy and cheap. A particular skill of his.

"No one to blame but yourself for that fact, Vesper," Grenoble said, offering her a sad-puppy expression that genuinely made her want to toss her drink in his face. He was handsome, she'd give him that, with auburn hair and arresting green eyes, broad shoulders, a wicked grin—but it was ruined for her by the knowledge of what a cad he was. She could practically *see* him undressing her with his eyes. It was frankly astonishing that she'd ever been attracted to this man.

She kept her smile firmly pinned in place. "I know," she said, all rueful embarrassment. "But I'm so pleased to have run into you—I desperately needed a night to blow off some sparks, you know?"

Out of the corner of her eye, she saw Ashbridge give the faintest eye roll at the magical expression, but she ignored him;

ideally, Ashbridge would say as little as possible to Grenoble, and they'd emerge from this conversation with no one bleeding.

"You seem to have managed that," Grenoble said, his smile turning arch and a bit knowing as he glanced at Ashbridge.

Vesper let out a titter. "Well, you know. It's not too difficult to find company, and I wanted to . . . take my mind off things." She offered a bit of a pout.

"Heard about your little mishap at Holloway's," Grenoble said, shaking his head. "Must have been a shock."

"Oh, it was nothing *too* serious—just a bit of excitement on a Friday evening. You were there, someone said?"

"I was," Grenoble agreed, with no sign of unease, which was disappointing, in terms of his likelihood of being a suspect. Still, Vesper decided to prod a bit.

"I didn't notice you," she said.

Grenoble—ugh—leered. "Looking for me, were you?"

"Well," Vesper said slowly, "it's nice to know one's . . . options."

Grenoble's self-satisfied smile grew even wider. Next to Vesper, Ashbridge had gone so still in his seat that she chanced a sideways glance to confirm that he was still breathing. He was—and he was regarding Grenoble with an expression of such open disdain that Vesper's breath caught in her throat.

Considering all she knew of Max Ashbridge, she suddenly saw Grenoble through his eyes: moneyed, magical, spoiled. A man who'd had every single thing in his life handed to him, and yet still wanted more.

Grenoble was the very worst sort of advertisement for the privileged magical elite, Vesper realized in a rush, and a hot burst of shame overtook her, startling in its suddenness and novelty. She was not one to often feel ashamed of anything.

"Where were you when your friend had his little incident?" asked Ashbridge now—with about as much subtlety as a hammer—and Grenoble jerked his gaze away from Vesper to focus on Ashbridge.

"Sorry, who the hell are you?" he asked.

"Ashbridge." He extended his hand, which Grenoble shook, still looking as though he were sizing Ashbridge up, trying to decide where to place him in some invisible pecking order. Men like Grenoble always were, Vesper thought with an internal sigh.

"He was at Cambridge with Freddie," Vesper put in, hoping that this would be sufficient context for Grenoble to lose interest.

Instead, Grenoble frowned. "Why does that name ring a bell?"

Ashbridge smiled thinly. "I couldn't tell you."

"He was a few years ahead of you, Edward, I doubt your paths crossed," Vesper said, eager to steer this conversation away from a direction in which Grenoble was giving too much thought to Ashbridge's presence.

"You didn't answer my question, though," Ashbridge said, leaning forward.

Grenoble's smile had become rather forced. "And what question was that?"

"Where were you," Ashbridge repeated, enunciating each word clearly, "when all hell broke loose at Miss Holloway's club?"

"What business is it of yours?" Grenoble asked, puffing out his chest a bit.

Vesper gave a tinkling little laugh, and then leaned over to press herself to Ashbridge's side, laying a hand on his chest. "None at all, of course—Ashbridge here just gets a bit protective of anything to do with me." She tilted her head back to peer up at Ashbridge through her lashes. "Isn't that right, crumpet?"

This close to Ashbridge, she could see the tension in his jaw, hear the slight inhale as she leaned toward him. He glanced down at her, his eyes unreadable, and then—

He *smiled.*

Not the kind of smile she had grown used to coaxing out of him, either—quick, fleeting, half-imagined things, gone as soon as they'd arrived. This was a proper smile, spreading slowly across his face, causing crinkles to form at the edges of his eyes. It was hypnotic; Vesper felt as though she were caught by a powerful magnetic force. She couldn't look away.

And then he slid his hand to her hip, squeezed, and leaned just close enough to give the impression of great intimacy. "Of course it is, teacake."

Vesper was gripped by a wild desire to laugh, but suppressed it, instead meeting his smile with a sultry one of her own. She leaned in closer.

At that moment, Grenoble made rather a show of dramatically clearing his throat, and Vesper blinked, then glanced up at him, as if she'd forgotten his presence.

"I was with Zelda McCourt," he said through a clenched jaw. His eyes were narrowed, taking in the scene of Vesper and Ashbridge. Ashbridge's thumb stroked a slow circle on her hip; the heat of it, even through the fabric of her dress, made it hard to think.

Vesper frowned, as if she'd forgotten what they were discussing entirely.

"At your club the other night," Grenoble said, looking even more annoyed. "We left . . . quite early." A bit of smugness had returned to his voice, though he was still viewing Ashbridge with considerable hostility. "As you two might consider," he added, a bit spitefully.

Ashbridge smiled at him, a thin, dangerous thing. "We'll take that under advisement."

"However . . ." Here, Grenoble leaned down, bracing one hand on the table so that he could loom over Vesper. She didn't gratify him by leaning back even a centimeter. "Vesper, if you're still feeling a bit shaken up about what happened, well, I'd love to help an old friend out, you know. Offer comfort in whatever way I can."

Vesper managed a sickly-sweet smile. "That's so kind of you."

"I do what I can." He reached out, chucked her under the chin, and gave her what he clearly considered to be an extremely seductive, nigh-impossible-to-resist smile. "You know where to find me." This was uttered in a low, intimate tone. Vesper resisted the urge to gag, but it was a near thing. Grenoble directed one last glare at Ashbridge, and a moment later had vanished into the crowd.

Vesper took a deep, fortifying breath—and then a deep, fortifying sip of her Warm and Fuzzy—before turning back to Ashbridge, whose hand had slipped from her hip the second Grenoble turned away. His expression was a bizarre combination of thunderous and amused, two emotions that Vesper had never considered natural bedfellows.

"You cannot be serious."

"I was *twenty-one*," she said. "No one makes intelligent decisions when they're twenty-one."

"That was my first year at Cambridge. Shall I let you take a look at my exam results?"

"If that's your idea of how to attract women, I imagine your bed must be a very cold and lonely one, Ashbridge."

"You really are astonishingly irritating when you set your mind to it, aren't you?" he asked conversationally.

Vesper could not help but be flattered; she didn't know *why* she wanted to be irritating to Ashbridge, except for some vague, ill-defined sense that she'd rather be annoying to him than nothing at all. This, she thought darkly, was likely how she'd ended up flinging herself at him in the first place, all those years ago.

A fact that she had *not* failed to notice had yet to be brought up. At least now she had a more recent memory of kissing him to replace her memories of that mortifying evening, she thought, trying to be philosophical about the whole thing. It was difficult to be entirely philosophical, however, when the memory of Ashbridge's kiss—the warmth of his mouth, the taste of him, the strength of his hands on her body—was so fresh in her mind.

It was distracting, and she couldn't really afford that at the moment.

"You know," she began, really settling into things and looking forward to a continued exchange of warm regards with Ashbridge, but before she could continue their convivial conversation, she was interrupted without warning by the rather unusual sight of a man directly opposite their table standing up and beginning to strip naked.

"Is this normal?" Ashbridge asked in an undertone, his eyes fixed on the man, who was behaving as though he were possessed, his movements frenzied, jerky, uncontrolled. "I know you said the potions lower inhibitions—"

"No," Vesper said, pressing her lips together. The man's companions were protesting—a couple even reached for his arms, as if to physically restrain him, but he shook them off with ease, as if possessed of supernatural strength. His chest was now bare, and he started on his trousers. Half the club was watching the spectacle by this point, a sort of embarrassed, fascinated horror having gripped the room. Edward Grenoble was at the man's side now, speaking to him in an undertone, but the man paid no more mind to him than he had to his friends, and within another half a minute, he was entirely nude.

And then, a second later, he slumped to the floor.

Chapter Thirteen

The club immediately descended into pandemonium.

There were several dramatic shrieks—one from close enough that Max's ears rang for several seconds afterward—and a woman at a nearby table slumped dramatically into the arms of the man next to her, though Vesper's muttered *"honestly"* made him suspect that the lady's distress might not have been entirely genuine.

Grenoble, predictably, was making a bit of an idiot of himself—loudly demanding to know what drink the unconscious man had been consuming, gesticulating wildly, but doing nothing whatsoever to deal with the body slumped at his feet.

Max was up in an instant, cutting through the crowd; moments later, he was crouching on the floor, reaching out to check for a pulse. Finding a fairly strong one, he exhaled; dealing with an unconscious body was a considerably less alarming prospect than reckoning with a dead one.

"Is he alive?" came Vesper's voice from behind him; he hadn't even noticed that she'd followed him, though he supposed he shouldn't have been surprised.

"Yes. I don't suppose you have smelling salts?" He didn't look at her as he spoke, his attention still focused on the man before him, who gave no sign of stirring. His breathing was shallow, his face very pale. "Or can someone telephone a doctor?"

Vesper was uncharacteristically silent for a prolonged moment, and Max glanced over his shoulder at her. "What is it?"

"Well . . . it's just. I've some Mackleworth's Rapid Revival."

Max met her eyes; he was familiar with the potion, as it had been commonplace before Forbiddance. He had found some in his mother's medicine cabinet once, even though his parents generally shied away from the use of any magical products.

Max moved back to allow her to press closer to the man on the floor. She rummaged in her beaded clutch and extracted a small gold vial that she unstopped. "Can you hold his mouth open?"

Max didn't bother with his scruples. Instead, he leaned forward, pinched the man's nostrils closed, and—when the man gasped through his mouth—tipped his head back slightly, allowing Vesper to pour a small, shimmering splash of a purple liquid between his lips.

Within a few seconds, the man's eyelashes were fluttering, even as he choked a bit on the potion. Max clamped a hand over his mouth. "Swallow it," he said, leaning forward to speak directly into the man's ear, and after a few more moments of coughing and spluttering, the man opened his eyes and met Max's gaze directly.

"Ashbridge?" he asked, blinking in confusion.

Vesper's head whipped around so fast it was amazing she didn't injure herself. "Do you *know* him?"

And it was only now, at this close proximity, that Max realized he did: it was Devon Finchley, whom he'd known both during the war and later at Cambridge. They'd served in the Royal Army Service Corps together in France; Max liked Finchley. His family was posh and wealthy and had once been magical, though these days were merely magic sympathizers, but for all that, Finchley was a decent chap.

Max reached forward and helped Finchley into a seated position. "Are you all right?"

Finchley nodded slowly, wincing and clutching at his head as soon as he'd done so. "What happened?"

"We were rather hoping you could answer that question," Vesper said, and Finchley's gaze slid to hers, his eyes widening.

"It's Miss Holloway, isn't it?" He glanced back at Max. "Ashbridge, I didn't realize you ran in these circles."

"Ashbridge contains hidden depths," Vesper said, and Max chose to ignore the very skeptical expression that Finchley, even in his weakened, confused state, managed to summon in reply. "What potion did you drink?" she added, her tone a bit more urgent now.

Finchley's brow wrinkled. "I—I don't know. I was speaking to a very pretty girl and she had a potion—said she didn't want the rest of it, and asked me if I'd like to finish it."

Max and Vesper glanced at each other, but were able to ask Finchley no further questions, as his friends intervened at this point; someone tossed his suit jacket onto his lap, preserving what was left of his dignity. Finchley seemed only at that precise moment to notice that he wasn't wearing any clothes, and turned a brilliant scarlet; in short order, he was ushered away to the toilets, where he could get dressed.

Edward Grenoble, meanwhile, was still blustering like a fool. ". . . can't account for someone not being able to handle his potions, I suppose!"

Next to Max, a woman with mousy hair and a feathered headband frowned. "I say, Grenoble—isn't this just what happened at Holloway's and at Plenus Venter?"

"Not in the slightest," Grenoble protested, looking offended at the comparison. "Those were clearly bad potions—Finchley here just overdid it."

"I don't think so," chimed in another man; he had brown skin and was wearing an immaculately tailored suit and tails in a rich burgundy color. "That was only his second potion—he has an early morning tomorrow and said he wasn't going to drink too much."

Max could tell that Grenoble was growing more irate by the moment. "Don't be absurd—this was just a mishap."

"But it's the third—no, fourth—in the past fortnight," the woman said, her frown deepening. "It happened again at Plenus Venter last night." Max glanced at Vesper, startled, and she nodded grimly back.

She stood on tiptoe to murmur in his ear, "Hazel told me at lunch today. Apparently it happened after we left."

This was growing serious, Max thought, faintly alarmed. Holloway's on Friday—then Plenus Venter last night, and Grenoble's tonight.

The woman with the feathered headband seemed to be

thinking along similar lines. "If there's something going wrong with the magic at three different clubs now, then I wonder if we should be drinking potions at all."

"I don't think there's any cause to panic," Vesper said quickly.

Grenoble, for once, seemed inclined to agree. "Just so, Vesper. In fact, I think the thing that would settle everyone's nerves right now is"—he pitched his voice louder, to be certain that everyone in the vicinity overheard—"a free round of potions for everyone."

Whatever misgivings the assembled crowd might have had in the wake of recent events were evidently not strong enough to outweigh the promise of free magic, and there was a veritable stampede for the bar. Vesper wasted no time in approaching Grenoble, who was watching the crowd swarming his bartenders with a slightly pained expression—no doubt calculating how much money that peacekeeping measure had just cost him.

"Edward." Grenoble glanced down, looking startled to see that Vesper had materialized at his side. "Do you still prepare your potions on-site?"

He scowled at her. "I don't think that's any business of yours."

"For the love of—" She reached out and poked him in the arm. "Don't be dense, I'm not trying to steal your trade secrets. I'm trying to work out how this could have happened."

He gazed at her petulantly for a long moment, rubbing at the spot on his arm where she'd prodded him, then nodded reluctantly. "It's just too much of a faff to do it elsewhere—especially given that it needs to be done every night, if we don't want the flavors to go off." He glanced over at Max now, catching him eavesdropping, and his scowl reappeared with a vengeance.

"I say, Vesper, I don't think you should be discussing this in front of"—he dropped his voice to a dramatic stage whisper—"a mundane."

"Don't be an ass, Edward," Vesper said, her voice as sharp as Max had ever heard it.

"I've realized why the name Ashbridge sounds familiar," Grenoble continued, undeterred. "Don't you work for the Home Office in some capacity?"

Max met his eyes without flinching, then gave a sort of disinterested shrug. "What of it?"

"You don't see why I might be a bit suspicious, to find you lurking here in my club?"

Vesper reached back to seize Max's hand; he twined his fingers through hers, drawing her toward him so that her back—all that bare, soft skin, so much of it on display in her skimpy gown—pressed against his chest. "I promise, your club isn't the main attraction this evening."

Grenoble's eyes narrowed at the sight of them standing together so intimately. "Right. I suppose she is a good enough time to make you forget whatever principles you thought you had."

Max stiffened at that, dropping Vesper's hand, but she stayed him with a hand on his forearm. She glanced over her shoulder at him—one quick, unspoken word: *Don't.*

She turned back to Grenoble. "Don't be a boor—and stop trying to provoke Ashbridge. Did you see the girl Finchley was speaking to?"

Grenoble shrugged. "Awful lot of girls here tonight, Vesper." He sounded smug, as if he labored under the impression that he was the reason for their presence.

Despite being unable to see Vesper's face at the moment, Max could feel her disdain. "The girl he was speaking to before he collapsed," she pressed. "She's evidently the one who gave him the potion he drank just beforehand."

Finchley himself reappeared just in time to hear this, now fully clothed and holding a glass of water. "Who was this?" Grenoble demanded.

Finchley took a seat at an unoccupied table, still looking a bit pale. "She was a brunette. Curly hair. A mole just beneath one eye, lovely long eyelashes—quite pretty."

"And you'd never met her before?" Vesper asked.

"What's this all about, Vesper?" Grenoble asked, stepping a bit closer to her before pausing at whatever he caught sight of in Max's expression.

"I'm just trying to piece together what happened—here, and at Holloway's."

Grenoble's expression turned so condescending that Max was tempted to punch him. "Vesper, darling. I think you'd better leave this to others to sort out—I'll have a word with my father. Perhaps we can convene some sort of meeting with all the families. I don't think you need to worry about this, though."

"Who oversees the day-to-day operations of Grenoble's?" Max interjected.

Grenoble blinked. "What's it to you?"

"Mere curiosity. I see you're here tonight, in lieu of your father—is that normally how the club operates?"

Grenoble's cheeks flushed. "Not... normally," he said through gritted teeth, as though the admission pained him. "My father had another engagement this evening, and asked me to step in."

"I see. Then it seems to me that since Miss Holloway does oversee the daily operations of her family's club, you are the one who needn't worry about this. Perhaps she can arrange the meeting you had in mind, and your father can tell you about it afterward."

"Now see here," Grenoble began, the flush on his cheeks deepening; Max ordinarily wouldn't give a damn about scoring a point against an ass like this, but for some reason, the sight of that angry flush was extremely satisfying.

"With whom?" Vesper interrupted, and both men turned to look at her.

"Sorry?" Grenoble asked, impatience writ clearly in his voice.

"Whom did your father have an engagement with this evening?"

Grenoble shrugged. "I don't know—none of my concern."

"Do you think you could find out?" Vesper pressed. "Without letting him know what you're about?"

"Why should I?"

"Well." Vesper took two steps closer, and when she spoke again, her voice had dropped to a quiet murmur. "If you do, then I'll consider not telling every woman I know that you were the worst man I've ever gone to bed with."

Grenoble paled, then attempted to rally. "They wouldn't believe you."

"All right," Vesper said, smiling sweetly. "If you'd care to chance it . . ." She shrugged, then glanced back at Max. "Ashbridge, I think I've had enough merriment for the evening—will you take me home?"

"Of course." He extended his arm, and Vesper pressed close to him, then glanced at Grenoble.

"Well, Edward, I suppose I'll tell you good night."

Max was surprised Grenoble didn't break a tooth, given how tightly his jaw was clenched. "All right!" he burst out. "Give me a day or so, and I'll see what I can find out."

Vesper gave him her most dazzling smile. "Brilliant. Thank you, Edward." And with that, she swanned off toward the exit without another word, leaving Max to trail admiringly in her wake.

Once they were safely on the street, buttoning their coats, Max slid her a sideways glance. "That was well played."

Vesper shrugged. "Easy enough, with a man like Grenoble. Men like that are so predictable—all he cares is what people think of him. He doesn't mind if he never satisfies a woman in his life, so long as no one knows it." Distaste practically dripped from her words. "But," she added, brightening, "hopefully he'll tell us who his father was meeting tonight, as that might be another angle to investigate."

"You think someone deliberately lured Grenoble Senior off the premises, so that they'd be more likely to be able to tamper with a potion unobserved?"

"It's not completely insane."

"No," he agreed, "but it would mean that we're dealing with at least two people here—someone to distract Grenoble, and another to do the actual tampering."

"Perhaps this mystery brunette?" she suggested. "But whoever's doing it is magical."

"Do we know that?" he asked, frowning; he hadn't considered the mundane-versus-magical angle when pondering the precise nature of what was being done. "Couldn't someone have just added an extra ingredient and made the potions go off?"

Vesper shook her head immediately. "No. If you botch a recipe, it doesn't work at all—nothing happens. The syrups are mixed very carefully and require a specific amount of dilution in order to work. It's more precise than it seems, magical bartending. But to make a potion or spell powder have unintended consequences—like whatever Finchley was doing tonight, before he collapsed—that's magical interference."

"Meaning?"

"If a family's Word is employed on a substance that has already been bespelled by a different family . . . unpredictable things can happen."

"So for the potions to be reacting like this—"

"Means someone is whispering a Word over them after they're made," Vesper concluded.

"So." Max tapped his chin. "We ought to compile a list of people from magical families who have been present for any of the incidents, then, and work from there."

Vesper suddenly looked as though she were trying not to smile.

"Yes?" he asked cautiously.

"Well," she said, still fighting a smile, "the top of your list ought to be me, then. Two out of four, isn't it? And we were at Plenus Venter the night of their second accident, so really it's three out of four."

He shook his head at her. "Somehow, I doubt you're trying to sabotage your own club."

"That's the sort of presumption that won't see you solving any mysteries!" she said in a scolding tone.

"Come on," he said, feeling very weary. "It's been a long night, and I fancy something to eat."

"Max Ashbridge, are you asking me out to *dinner*?"

"If you count a late-night visit to a chippy, then certainly," he said dryly.

"Be still, my beating heart," she said over her shoulder. As he watched her slender, golden-haired figure slipping down the street a few steps ahead of him, occasionally tossing a teasing glance back at him, he was very much afraid that he needed to tell his own heart the same.

Chapter Fourteen

The next day was Friday, which meant that Vesper, unfortunately, had to face her family once again.

"There she is," Freddie said, as soon as she materialized in the drawing room. "The temptress herself."

Vesper scowled at her brother on instinct, despite not having the faintest notion what he was talking about. Bypassing the human inhabitants of the room entirely, she made a beeline for the bar cart in the corner. She seized the champagne bottle as though it were a life raft and poured herself a healthy glass.

"What are you on about?"

Freddie smiled innocently at her, which immediately set her on edge. "You and Ashbridge. Looking quite cozy at Grenoble's, I hear."

Quite cozy, Vesper thought, was an understatement—not that Freddie needed to know that. Or the fact that she'd replayed the memory of Ashbridge's kiss more than once last night before falling asleep.

"Merely trying to keep our cover story intact," she said airily, flopping inelegantly into an armchair next to Simon, who at the very least could be counted on to be a neutral party. Tonight, he had George on his knee; the latter was concentrating very hard on a thick volume that, despite his precociousness, Vesper was certain he could not possibly read.

Vesper jerked her chin at the book. "What's this, then?"

Simon sighed the long-suffering sigh of parents everywhere. "*The Iliad* in the original Greek."

"Ah," Vesper said, nodding, as if this were a perfectly normal thing for a five-year-old to be engrossed in. "Fluent, is he?"

"Give it a year or two," Simon said darkly. He leaned toward Vesper conspiratorially. "He's angry that he hasn't learned to read yet, so I've given him this—seemed safer than anything in English, since he might *actually* teach himself to read that."

"And what are you going to do if he somehow teaches himself to read Greek?"

"Send him to scientists to be studied," Simon said, looking unconcerned.

Vesper gave her brother-in-law a jaundiced look, and took a healthy sip of champagne.

"What about you and Ashbridge, then?" he asked, and her look turned to one of betrayal.

"Not you too!"

"I'm curious," he said with a shrug.

"You've been in the family too long. We've had a bad influence on you."

"Undoubtedly."

"Vesper, stop stalling and tell us what you and Ashbridge

learned," Cecily called from her spot on the sofa next to their mother, where they had their heads bent together, having previously been deep in discussion; Cecily had always had an annoying knack for keeping an ear on other people's conversations, even while conducting her own. "I heard about the poor chap last night."

"In a frenzy stripping naked, was he?" her father added, looking more satisfied than was remotely seemly. "I wish I could have seen Anthony Grenoble's face—"

"He wasn't there," Vesper said. "Just Edward."

She and Cecily exchanged grimaces.

Their father's face darkened. "If that young upstart so much as laid a finger on you—"

"Daddy, please, let's not do this." Being the youngest was very exhausting at times. "Besides, Ashbridge was there."

"And that's reassuring, is it?" Cecily asked, bearing a striking resemblance to a lion about to pounce.

"Yes, actually," Vesper said, feeling a bit defensive on Ashbridge's behalf. "If Edward Grenoble had tried any funny business, I'm fairly confident Ashbridge would have knocked him flat. I can trust him on that count."

"And that count alone," Lucian murmured, taking a sip of his own champagne. Vesper frowned; a week ago, she would have agreed with her father in this assessment of Ashbridge. But now . . .

She wasn't so certain.

"Let's please not lose focus," Amelia said briskly. "This isn't good. That's four accidents at the clubs in less than a fortnight. Word's beginning to spread."

"Is it?" Vesper asked, jerking her head up.

Amelia nodded, her expression concerned. "I had lunch with Lady Adele today."

Vesper frowned. "Who?"

Amelia now looked a bit exasperated, as she always did whenever someone couldn't keep up with her seemingly infinite social sphere. "Adele Audley. Mundane. Her brother is a duke. She was saying that she'd heard about what happened at Grenoble's last night—and that was only at *lunchtime* today. If word's spreading that fast . . ." She trailed off. This, Vesper thought, was precisely why her investigation with Ashbridge was important. If people began to fear that each time they drank a potion or inhaled some spell powder, they'd find themselves spinning around the chandelier or stripping naked in company, they'd become less willing to risk it.

And *that* would be very bad for business.

Vesper frowned into her drink.

Echoing her thoughts, her father said, "I don't like this. Simon, what's been said about it among the MPs?"

"Nothing so far," Simon said. "But if word is spreading this quickly, then I expect that will change—the second Finlay hears about this, he'll be like a predator scenting blood."

"The bill's going to be read in a fortnight," Cecily said, mirroring her father's frown. "And if things continue in this vein—or something actually dangerous happens—"

Vesper raised her chin. "Ashbridge and I are doing our best, you know."

Everyone blinked at her. "Of course you are, darling," Amelia said, in the same tone she'd employed to comfort Vesper when she'd fallen off her bicycle as a girl. Vesper—as so often seemed to be the case when she was around her family lately—wanted to scream with frustration. Why did everyone insist on treating her as though she were still a child? She was twenty-five! It was this vague feeling of resentment, which had been simmering within her for the past week or more, that propelled the next words out of her mouth—ones that, perhaps, she might have considered a bit more carefully before uttering them:

"And we're going to investigate the Duke and Earl next."

Silence fell at this pronouncement, as well it might.

"You . . . are?" Freddie asked, raising an eyebrow. "*You*, Vesper."

There was nothing for it at this point but to brazen it out, obviously.

"*I* am, yes, Frederick."

"And how, precisely, do you intend to do that?" Cecily asked, sounding amused.

"Freddie has a membership, if I recall," Vesper said, as if membership was the biggest obstacle.

"I do," Freddie agreed. "Though I think they might notice if I suddenly grow a pair of—"

"*Frederick Leighton Holloway*." That was Amelia, who was perfectly content to be appallingly bawdy with her friends—particularly once she'd had a glass or two—but who was rather capricious when it came to her children's language and manners.

Freddie, abashed, fell silent.

"Thank you, Freddie, for stating the obvious," Vesper interjected into the silence that had fallen. "I'm aware they don't allow women. But fortunately for all of us, I have a plan."

"I see. And I suppose you've informed Ashbridge of this plan already?"

"I have, yes," Vesper agreed. She'd always been a very confident liar—*too* confident, as more than one exasperated childhood nanny and governess had informed her parents on various occasions.

It wasn't *really* a lie, after all. It *would* be true—just as soon as she told Ashbridge that their next quest would involve a bit of cross-dressing.

What cause could he possibly have for complaint?

◆

That evening, just before bed, Vesper received a note from Edward Grenoble.

It was delivered to her by a member of the Grenoble family staff, who appeared at her door at half past midnight—Vesper had only been home from the club for a short while, but the boy at the door didn't appear to find it the slightest bit odd to be delivering a note to a woman in the wee hours of the morning. Vesper imagined that Grenoble kept him quite busy with such tasks, grimaced, and sent the boy off with a coin for his troubles.

The missive, on engraved stationery that featured a bit more gold foil than was to Vesper's taste, was brief:

V—

My father was out to dinner last night with Jacob Finlay, the mundane MP. I trust you'll keep your word.

—E

Vesper stared down at the words on the paper, her mind churning. Jacob Finlay: Simon's rival in Parliament. The architect of Forbiddance. As strong an anti-magic voice as there was to be found in the country these days. Why had *he* wanted to take Anthony Grenoble out to dinner? She supposed there must be some sort of greasing of palms happening; it was common enough practice, the cost of doing business now that magic was illegal, but she was a bit surprised to learn that Finlay partook. She'd always got the impression that he considered himself so principled as to be above this sort of thing—"maddeningly sanctimonious" was how Simon had once described him.

She supposed she should stop acting like a naive girl, and simply accept that this was how the world worked. And yet, as she got ready for bed and slid between her warm sheets, listening to the wind gust outside, she puzzled over the matter, something about this seeming not quite right.

She was still wondering about it when she finally fell asleep.

◆

Ashbridge lived in a cozy little flat in Hampstead village, within a stone's throw of the heath. Vesper had procured the address through her usual means—asking around.

The building was a red-brick Victorian with bay windows that must have been carved up into flats after its original owners sold the house. There was a small, neat garden between the front door and the street, hidden from view by a high wall and a wrought-iron gate that wasn't locked. She walked to the blue front door, took a breath, and then pressed the buzzer with a neat, handwritten label next to it that read TOP FLOOR – M. ASHBRIDGE.

There was a wait of perhaps thirty seconds, and then the door opened to reveal Ashbridge, wearing an expression of such honest astonishment that Vesper nearly laughed. As it was fairly early—not quite ten on a weekend—he was looking rather casual, dressed in a pair of gray wool trousers and what looked to be a hand-knit jumper of a deep forest green.

"Vesper," he said, his tone as startled as his expression, but he recovered quickly. "I wasn't aware you knew the hours before noon existed."

"Is this the bit where I'm meant to laugh at your wit?"

"Did we have an appointment I've forgotten?"

"Why don't you invite me in, rather than discussing this on the doorstep?"

She could see, for a split second, his wariness at war with his innate good manners, but the latter won out. He beckoned her into the tiny entryway and then led her up a couple of narrow flights of stairs before they emerged on a landing on the top floor. He opened the door to his flat and said, a bit wryly, "After you."

Vesper realized, as her gaze greedily took in the contents of Ashbridge's flat, that she was more curious than she might have liked to admit. It was small and tidy, composed of a sitting room, a little nook into which he'd set a table and two chairs, and a kitchen. There was another doorway, its wooden door shut, that Vesper presumed led to his bedroom.

Naturally, she made a beeline for that.

"Excuse me?" he asked, sounding nonplussed.

She cracked the door open and peeked inside. It was painted a serene white; the bed was tidily made with a dark blue quilt; a green rug covered the bare boards of the floor; atop a wooden dresser, she could see a framed photograph of a couple who she suspected must be his mother and stepfather. She had not expected the art on the walls, however: A large painting of the sea, done on canvas and framed, was over his bed; above his dresser, a series of still lifes in muted colors; on another wall, a rather charming sort of gallery display of framed advertisements from approximately twenty or thirty years earlier.

She stepped back into the sitting room, considering, and realized that these walls were similarly adorned: There were a couple of landscape paintings above the blue sofa; a mishmash of portraits and still lifes on the wall above the fireplace; even what appeared to be a collection of children's storybook illustrations.

Vesper blinked, feeling almost *charmed*. By *Ashbridge*. What on earth.

"Have you lost your mind?" he asked now, conversationally, and she startled a bit, having nearly forgotten he was there.

"We've discussed the warmth, or lack thereof, of your bed enough that I wanted to observe it for myself," she said, recovering her sangfroid, though she thought that it was a slightly weak effort, not sounding as carefree and breezy as she might have liked. "It doesn't look half as spartan as I expected."

"I'm flattered."

She grinned at him suddenly, unable to help herself. He was considerably more amusing than she'd first given him credit for. Something inscrutable crept across his face at the sight of her smile, but she didn't know how to decipher it.

"Ashbridge, you never said you loved art so much," she said, instead of puzzling over this further. "You don't strike me as the sort."

He shrugged, rubbing at the back of his neck, which she had come to recognize as a small tell—he only did it when he was embarrassed, or uncomfortable. "My mum used to take me to the museums—to the Victoria and Albert, and to the Tate Gallery, the National Gallery . . . I think she thought that just because we—well, just because we didn't have a lot of money didn't mean I shouldn't be exposed to some culture. And I loved it—could've stayed all day, even as a boy. I'd never traveled anywhere beyond the seaside in Kent, and it opened my eyes to the rest of the world. I would look at paintings of the canals of Venice, and imagine that I was there, too—it made the world feel so much larger. Of course," he added, his voice turning slightly bitter, "I *did* end up seeing a bit of the world, thanks to the war. It wasn't quite what I'd imagined."

Vesper moved closer to him as he spoke, strangely riveted. He was looking at her, but she had the strangest sensation that he wasn't seeing *her* at all in that moment. He blinked and met her eyes, a smile crossing his face. Combined with his mussed hair, and his jumper, and the fact that a quick glance down confirmed that he was in his stocking feet . . .

Well, he didn't look like Ashbridge at all.

Even his gray eyes seemed warmer, less unreadable.

Vesper thought, a bit wildly, that it was probably for the best that *this* Ashbridge seemed to exist only in the privacy of his own home, before noon on weekends, and not anywhere else.

"Are you going to tell me what the ever-loving hell you're doing here, now?" He broke the spell.

"I have devised a plan," she announced. She dropped her handbag onto the battered wood coffee table, shed her coat onto an armchair, and sank onto his sofa. It was surprisingly comfortable—Sheep would have approved.

"Oh, no," he said.

"Oh, yes," she confirmed. "You're not going to like it, and I'd wager you're going to pitch a bit of a fit about it, so why don't you spare me the bother of having to listen to all that and instead leap to the point where you agree to go along with it?"

"No," he said, crossing his arms. "I expect I'm going to be very wedded to that bit in the middle, actually."

She sighed. "It was worth a try. We're going to go to the Duke and Earl."

He blinked. "The—wait." A look of dark suspicion crossed his face. "Isn't that the one club left that's men only?"

"*Gentlemen* only," Vesper corrected him, in her poshest voice. She was attempting to sound like a combination of her grandmother and the Prince of Wales, but merely succeeded in sounding like she was a lifelong smoker with some sort of lung infection.

"And how, precisely, do you propose we sneak our way in there?" he asked. He was still standing, arms crossed, staring down at Vesper in a bemused sort of way that clearly conveyed that he had no notion of how his peaceful Saturday morning had gone so far wrong.

"You might have noticed that Freddie and I look rather similar," Vesper informed him cheerfully, and his expression darkened further.

"Vesper—"

"*And* Freddie has a membership."

"Freddie is also about six inches taller than you are, and lacking in certain—er—"

Here, he broke off, and Vesper leaned forward, delighted. He was blushing; the color was high in his cheeks, and he tugged at the collar of his jumper as if it were suddenly choking him.

"Yes, Freddie hasn't got breasts, thank you Ashbridge, I'm aware. I expect I'll manage to work around this problem with a bit of clever dressing."

He was blushing more furiously now at the word "breasts," which Vesper found a bit bemusing, considering he had, in fact, once *seen* the breasts in question, under less-than-ideal circumstances. Shouldn't *she* be the one blushing? Only one of them had humiliated themselves that night, after all.

"Why do we need to go there, particularly?" he asked now, recovering enough to speak, though not quite meeting her gaze.

She somehow didn't think *because I impulsively told my family we were going and now we've got to do it so that they'll think I'm Crafty and Competent and A Woman with a Plan* would go over well with this particular audience, so instead, she said, "I've been thinking, about which of the clubs *haven't* been hit yet, and it made me wonder—what if we ought to investigate the *least* likely candidate? The Duke and Earl is stodgy as hell; its owners are known to be friends with loads of mundane politicians, in fact. Nothing interesting *ever* happens there—which means *they'll* be the ones benefiting if business begins to dwindle at the other clubs."

It was the sort of place where nothing at all scandalous ever occurred. Vesper had been mildly surprised that the owners—a pair of elderly brothers of her grandmother's generation who flatly refused to pass the ownership down to their daughters—had elected to keep the club running once Forbiddance came into effect, but it seemed their obsession with propriety did not extend to the point of allowing their own business to be shut down, though their offerings continued to be considerably less flashy than those of the other clubs. Freddie had told her once that one of their menu items was a finger of whisky combined with a teaspoon of spell powder, and its sole effect was to cause the imbiber to grow a particularly bushy moustache for precisely six hours.

Ashbridge, meanwhile, still looked unconvinced. "I don't think—"

"Ashbridge, it's been a week since the attack at Holloway's, and my mother says gossip is beginning to spread. We need to take bolder action."

"And by 'bolder action,' you mean you in trousers."

"I look quite enticing in trousers, I'll have you know."

"I've no doubt," he said absently. "So you think . . . what? The owners of the Duke and Earl are somehow orchestrating this? Sending someone to infiltrate the other clubs and tamper with their magic?"

"Perhaps," she said, and leaned forward. "Grenoble sent me a note last night—his father was at dinner with Jacob Finlay."

Ashbridge's brow wrinkled. "You can't be serious. Finlay won't have anything to do with the magical world."

Vesper shrugged. "I thought it was odd myself—odd enough to be worth investigating. If he's mixed up in this somehow . . ." She shook her head. "It's all the more reason to go to the Duke and Earl—if there are any club owners who would be likely to know Finlay, it's them. They're very old-fashioned, just Finlay's sort of chaps."

"Except for the bit where they're magical," Ashbridge said, sounding a bit skeptical.

Vesper sighed. "It's as good an idea as any other. It's not as though we're making much progress."

"We've only been at it a week. I didn't expect us to sort it out overnight."

"But the longer this goes on, the more likely word is to spread. My mother heard gossip from a mundane friend yesterday."

"Didn't know you had those."

Vesper's temper flared. "You know, Ashbridge, you *might* pause to consider that you don't actually know all that much about us, if you think we're so prejudiced that we wouldn't have any mundane friends. Last I checked, *you're* the one who seems to have a problem associating with anyone magical; my family doesn't mind about that at all when choosing our friends. Or have you forgotten the years that you and Freddie were best mates?"

Ashbridge went very still at the mention of her brother's name. "I don't want to talk about Freddie."

"Of course you don't," she muttered. "Just as he never wants to talk about you, or whatever it was that you two quarreled about, because Merlin forbid he have to admit that he misses you."

Ashbridge's jaw tensed. "I doubt it. I can't imagine a mighty Holloway missing an Ashbridge all that much." Without thinking, Vesper reached out a hand and laid it atop his. His gaze dropped to her fingers pressing into his skin, then slowly raised to her face. His gray eyes were intent on hers.

"You don't rate yourself highly enough, then," Vesper said, speaking very clearly, "if you think that your friendship wouldn't be missed." No sooner were the words out of her mouth than she felt itchy with the sudden, unvarnished honesty of them.

Ashbridge was silent for a long moment, never breaking eye contact, before at last saying quietly, "I wasn't trying to start a quarrel with you." He flipped his palm up to wrap around her fingers, giving them a quick squeeze.

Vesper dropped his hand, feeling oddly flustered. "My point was, originally, that we need to make progress on this investigation, or it's going to hurt business—and, presumably, someone else from the Fleas—"

"F.L.E.A."

"—will get involved."

He raised a dark brow. "And that would be so terrible." He, apparently unconsciously, rubbed at the spot on his hand that Vesper had gripped.

Vesper curled her fingers into her palm. "Yes," she said lightly. "I've rather got used to you by now." She leaned closer. "Did you just roll your eyes? Max Ashbridge, I am *delighted*, I thought you were far too polite!"

"Growing less polite with each moment I'm forced to spend in your company," he murmured, but there was the smallest of smiles curving at the corner of his mouth, and she knew he didn't mean it, even before he added, with a sideways glance at her, "You know I'm only joking. This has been—"

"Thrilling?" Vesper suggested. "Invigorating? Stimulating? Eye-opening?"

"Not as much of a catastrophe as I initially expected," he replied, and Vesper decided, on the whole, that she was going to take that as a compliment.

Chapter Fifteen

Max had known he was going to regret this scheme, but he hadn't been quite prepared for *how* quickly he'd regret it.

"This is never going to work," he pronounced, the moment he met Vesper at the corner of Blandford Street and Marylebone High Street later that evening.

"Stop being hysterical—*you're* going to give us away, carrying on like this," Vesper protested.

"Yes, 'hysterical' *is* often an adjective that is applied to me," he agreed, shaking his head. "Your brother has at least four inches on you."

"How fortunate, then, that he's not standing next to me for people to compare me with," she said. She did, he had to admit, bear more of a resemblance to Freddie than he might have expected; she was wearing a pair of black trousers and a well-tailored black jacket, complete with a tie, and she'd hidden her own hair beneath a wig (he assumed—otherwise, she'd had a very dramatic haircut at some point in the past ten hours). He wondered, briefly, how on earth she had produced all of this on such short notice; there was no telltale sheen around the hairline indicating she'd consumed anything magical, leaving him all the more (reluctantly) impressed.

"Ready?" he asked wearily.

"Of course I am," she said, and began to walk down the street.

Max watched her for a moment, then caught up to her in a couple of long strides. "Er," he said politely. "What's this, then?"

Vesper glanced up at him. "I'm walking."

He shook his head. "No, you're . . . swaggering? Your brother doesn't walk like that. *Men* don't walk like that."

"Yes, they do." She took another oddly swaying step. He noticed that she was walking a bit bandy-legged, as if to accommodate the enormous size of the male anatomy she allegedly possessed, and he felt the strangest urge to laugh.

He reached out to grasp her elbow and draw her to a halt. "Here—just watch me walk for a moment." He took a few steps down the street, feeling oddly self-conscious now that he knew her eyes were on him. He stopped and turned. "See?"

"That's what I was doing."

"I can promise you it isn't. Try again."

She tried again, doing better this time—at the very least, she looked less likely to drunkenly stagger into a lamppost.

He sighed. "That'll do."

Around the next corner was the Duke and Earl; Max realized, as they drew up to its imposing oak doors, that he'd passed it multiple times without clocking what it was. It was stodgy-enough looking to be a bank—or, at the very least, a mundane club, though its presence in Marylebone clearly implied the contrary.

An elderly man in a somber black suit and top hat was standing at the front entrance. Max inhaled slowly, then—against his better judgment—allowed Vesper to take the lead.

"Hello, old chap," she said to the man at the door, her voice a full octave lower than usual. It should have sounded ridiculous but she was actually, Max had to concede, a decent mimic; her walking might have been atrocious, but she did have something of her brother's mannerisms, and she didn't sound entirely unlike him.

Reaching into her coat pocket, she produced a card. The elderly man inspected it through enormous spectacles, then nodded. "Very good, sir, and welcome."

"This fellow's with me," Vesper added, jerking her head in Max's direction, and the doorman nodded reverently.

"Of course, sir. Enjoy your evening, sirs."

And, as simple as that, they were in.

"I knew it," Vesper hissed, as soon as they were through the doors.

"Be quiet," Max muttered, though a smile tugged at his own lips. "We're just lucky they're employing a doorman who's half blind. You could have waltzed in wearing a ball gown and he likely would have allowed you entry."

"Freddie does look quite fetching in a dress," she confided. "Looks rather like me, in fact," she added, preening, and Max gave her a severe look.

"If you're fishing for a compliment, find a different pond."

"I should never dream of it, dear Ashbridge," she said, and then led him deeper into the club. It was a rather different atmosphere here, compared to others they'd visited; if he'd walked in unknowing, he wouldn't have guessed that there was anything magical about the place. They passed through room after room done in wooden paneling, the floors covered in heavy Oriental rugs. There was a fire crackling in every fireplace, the windows were covered by thick curtains in shades of dark red and blue, and everywhere there were men—an older set, here—drinking glasses of amber liquid and deep in murmured conversation, looking solemn. The lack of women was a bit of a weight upon the room, Max thought, making it feel like a relic from the previous century. He disliked it immediately.

"Stop scowling," Vesper murmured as they made their way to the back corner of the lounge, where there was a small door at the edge of the bar. She leaned toward it, clearly stated, "Frederick Holloway," and the door unlocked itself with a faint *click* and silently opened.

Max tried not to gape. "Another residual spell?" he asked quietly, as he followed her through the doorway.

"Precisely. We're lucky it's not one of the ones that recognizes fingerprints, or we'd be in a real pickle."

"Recognizes—hmm. That actually sounds useful."

Vesper shot him a speaking sort of look over her shoulder. "Yes. Magic generally is, if half the population could bother to pull their heads out of their own arses and see it."

He didn't have a good reply to that, so instead he looked around the room they'd entered. At first glance, it didn't appear any different from the rest of the club—more oak paneling, a marble fireplace, squashy leather armchairs arranged before it. There was a long bar against one wall, seemingly identical to the one in the room they'd just passed through, the dark wood gleaming in the firelight and the old-fashioned gas lamps on the wall. However, Max could see the telltale glimmer at the hairlines of most of the room's occupants that indicated they were consuming more than mere spirits.

"What was this room for, originally?" he asked curiously. "Why the spell on the door?"

"Private parties, I think," Vesper replied. "Though the idea of going to a private party with this set seems rather . . ." She trailed off with a grimace, her gaze on a group by the fire. It comprised five men, gathered in chairs in a loose circle, their heads alternately gray and bald, each sporting an impressive set of whiskers. It did not, he had to admit, seem like an atmosphere conducive to raucous debauchery.

"Dull," he suggested.

"To say the least. I don't think Freddie ever comes here."

"It doesn't quite seem like his sort of place," Max agreed.

She cast him a look. "Are you two going to attempt to become friends again?"

"What? No."

"It's just—" She broke off, shaking her head. "I don't know why I'm bothering to try to convince men to admit they have feelings about something. But you clearly knew each other quite well, once."

"We did," he agreed. "Once."

"Are you still angry with him about whatever it is that you fell out over?"

"I—" He stopped, taking a moment to consider the question properly. "I don't know," he admitted.

"Hmm," she said, tilting her head at him. "I don't think he knows, either."

Silence fell, and Vesper evidently decided not to push him further. Instead, she led the way to the bar, where she ordered, in that ridiculous-and-yet-somehow-not-as-ridiculous-as-it-should-have-been attempt at Freddie's voice, a glass of champagne, a glass of whisky, and a packet of something called the Fact Checker, which she selected after a casual perusal of the menu, which was on heavy, embossed paper that Max guessed had cost the entirety of one of his paychecks.

Claiming their drinks and the brown envelope sealed with a wax crest, they retreated to a pair of armchairs situated before a small occasional table. They set their drinks down on the table, and then Max watched with considerable amusement as Vesper flung herself into a chair and proceeded to spread her legs with wild abandon.

"This is *incredible*," she said, practically in raptures. "I don't think I've a single dress that would even stretch this wide."

"You look ridiculous," he said, trying to be severe but spoiling the effect when he failed to prevent a small smile from twitching at his mouth. He did not consider himself an easily amused man, generally speaking; one of his university friends had once told him that he considered it a great victory when he managed to make Max laugh. But with Vesper, even when she wasn't in disguise as her brother and spreading her legs like a threepenny whore, he found himself smiling more readily than he had in quite some time.

She straightened in her seat a bit, though she still kept her legs spread far more than would be considered polite for a woman, and leaned forward to snatch up the paper packet she'd procured at the bar.

"What does that one do?" Max asked warily, though he couldn't imagine the magic sold at a place like this could be all that dangerous. This simply didn't seem like the clientele for anything risky.

Vesper ripped the packet open, breaking the wax seal. "It's supposed to give you specific knowledge regarding a topic your companions are conversing on."

Max blinked. "So if I say—"

"Wait, wait, let me take a bit," Vesper protested, tipping the packet into her champagne and swirling it around. It dissolved easily, and he watched as she took a healthy gulp.

"You don't like to lick it?" he asked, and then immediately realized how that question sounded, out of context.

Vesper cackled. "I do, frequently," she assured him with mock gravity, her eyes twinkling. "But for spell powder, I prefer it in drinks." She wrinkled her nose. "The people who snort it are mad."

"That makes it take effect more quickly?"

"Yes. But it'll give you a nosebleed, more often than not, and occasionally it reacts to that method of consumption in . . . unpredictable ways."

"Such as?"

"Since it speeds things up, it can sometimes make the effects occur so quickly that it's dangerous—or ruins the fun, at least." They sipped their drinks companionably for a few minutes, and then Vesper nodded at him. "Go on, then."

He looked at her consideringly for a moment, then crossed

an ankle over a knee, holding his glass up to the light. "This is a nice vintage of scotch—a fifteen-year, I think."

"Twenty-one, actually," Vesper said immediately, with a decisive nod. "Aged in an oak cask in the Inner Hebrides. That one's particularly known for its notes of pepper and anise."

Max shook his head. "It does lead to an interesting conversation, I suppose."

"Depends on what your drinking companions want to talk about," Vesper said, looking unconvinced. She took another sip of champagne. "It's making this champagne taste odd, too. This is why I prefer making proper potions—you can select flavors for the syrup that interact nicely together, and you can tailor the ingredients used in the potion until you find something that works properly *and* tastes lovely. But if you just dump spell powder in a glass of whatever you're drinking, it's not as nice."

"Why don't they do potions here, then?"

"Too flashy and modern. They're very stuck in their ways."

"You don't say." He leaned back and surveyed the room, trying to project the sort of casual comfort that never came naturally to him in places like this. He could never quite forget that he was the out-of-wedlock product of a liaison across class lines and that he'd been raised relatively modestly. He'd gone to school on a scholarship—Cambridge, too. He'd considered turning down his spot, since that was where his father had gone, but his mum had intervened, telling him that she couldn't bear the thought of him passing up such an opportunity simply to spite the man who'd fathered him.

"Succeed in his world, darling, that's the best revenge."

And now, here he was, working a job that he was growing

less certain that he entirely agreed with, philosophically speaking, and one he knew perfectly well his father would despise—that was the entire reason he'd taken it.

"I can't work you out."

He met Vesper's eyes, realizing that she was considering him thoughtfully. It seemed like a non sequitur, and yet somehow didn't, at the same time. "How so?"

She shook her head without breaking his gaze. "I don't know. It's very annoying—men are usually so easy to figure out. They're either terrified of you, or they want to go to bed with you, or they think you're a chum, or they're . . . completely disinterested." She shrugged. "It's usually easy enough to work out which category men are sorting you into. But you . . . I can't tell."

"Do I strike you as being terrified?"

"No," she said, her mouth quirking up at the corners. "It might make my life easier if you were."

"I don't find myself terribly interested in making your life easier." He meant it to sound light, teasing, but something about his tone was too warm. He sounded . . . fond. He was many things in regard to Vesper Holloway: irritated; frustrated; yes, damn it, attracted. But fond, somehow, felt by far the most dangerous.

"I've noticed," she said, very dry, and he couldn't help the laugh that escaped him. "Well, then, which one is it?"

"Which what?" he asked, his voice coming out a bit hoarse.

"Which category," she said, very deliberately. She leaned forward in her seat, bracing her elbows on her knees. "Which category do you think you'd put me into, if you're not terrified?"

"Nor," he said evenly, "completely disinterested." The

memory of the kiss at Grenoble's hovered between them, unacknowledged—a kiss that should have meant nothing, and yet one that he couldn't get out of his head. He looked at her, and she looked at him, and for a long moment silence stretched between them, like an elastic band slowly being pulled until it was taut.

"Well," she said at last, leaning back in her seat and breaking the spell, "I suppose I'll just have to work it out for myself."

Chapter Sixteen

An hour later, Vesper was growing weary of both pretending to be Freddie and suddenly finding her mind filled with useless facts on arcane topics. Ashbridge seemed to be getting a great deal of entertainment out of offering seemingly innocuous opinions on fairly niche subjects—his most recent opening gambit had been, "I wonder if tennis scoring ought to eliminate deuce," and then Vesper had found herself, against her will, being suddenly overcome by a desperate urge to go on a lengthy tirade in defense of the mystifying scoring system of a sport she didn't care two figs for. She, who had no use for any sort of sport, except for the bit where she wore a nice dress to Wimbledon each summer, got drunk on ill-advised quantities of champagne by the early afternoon, and inevitably returned home with a sunburn.

It was an entertaining enough way to pass the time, though—for Ashbridge, at least. Vesper's throat was growing sore from talking so much, though he'd taken pity on her a little while back and gone to the bar to request a large glass of water, which she'd accepted gratefully. However, they had whiled away enough time now that it seemed safe to say that no one appeared concerned by—or had even taken note of—their presence. This meant that the time had come to do a bit of poking around.

"I'm going to find the toilet," she said, standing up, and then nearly laughing at the look that crossed Ashbridge's face at this announcement, which was downright alarmed.

"I . . . do not think that's a good idea," he said, his voice nearly strangled.

Vesper, curious to see how much she could horrify him, decided to press on. "It's not as though I've never seen a penis before, Ashbridge."

Ah, yes, that did the trick. He had gone scarlet, and was looking so scandalized that if someone had put him in a gown and a feathered headdress, he could have easily passed for a society mama from the previous century.

"That's hardly the point," he hissed, casting a furtive glance around as though expecting eavesdroppers to be skulking behind their armchairs. "What are you going to do—pop in and then just lurk about, pretending to need to piss but mysteriously not unbuttoning your trousers?"

"Have you lost your mind?" Vesper asked, exasperated. "Obviously I'm not *actually going to the toilets, Ashbridge*, I just need an excuse if anyone catches me prowling around a corridor that's supposed to be private."

"Oh." He leaned back in his seat, his blush fading a bit. "Shall I come with you?"

"No—it'll look too suspicious if we're caught back there together. Just . . . try to sit here and act remotely natural, will you?"

"What do you call what I've been doing for the past hour?" he asked, looking offended.

"I am not certain it has a name," she said.

Upon making her way back through the enchanted door, she moved quickly past the mundane bar and out into a quiet corridor, done in yet more wood paneling.

There was no one in sight, and she paused for a moment, considering her options. She began a slow progress down the corridor, trying doorknobs and preparing to act extremely intoxicated and confused if anyone questioned her about what she was doing. After a moment, a youngish man emerged from one of the doorways ahead and slumped against the wall, exhaling heavily. She clocked the waistcoat—woven with threads of dark green in a subtle ivy pattern—and realized he worked for the club. She wished, for a moment, that she weren't in disguise; men were so easy to get to speak if one was blonde and pretty and female. Though she supposed she could try using her wiles in disguise as Freddie instead.

She took a breath, and then began to walk toward him, altering her stance a bit to imply a sort of looseness, if not outright drunkenness. Given Ashbridge's critique of earlier in the evening, she was careful not to veer too far into—how had he phrased it? *Swaggering?*

The man took notice of her and straightened. The exhausted expression on his face was replaced with something more distantly polite.

Vesper waved a hand. "Don't stand up on my account." She

shook her head, and reached out a hand to brace herself. "Might join you, in fact." She kept a careful amount of space between them as she leaned back against the wall, tipping her head back to look at the ceiling.

She could feel his eyes on her.

"Is there anything I can do for you, sir? Someone I should fetch?"

She shook her head. "Just been a rather long night. You know how it is. All the . . . brandy, eh? And talk of politics? It can be wearying."

"As you say, sir," he said, sounding uncertain.

"I expect you hear that complaint all the time," she attempted now, seeking some sort of natural entry into conversation with him, something that might set him a bit more at ease.

"I believe that our patrons are very fond of brandy and politics, sir," he said diplomatically, and Vesper's mouth twitched.

"Aren't they just," she murmured, and a quick glance out of the corner of her eye revealed a small, matching smile of his own. Seeing it, she decided to attempt a bit of detective work. "At least no one here has started tearing his clothing off or spinning from the ceiling."

A quiet huff of laughter; she didn't look at him after she spoke, careful not to appear too interested, eager to give the impression that this was idle, tipsy chitchat.

"I wouldn't mind something livening things up around here—the owners are nearly pissing themselves about it, though."

"Are they?" Vesper asked, frowning up at the ceiling. "Nothing's happened here, though, has it?"

"No." She saw a flicker of movement out of the corner of her eye: he was shaking his head. "But with all the gossip, they're worried that we're next. Whoever's doing this . . . they don't seem like they plan on stopping anytime soon."

"Do you know what else is being said about it?" Vesper asked. "I mean, do you hear things from friends at the other clubs?" Recalling her disguise, she added, in careless tones, "Most of my mates seem to think it's all a bit of a laugh."

"They're mostly just worried that if any of the clubs close, we'll all be out of work," he said frankly, and Vesper schooled her features into a contrite expression, as if such a possibility had never occurred to her.

"I hear they're attempting to repeal Forbiddance in Parliament, though," she said, curious to hear his thoughts on the matter; she realized, incredibly belatedly, that, as good a relationship as she had with the staff at Holloway's, they might not feel entirely comfortable speaking freely before her. She was interested in the opinion of someone who didn't realize that he was speaking to a daughter of the storied Holloway family.

He shrugged. "I heard that, too—one of my mates is involved with one of those groups that distributes the pamphlets and whatnot." He didn't sound as though he considered this terribly impressive political activism, which nearly made Vesper grin, thinking of Freddie. "I don't see how that'll help, though, if people are still being sick every time they drink a potion—no one'll want to come to the clubs then, even if it's legal."

He was right, of course—though Vesper had her doubts that Simon's bill could even pass, not if matters continued on as they had for the past week and a half. People would grow edgy; the public would stop trusting magic entirely.

"Besides," he added, "it's not as if Forbiddance is stopping anyone, for all they'd have you believe. Seems to me that everyone's using magic, regardless of what they say publicly."

"Is there anyone particular you've spotted?" she asked, trying to merely sound idly curious so as not to spook him.

"Let's just say that some of the voices shouting the loudest about Forbiddance have been seen here more than once." He jerked his head over his shoulder, in the direction of the loos. Vesper's gaze flicked in that direction, and she nodded.

"Interesting," she said slowly, and he shrugged.

"I hate some of those goddamn hypocrites in Parliament." He pushed himself off the wall with his foot. "I ought to get back to work." He looked at Vesper for a moment, seeming to be considering something, then leaned down and, in an even lower voice, said, "I wouldn't push my luck, if I were you. I think the rule barring women is stupid, but they're very committed to it."

Vesper blanched. "I've no idea what you mean."

"Of course you don't," he agreed, all amiability, and then with a last, curious glance at her, he was off.

She remained where she stood, considering her options. She could return to Ashbridge, but she was suddenly desperately curious to see who might be in the loos that would be of interest. She was weighing Ashbridge's—clearly not unreasonable—fears about her giving herself away when a distant motion caught her eye. Down the hallway, emerging from the toilets, was a man about Vesper's father's age, lean and cunning-looking, with a head of gray hair that was still impressively thick. After a moment, she recognized him: Jacob Finlay.

What was he doing at a magical club?

Finlay, thankfully, didn't notice her, instead vanishing through a nondescript door that Vesper had thought, upon passing, was merely for staff. She waited approximately five seconds, then scampered down the hallway and yanked the door open. It revealed what appeared to be a servants' staircase; crossing the landing and peering down a flight of stairs, she was just in time to see a door on the ground floor swing shut, offering the merest glimpse of a back alley.

Deciding not to push her luck any further, she retreated, and two minutes later, she was sliding into a seat next to Ashbridge, who was slumped in his chair, drumming his fingers in an impatient rhythm on the arm. She reached for the fresh glass of champagne he must have procured in her absence, enjoying the taste of it unmarred by spell powder this time.

He was scanning the room, clearly seeking out anything out of the ordinary. Sipping her champagne, Vesper followed his gaze, her own landing on a man across the room who was settling into a seat, reaching for a menu. The man, tall and broad-shouldered and gray-haired, was immaculately dressed in a dark suit jacket and tie, the jacket unbuttoned to reveal a peacock-blue waistcoat. After a second, Vesper recognized him as Augustus Grimme-Nox, owner of the Grimoire. He and her father had been friendlier in their younger days, but there had been some sort of falling-out. Vesper couldn't remember the story—her father had so many dramatic anecdotes from his largely misspent youth that she had started to tune them out at a certain point.

Not spotting anyone else she recognized, however, she felt safe to lean closer to Ashbridge and ask, "Did I miss anything?"

He took a moment to answer, his gaze still distant, but eventually he glanced down at her. "Nothing other than a load of men at the next table discussing investment strategies and fox hunting." Distaste practically dripped from the words; he reached for his whisky, his jaw tense. "What did you learn in your sneaking about?" He took a sip of his drink.

"Well," she said, trying to keep a note of triumph from her voice. "Not much. Unless you count the fact that Jacob Finlay is here."

Ashbridge stilled, then set down his glass very deliberately and turned to her. "Excuse me?"

"Finlay. He was in the loos."

"Vesper." He pinched the bridge of his nose. "Please tell me that you didn't actually go—"

"For Merlin's sake, Ashbridge, focus!" Vesper was growing cross. "Jacob Finlay, one of the architects of Forbiddance, is here. What's he doing here?"

"Being a raging hypocrite?" Ashbridge suggested.

There were legions of men who complained about magic in their speeches in Parliament but who reliably haunted the streets of Marylebone in the evenings. However, Vesper had always been under the impression that Finlay genuinely believed in his public stance against magic.

"It seems very odd to me," she said. "Especially since he just went to dinner with Anthony Grenoble."

"Two confirmed encounters with the magical world in three nights," Ashbridge agreed, clearly deep in thought. "It's beginning to seem plausible that he could be mixed up in all of this somehow."

"It could just be a coincidence," Vesper pointed out in the interest of fairness. "Or he might be trying to meddle in the magical world in some other capacity. After all, it's not as though he could be the one directly tampering with the potions—he hasn't got any magical ability himself. And I can't see anyone magical wanting to ally themselves with Finlay—all of us hate Forbiddance, after all."

Ashbridge shook his head, still frowning. "There's something we're missing—some connection. There has to be."

"I thought I might ask Cecily to look into it," Vesper said. "She knows everyone, and is a genius at digging up sources. If anyone can find dirt on Finlay, it would be her."

"Good idea. I can speak to my friend Will, too—he's a reporter at *The Times.*" He still sounded a bit distracted, his gaze occasionally flicking around the room.

"I spoke to a member of staff, too, while I was poking around—he says the owners are panicking about the attacks at the other clubs. It could all be an act, I suppose, but—"

"But if it's not, then they're unlikely to be behind it," he finished for her.

"I wonder if we ought to consider one of the pubs," she said thoughtfully. "We've been focused on the clubs, but what if it's one of the magical pubs that's trying to drive us out of business?"

"That's certainly possible," he allowed, his brow furrowing slightly. "There are also a few more clubs we've not visited yet, right?"

"Just two," she said. "There's the Grimoire—we could pay them a visit this week, I suppose—and also the Secret Garden.

They're closed for the season, though, and won't reopen till the spring. . . ."

"I'll speak to Will, and you speak to Cecily, and we'll sort a plan from there." He knocked back the rest of his whisky, and set down his glass. "I think this is quite enough for tonight, though." He appeared to be positively itching to leave the club, not that Vesper could blame him. They rose to their feet, and made for the bespelled door; a couple of minutes later, they were breathing in cold night air, the headlights, laughter, and music of a Marylebone Saturday night surrounding them. Vesper stomped her feet against the chill, and looked up at Ashbridge. "I'm going to get a taxi—it's too cold to walk. Want to share?" She raised her hand at an approaching cab, which slowed.

He looked down at her for a long moment, then shook his head. "I'll walk to the Tube—I want to clear my head." The cab Vesper had hailed pulled up before her, and Ashbridge opened the door, allowing her to slide inside. He hesitated, and then the smallest hint of a smile curved at the corner of his mouth. "Nice work tonight, Holloway, old chap." He slammed the cab door shut with a last nod of farewell.

And Vesper, watching his retreating shoulders, could not stop the helpless smile that crept over her face.

Chapter Seventeen

Max wished like hell the next morning that he'd not agreed to have lunch with his parents.

He'd walked the streets of Marylebone for a while the night before, eventually making his way to Warren Street to catch the Underground to Hampstead. It was past midnight by the time he walked through the door of his flat, but sleep was a long time in finding him. At least this time, he'd learned his lesson, and hadn't had another drink at home—his head was thanking him for that this morning.

The weather seemed to echo his unsettled mood, the sky outside his window overcast, the clouds scuttling overhead on a stiff breeze, rain occasionally spitting against the pane. The oak tree in the back garden was radiant shades of red and yellow, its branches quivering in the wind. After a fitful morning spent at home, unable to settle to anything, he seized his coat at half twelve and set out into the chill fog.

His mother and stepfather lived a quarter hour's walk away,

still in the same small terraced house they'd bought when Max had been a young boy. The purchase had been a stretch on their limited resources at the time, but they'd been able to slowly renovate it over the years, and the result was charmingly cozy. Max didn't bother with the doorbell, instead popping round through the garden to poke his head through the kitchen door, even as he began toeing off his wet shoes.

"It's only me," he called, and his mother materialized in the doorway leading from the dining room a moment later.

She squinted at him. "Are my eyes failing me, or is that my firstborn son, in the flesh?"

"Hi, Mum."

"He calls me 'Mum,' it must be him, and yet the sight has grown so unfamiliar in recent weeks that I really can't be certain. Paul," she called over her shoulder now, "fetch those binoculars you use for bird-watching on the heath, please, I want to see if this really is a rare species materializing in our kitchen—'adult human son come to visit his family.'"

"Right away, my love," came Paul's unconcerned reply.

Max shook his head as, now shoeless, he padded across the checkerboard tiles of the kitchen floor and dropped a kiss on his mother's cheek. Florence Ashbridge was well past her fiftieth birthday, but as lovely as ever—lithe and petite, with the dark hair (now liberally streaked with gray, which on her looked quite elegant) and gray eyes that she'd passed on to him, even if his build—the height, the broad shoulders—was all his father. He had never cared much about his appearance, other than the faint satisfaction he got when he looked in the mirror and saw his mother's face looking back at him.

It was still his favorite face, he thought—even as, at the back of his mind, another face, green-eyed and golden-haired and with a mischievous upturned nose, lurked quietly.

His mother grasped him by the elbows when he would have pulled away, her eyes searching his face in the way that always made him slightly uncomfortable, since it gave the distinct impression that she was seeing more than he would wish her to.

"Are you all right?" she asked, more quietly now.

He nodded, forcing a smile, and she seemed reluctantly mollified, if not entirely convinced. He moved past her, through the dining room and into the sitting room, where his siblings awaited. He hadn't been certain the twins would be here today—they were terribly busy of late, and Jamie was living south of the river in a cramped flat with one of his mates now that he had started working as a clerk on Fleet Street—but there they were on the couch splayed out like beached whales, legs intertwined as ever. The fact that they were twins went a long way to explaining their closeness, but Max knew that they would have felt separate from him even if they'd not been twins; a full decade separated him from them in age.

"Max!" Maud disentangled herself from Jamie and flung herself at Max, all long limbs and blond hair—the twins both bore a strong physical resemblance to Max's stepfather. At nineteen, she was exceedingly lovely, albeit something of a terror to both of her brothers, whom she harassed relentlessly. She was wearing a simple white shirtwaist and blue wool skirt, and her long hair was in a plait over one shoulder, though she often pinned it up in a faux bob before going out, her solution to the fact that she was too emotionally attached to her long hair to cut it for the whims of fashion.

He spat out a mouthful of her hair and hugged her back, nodding at Jamie over her shoulder.

"I didn't know if you'd make it home for Sunday lunch."

"I've been home all weekend. Couldn't resist the chance for two days of free meals." Jamie looked at his sister. "Maud, let him breathe."

"I haven't seen him in *weeks*," Maud protested, though she did loosen her grip from around Max's neck and step back, tugging at his hand until he had no choice but to join the twins on the sofa that was, strictly speaking, not entirely large enough for three tallish adults.

"Whose fault is that?" Max objected. "Last time I came by, you were out to lunch with . . . one of the 'ie' ones."

"Elsie? Nellie? Sophie?"

"There are so many, I can't remember who's who."

Maud shook her head in disgust. "I can see why Mum complains about men so much," she said, with all the worldly wisdom of a nineteen-year-old. "Though it *is* nice that this one deigned to remember we exist." She nodded at Jamie.

"I take you to lunch *every week*," Jamie objected, poking his sister in the side, and she stuck out her tongue at him.

"Where've you been, Max?" Maud said, turning back to him. "It's been three Sunday lunches in a row that you've missed."

"Work has been busy," he said, which was true, but felt like an evasion, because it wasn't work in general that was busy—it was one specific preoccupation.

"Is that Raffles woman giving you a hard time?" Maud asked,

looking a little *too* interested, Max thought with some wariness. She had seen a photograph of Raffles in the newspaper soon after Max was hired, and had been exceedingly interested in his professional life ever since. He expected to have aged approximately one hundred years by the time Maud got married, though fortunately, she was so obsessed with books—and so preoccupied with the job she'd got as a shopgirl at a bookshop in the village—that she had little time left for romantic exploits.

"Even if she weren't married, she'd be too old for you," he informed his sister sternly.

"She's not that old. She can't be forty yet."

"And you're not yet twenty, so I recommend you look elsewhere." Max patted his sister on the head, the gesture designed purely to annoy her, and it had its intended effect, as she scowled at him.

"Ah, Max, there you are," said his dad, wandering into the room with a newspaper in hand. He looked his usual vague sort of self—blond-haired, yet to go fully gray, which made him look oddly boyish; slender and long-limbed, just like the twins.

"Just attempting to convince your daughter to stop pining after inappropriately aged women," Max offered with a nod.

His dad looked unconcerned. "Better pining than actively chasing." He slid a sly glance at Jamie, who was slumped next to Max on the couch, listlessly contemplating the ceiling, and who did not even appear to be able to muster the energy to object to this.

"Without much success," Maud added cheerfully, which did provoke an indignant "Oi!" from her twin.

Max's dad reached out to ruffle his hair affectionately. "I'm glad you're home—your mother's been fretting since we've not seen you in a while. She started counting backward last night before bed, trying to work out how many days it had been, and you know how much she despises maths."

"What about *me*?" Jamie objected. "Doesn't anyone fret about *me*?"

Max, Maud, and Paul contemplated him for a moment, and then said in unison, "No."

"Tossers," Jamie muttered, crossing his arms over his chest.

At that moment, they were interrupted by alarming noises from the kitchen, which prompted Paul to go a bit pale and vanish. "I suppose we ought to help," Max said, nudging the twins with his feet in turn, and, heaving melodramatic sighs, both twins joined him in rising and following the smell of slightly burning . . . something.

In the end, nothing was too terribly singed—Max's mum was a good cook, but she was very fond of experimenting in the kitchen, which Max's dad had tried to discourage over the years, with limited success. This Sunday it was a standard roast chicken with all the trimmings, with only one (1) single parsnip that had caught fire in the oven.

It was while they were eating their sticky toffee pudding and custard that Max's mother chose her moment.

"I hear you've been seen with the Holloway girl," she said casually, adding a bit more custard to her bowl as if she had not just uttered anything remotely interesting.

Maud's spoon dropped with a clatter. "What?"

Max set his own spoon down in a more dignified fashion. "Where did you hear that?"

"I ran into her mother in the food hall at Harrods the other day when I was buying paté."

"Have we recently come into a small fortune?" Paul wondered to the table at large. "How thrilling. I shall have to purchase myself a new top hat to celebrate."

"You don't wear top hats," Maud informed him.

"Perhaps, daughter of mine, I am going to start, now that I have learned that I am a man of means."

"It was for last night's recital at the school, stop being ridiculous," Florence retorted with a dismissive wave of the hand. Over the past decade, her small ballet school had seen ever-increasing numbers of pupils, as ballet became more established within the country—gone were the days when the only talent to be found in the field came from France or Russia. In light of the school's success, the clientele had grown considerably more upscale.

"I didn't know you knew each other," Max said, largely to buy himself time.

"We met at some party or other years ago, when you and the son—Frederick, is it?—were friends. But I hear it's not the *son* who's caught your attention at the moment."

"Aren't the Holloways magical?" Jamie asked, then proceeded to take a revoltingly large spoonful of pudding, which he seemed to inhale largely without chewing. He had also eaten a third helping of everything served for lunch. Max didn't often feel *that* old, but he'd forgotten how hungry he'd been when he was a decade younger.

"Yes." The reply was curt, and did not invite further questions.

This, naturally, did not deter anyone present.

"I didn't know you would deign to associate with *anyone* magical, Max," Maud said. "I thought you considered them all a bunch of—what did you call them?"

"Posh wankers," Jamie informed her helpfully.

"No—well, yes, he's said that too, but there was another one, a bit more colorful . . ."

"Inbred hedge witches," her father said, and she snapped her fingers.

"That's the one!"

"I'm sorry, have you all gone mad? I didn't realize I was sitting at a table full of magical sympathizers," Max said waspishly, though he was well aware that his own sentiments toward the entire magical system, and the families who practiced it, were much stronger than those of his family.

Maud gave him a pitying look. "Max, you really don't know how to have any fun at all."

" 'Specially now that he's a Flea," Jamie said with a sad shake of the head. The words came out a bit muffled, due to the large quantity of sticky toffee pudding currently in his mouth, but Max was unfortunately still able to easily understand him.

"F.L.E.A."

"That's what I said."

"No, it isn't—why am I bothering to argue with you?"

"I think the *real* question is why you have a job as a professional killjoy," Maud said, licking her spoon.

"The magical families are coasting along on centuries of privilege and are now gleefully flouting the law—"

"Yes, yes, we've heard it all before," Maud said, sounding

terribly jaded and disillusioned for someone who was not yet twenty. "That still doesn't explain why *you* have to be the one to uphold this ridiculous law."

"Maud, leave your brother alone," Paul said quietly. He tended to keep largely out of family squabbles, being easily the mildest-tempered of the Ashbridge clan, but he was perceptive enough to recognize when someone was pressing on a nerve.

"If this has to do with your father," Florence began, but Max interrupted.

"Dad is the only father I care to have." He jerked his chin at Paul, whose expression softened as he looked back at him. "And it's not a ridiculous law," he added for Maud's benefit, though he realized as he spoke that he didn't feel quite as fervent about this as he had a fortnight earlier. "I think everyone's rubbing along perfectly fine without magic, anyway."

"Speak for yourself," Maud said, pouting. "I'm desperate to try one of those appearance-modifying potions—Elsie said every time she drinks one, no matter who she ends up looking like, she has the most adorable dimples in one cheek. *I* wouldn't mind dimples."

"You don't need dimples," her father informed her. "You're going to cause us enough sleepless nights as it is, I expect."

Something niggled at the edge of Max's mind, just out of reach. Something that felt . . . important.

His mother, clearly torn between pressing on this further and letting things lie, gave him an anxious sort of look, but then redirected the conversation to what she obviously *really* wanted to discuss:

Romance.

"Leaving all that aside, then, what are you doing with the Holloway girl?"

"Vesper."

"Ah, that's right," she said vaguely, though Max was unconvinced; his mother had an excellent memory for faces and names, and Max didn't believe for a second that she'd forgotten Vesper's.

"It's for work," he said shortly. "And I can't say anything else about it." Which was true, more or less—and God knew he didn't trust the twins not to have loose tongues, fond as he was of them—but it was also a convenient excuse to end a conversation whose direction he didn't like one bit.

"Hmmm," said his mother.

"Hmmm," said Maud.

"Hmmm," said his dad.

"Is there any more pudding?" said Jamie.

◆

Later that evening, Max found himself in Marylebone, with no good reason to be there.

It wasn't too late—only around eight—but as it was a Sunday, and the weather continued to be poor, the fog having thickened over the course of the afternoon, the crowds on the streets were thin, most people at home, tucked up cozily before the fire with their nearest and dearest. Max had lingered at his parents' house into the early evening, reluctant to return to the quiet of his flat, which always felt particularly noticeable after an afternoon spent at home, especially when the twins were present.

When it had finally come time to leave, he'd walked out the door, paused—and then, instead of turning his steps toward home, he'd walked to Hampstead station and caught the Underground to Baker Street. Which was how he found himself here, in the quiet cobblestoned mews that housed Vesper's flat. He stood outside her green door, hesitating, feeling more foolish by the moment. He wasn't used to uncertainty; he made up his mind about things, and moved forward. The habit had always served him well, particularly at work. But now he felt unsure—he and Vesper were meant to be working together, nothing more, and yet he knew, if he were honest with himself, that describing their relationship as strictly professional would not be entirely accurate. There had been that kiss at Grenoble's, of course; a kiss that had kept him awake at night as he replayed it in his mind, recalling the heat of her mouth, the softness of her skin, the faint, urgent sounds at the back of her throat. But, equally, there had also simply been . . . moments.

Moments when their eyes caught, or when her mouth quirked into a smile; moments when she teased him, but with affection in her tone that he didn't think he was imagining.

Moments that made him wonder, now, if being alone with her again in her flat was a good idea.

However, foolish as he was beginning to feel, he would feel even more foolish if he were to turn around without knocking and make his way home again—it would have been a waste of Tube fare, to start. So instead, he knocked, not certain whether he hoped she would answer or whether he hoped she wouldn't.

Several long seconds later, she was at the door, her eyebrows raising at the sight of him. She clearly hadn't been expecting company—her blond hair was damp from the bath, beginning to curl a bit around her chin, the unruly curl near her ear having already started to frizz, and she was wearing a dressing gown made of green silk that matched her eyes. He tried not to look at the hint of her collarbone that was visible, or notice the crescent-moon-shaped birthmark just above it that he'd spotted once before.

"Ashbridge. This is—"

"Rude of me, I know. I wanted to speak with you, though."

"I was going to say 'unexpected,' but come in."

She stepped back, allowing him to walk through the doorway and into her flat, which felt smaller, somehow, when she was not fully clothed. No sooner had the door shut behind them than there was an inquisitive mewl, and he looked down to see the sheep-cat winding its way about his legs.

"Traitor," Vesper muttered, reaching down to extract the livestock/pet and scoop it up in her arms. She placed a kiss atop the cat's head; based on the creature's baleful expression, Max was not sure whether or not this gesture had been positively received.

"Not at the club tonight?" he asked.

She shook her head. "My father's there—someone else from the family goes one night a week so I can have an evening off. Anyway, I was there this afternoon, training a new hire."

He blinked. He supposed business had to go on, and the club couldn't afford to be short-staffed, but . . . "Weren't you nervous about hiring someone new, given . . ." He offered a broad gesture meant to encompass the current state of affairs in the magical world.

Vesper shrugged, looking a bit sheepish; Sheep the cat offered a chirp in protest. "It was Gus—the bartender from Plenus Venter."

Max stared at her. "I thought you said the clubs didn't like to hire from other clubs."

"We don't, but—well, none of it feels fair, him losing his place. I thought it was the least I could do."

She turned, still clutching the cat, and led him into the sitting room; Max trailed behind her, his gaze fixed on her slender figure, wondering if he would ever stop being surprised by Vesper Holloway.

Vesper, not privy to the complex tangle of his thoughts, invited him to take a seat on the sofa, deposited the cat next to him, and vanished into the kitchen, where he heard some clattering and splashing.

"Do you like chocolate?" she called.

"Er. Yes," he said, distracted by the unnerving eye contact the cat was offering him. After a moment, it climbed onto his lap, and he held his breath, not liking the look of those claws one bit. However, his fears were for naught, because the cat curled up on his lap and, after a moment, began emitting a sound like a rusty motor that he belatedly identified as a purr.

Vesper reappeared, clutching two mugs in a shade of yellow that reminded him of the Mediterranean sun. Her eyes landed on the cat on his lap, and she looked amused.

"It's making friendly advances," he informed her, accepting a mug from her and trying to take a subtle sniff of it.

Apparently not subtle enough. "It's not poisoned, you know."

"Just wanted to know what you were attempting to ply me

with," he said, taking a cautious sip. It was hot chocolate, thick and rich. "Did you make this with cream?"

"*Double* cream," she said, a blissful expression on her face. "Milk, sugar, cocoa, cinnamon, a pinch of salt, and double cream to finish."

He took another sip. "It's quite nice."

"You needn't sound so surprised."

"*You're* the one who admitted your parents' cook worries that you can't feed yourself."

"Well, this isn't feeding, strictly speaking," she said, and took a sip from her own mug. "Besides, I don't think men who show up unexpectedly at my door on foggy nights are in any position to complain about what I serve them."

"I don't believe I was complaining," he retorted, and knew, just from the expression on her face, that she was about to mock him.

"*I don't believe I was complaining*," she mimicked, in what he could not help but sourly note was a considerably worse approximation of his voice than her attempt at Freddie's had been. "Are you going to tell me what you're doing here?"

He bought himself some time by taking another sip of his cocoa, but she seemed prepared to wait him out, settling into the corner of the sofa more comfortably and tucking her feet beneath her. He got a brief flash of one smooth, fair knee, and tried very hard to immediately forget what he'd seen, because he could not imagine that anything good could come from him having any sort of familiarity with Vesper Holloway's knees.

"I've been thinking about what our next steps should be," he said at last, and she arched an eyebrow at him. He was starting to feel it in his cock, every time she arched that brow at him. This could not possibly be normal.

"I thought we agreed on that last night."

They had, of course. But he couldn't admit that—could barely admit, even to himself, that the reasons he was here had nothing whatsoever to do with their investigation, and everything to do with the fact that he hadn't wanted to return to his quiet, empty flat, where he would have spent his evening with her face in his mind.

So, instead he said, "I think we're missing something obvious. And if we don't work it out soon, Raffles is going to bring in Scotland Yard, and the situation will be out of our hands." He felt unexpectedly grim at the prospect; when the police raided illegal mundane nightclubs that were selling alcohol out of licensing hours, the clubs tended to spring up in new locations within a matter of days, like particularly determined mushrooms. He had no doubt that the magical clubs would prove similarly crafty, but now that he'd visited a handful of them, the difference between these storied establishments, full of history, and the seedy nightclubs serving champagne at two in the morning for quadruple its worth seemed suddenly stark. The idea of them vanishing, being forced to start from scratch, was not as appealing as he'd have found it a fortnight earlier.

"There has to be something else that the accidents all have in common," Vesper said thoughtfully. "I think if we could work that out, we'd be on the right track." She sighed. "It's a shame there hasn't been a mysterious buxom and dimpled redhead hovering by the bar in all the instances, something obvious like that."

"Ha," Max said, but then his mind snagged on the word *dimpled*—and returned to something his sister had said earlier.

Every time she drinks one, no matter who she ends up looking like, she has the most adorable dimples in one cheek.

"Vesper," he said slowly, "how do the potions at the Grimoire work?"

Vesper blinked at this non sequitur. "Well—they have several on offer. They all change your appearance in some way, obviously. Some will give you a rapid-fire succession of different faces; some let you swap genders; some change your hair color—"

"Do they—do they have any . . . consistencies?" he asked. He felt all at once frustrated by his lack of magical knowledge. This was never something he had considered to be a disadvantage before, and yet now he suddenly became conscious of the reality of a large, intricate component to the world that he didn't understand—and had never tried to. "I mean, if you use a potion, is there anything that stays the same?"

"Well—yes, actually." Vesper sounded a bit surprised. "It's one of the quirks of the Grimme-Nox magic—there's always one new feature that's consistent, no matter what your face or body does. I always get the most annoying cowlick that is absolutely impossible to hide, but some people have the same nose . . . or the same freckles . . . or their ears stick out . . . or—"

"Particularly long eyelashes?" Max suggested. Vesper looked at him, eyes wide. "At Plenus Venter, and Holloway's, *and* Grenoble's, the people handing off the drinks had extremely long eyelashes—long enough that someone noticed, each time. Almost as if—"

"It was the same person, taking an appearance-changing potion," Vesper finished for him. "Merlin. Do you think—"

"What *I* think," Max said, feeling grimly satisfied, "is that we should break into the Grimoire."

"Is there a reason that we can't simply visit it one evening, as we have done all the others?"

"I'd rather Augustus Grimme-Nox didn't know I was there."

"And why's that?"

He took a breath, weighing his words—but, really, there was only one way to explain it.

"Because he's my father."

Chapter Eighteen

Vesper wasn't often at a loss for words, but for several long moments, she could do nothing more than gape at Ashbridge, her mug of cocoa suspended halfway to her mouth.

"I wish you'd say something," he said after half a minute or so of wary contemplation of whatever expression was on her face.

Vesper found her voice. "Well, *I* wish you'd seen fit to share this little morsel of information at—oh, I don't know, any point in our investigation up till now."

"It wasn't relevant."

"Bollocks. You *know* it was."

"My father and I—Grimme-Nox, I mean—we don't speak."

"You still might've mentioned that you're the illegitimate offspring of one of the magical families, just so I knew what I was getting myself into." She was growing more indignant by the moment; give her another couple of minutes, and she could work herself into a proper fury.

"I have not allowed anything about my . . . my personal politics to impact my judgment." His voice was cool and measured, and he set down his mug with a *thunk*, as if the conversation were too serious to be conducted while one was drinking a cozy warming beverage. The impression of getting down to business, settling into the meat of the discussion, was somewhat ruined by the fact that he still had a faintly purring Sheep on his lap.

"No," she said, not bothering to disguise the curtness of her voice. "Of course you wouldn't let anything *personal* be a consideration for even a single second."

"What is that supposed to mean?"

"When you came to Holloway's that first night, did you feel even the faintest bit of guilt about what you planned to do?" Vesper asked—the question she'd been wanting to pose to him for the past ten days.

"It was an assignment," he said evenly.

"And I don't suppose you paused for even a single second to reflect on the fact that it was a bit dreadful of you to waltz into the business of a family you had once known and try to shut it down?"

"I did, actually," he said, his voice quiet. He didn't get loud when he grew angry, she had noticed; he merely grew even more self-contained. "But it was made clear to me that my connection to the family was—"

"Was what?" she asked sharply.

"Was considered an advantage." His gaze was lowered, seemingly on Sheep, who was still purring away happily and no doubt shedding approximately half a ton of cat hair onto his trousers. After a moment, however, he looked up and met her eyes.

"I didn't like it," he said, frustration in his voice. "It felt like a piss-poor way to repay your family, when they'd never been anything other than kind to me—your father took me and Freddie to lunch, you know, that weekend of Freddie's birthday."

Vesper didn't need to ask which birthday this was; it was a relief to know that particular weekend clearly lingered vividly in Ashbridge's mind as well.

"I was nervous beforehand," he continued. "Based on my experiences with my father . . . I wasn't sure what to expect from yours. But he was brilliant—never made me feel less than, for being mundane."

"Because we don't consider you less than," Vesper said, fury rising in her once again. "*You've* decided this about the magical world, based on—"

"Based on my experience of it," Ashbridge interjected. "If your introduction to magic had come courtesy of my father, I don't think you'd feel so rosy toward it, either."

It struck her, then, that she and Ashbridge were not so unalike; both had strongly held feelings about magic and Forbiddance based, as he said, only on their own experiences. The gap between them—which she had felt narrowing in recent days—suddenly felt like a chasm.

"Why did you and Freddie quarrel?" she asked, and Ashbridge blinked, clearly not having expected the question.

He considered her for a long moment. "At Cambridge, I could . . . pretend. It was after the war—we were all glad to be alive, and the magical-versus-mundane distinction felt . . . irrelevant. It was like we lived in an enchanted kingdom, but after moving to London in the wake of the Forbiddance law . . . I realized that Freddie and I lived in different worlds."

"How so?" she pressed.

Ashbridge was silent for another few seconds, long enough that she began to wonder whether he was going to answer her at all. "The first night I saw Freddie, after we'd both moved back to town, I had spent the day sending letters of introduction to various departments within the Foreign Office for civil service positions. After the war, I thought it would be good to have principled people working for the government, trying to ensure nothing like it ever happened again. I was particularly interested in the Foreign Office, but I saw that the Home Office was hiring someone for the F.L.E.A.—it was quite newly formed then—and I . . . well, I considered applying. I needed work—I was staying with my parents, because I didn't have a paycheck yet. After the war, and going away to university, it was quite an adjustment to return to my parents' house, with my siblings pestering me around every corner. We were all working each other's last nerve. So when Freddie invited me for a night out, I accepted without asking what he had in mind."

"Magic?" Vesper guessed.

"Magic," Ashbridge confirmed. "He had me meet him at Holloway's, but the evening went wrong almost from the start—I wouldn't go into the backdoor bar with him, which annoyed him immediately. I was tired, and frustrated, and just wanted a bloody job that would pay me enough to let me get my own flat while also putting to use the degree I'd worked so hard for, and Freddie waltzed in having spent the entire time since he'd arrived in town going to auditions and fucking half of London, it seemed, and then I mentioned that I was considering applying to the F.L.E.A., which went down as well as you'd imagine with him . . ."

Vesper shook her head, able to imagine it all too well. Freddie had a quick temper, which had been even worse when he was younger. She could see it so clearly: Ashbridge, distrustful of magic, frustrated by his circumstances, walking into Holloway's and despising everything it stood for. Everything her family—with its name and money and conviction that a silly law wasn't going to stop *them*—stood for.

"In hindsight, I might've picked the fight," Ashbridge said, sounding thoughtful now. "Mentioning it while I was at Holloway's with him—it was stupid. But once we'd started arguing about it, I wasn't going to back down, and we were both too stubborn to apologize after we'd cooled off."

"But you didn't even go to work for the Fleas—not then, at least."

Max shook his head. "I got an interview with the Passport Office first, and was only too happy to take the position they offered me."

"Then *why*," Vesper asked, frustration creeping into her voice, "did you end up with the Fleas in the end?" Ashbridge suddenly cut his gaze away, and comprehension dawned. "It's your father—that's what *all* of this is about, isn't it? You've got me sucked into some scheme in which you wind up shutting down the Grimoire?"

Heat flashed in Ashbridge's gaze, and Vesper found the sight rewarding. He was so cool, so impassive, so difficult to rile that it was maddening, when she so often felt as though she wasn't entirely in control of her emotions, and how she reacted to them. She wanted him to be angry.

"Last I checked, I was trying to help you, and the Grimoire

didn't have a damn thing to do with it." He sounded weary, which Vesper found infuriating—*he* was the one who'd shown up here on a Sunday night, while she was fresh out of the bath, and he was looking particularly handsome. He had on a cozy cable-knit white jumper, and a pair of brown wool trousers that had clearly seen some wear. Evening stubble shadowed his jaw. His dark hair was a bit unruly; he had a cowlick, she saw now, that he must ordinarily keep ruthlessly suppressed with pomade. She liked this version of him far too much.

"I don't think I believe you. I think you've got me swept up in some sort of demented scheme for revenge—"

"Don't make this sound like a cheap novel, Vesper. I'm trying to *help* you—"

"By using me to gain entry to clubs you'd never be able to set foot in?" she interrupted. "Oh, yes, what an enormous help you've been. And I suppose that eventually you'd oh-so-casually suggest that we go to the Grimoire, and the next thing I knew you'd be telephoning your friends at Scotland Yard and putting them out of business—"

"I gave you my word that I wouldn't," he interrupted, his voice flat.

"You did," she agreed. "And now I'm thinking that I was the biggest idiot in London to trust it."

"You didn't simply have to trust it, though," he said. "Or did you forget about that envelope I gave you?"

Vesper blinked; she *had* forgotten, locked away in her desk as it had been. Understanding dawned. "Is *this* what you wrote on that piece of paper?" she asked. "That Grimme-Nox is your father?"

He nodded once, a single, sharp gesture. "If word got round at the F.L.E.A. that I was the natural son of one of the most powerful men in Marylebone, I don't think I'd be trusted ever again. It's one thing to have been friends with Freddie at university; if they knew Grimme-Nox was my father, however, they'd never have thought I was anything other than some sort of spy on behalf of the magical world."

"And I suppose no part of you hoped that our investigation *would* find out something incriminating about Grimme-Nox? You weren't hoping at all that you'd have an excuse to shut down the Grimoire?"

He was silent, his eyes locked on hers, frustration written into every line of his body. "I don't *know* how I feel anymore, Vesper. It's all grown . . . complicated."

She let out a sharp laugh. "It hasn't *grown* complicated—it's been that way from the start, from the moment you showed up at my club. How else would you describe your history with my family, after all? I'm not sure what the appropriate adjective is to describe a relationship whose history involves friendship, a row, a brief moment of champagne-fueled insanity, and me with my top off."

And there it was, at last: their prior meeting, acknowledged. She felt as though they'd been tiptoeing around it, both wary of giving voice to their past. It was almost a relief to lay it bare.

Ashbridge, meanwhile, was looking angry—*properly* angry, not merely stern. A deep line formed between his eyebrows, and his gray eyes flashed with an electric spark of fury that Vesper had not previously seen.

"How would I describe it?" he repeated, his voice quiet but

something in his tone enough to set Vesper on edge. Sheep evidently sensed it, too, as she looked up at him with a somewhat disquieted expression and offered an inquisitive "*Meow?*"

Ashbridge rested his hand almost absently on the cat's head; this was evidently sufficient to smooth Sheep's ruffled feathers, but Vesper was still feeling quite ruffled, and didn't fancy a head scratch to soothe her.

"I would describe it as: I had a career that I was perfectly satisfied with until six months ago, when my father sought me out for the first time in years, we had a blazing row, and I quit my job and joined the Licensing Agency out of some Shakespearean quest for revenge, and instead I find myself assigned to some sort of—of *fact-finding* mission, based on the fact that my superior knows I'm well-connected, and so I walked into Holloway's dreading seeing anything that would give me cause to report the club and arrange a raid, because one of the best friends I ever had was a member of the family that owned it—and so, too, was his sister, who had lingered in my mind for the better part of seven years, because she was maddening and beautiful and spoiled and overprivileged and everything that I'm meant to despise, but somehow can't work up to it properly where she's involved because you Holloways are just . . . *just* . . . Holloways! And it drives me bloody mad."

He came to the end of this quite astonishing speech without any enormous displays of emotion—he had not raised his voice, or gesticulated wildly. He had not moved from his seat, remaining still enough to allow Sheep to commence her lengthy personal grooming routine (currently involving licking her stomach in an undignified fashion) without being disturbed. The only hint at any emotion on his part came from the color rising in his cheeks—and, too, in the look in those usually inscrutable gray eyes as they remained locked on hers, unrelenting.

Vesper found her voice; the search took a second longer than it usually did. She was used to men calling her beautiful; she wasn't at all used to them sounding quite so anguished about it.

And she wasn't used to it *mattering* to her quite so much.

But she needed to focus on what was important—which wasn't the history between her and Ashbridge, or even that between Ashbridge and Freddie. It was this: the club. The anxious air that had descended upon Marylebone, everyone sensing the ease with which what seemed like a few harmless accidents could slip into something more severe—something that threatened the magic and traditions that they had worked so hard to protect.

So, instead of addressing several of the most interesting points he had just made—ones which she would have greatly enjoyed a prolonged discussion of, in fact—she merely said, "What did your father say to you, to make you become a Flea?"

"F.L.E.—oh, for fuck's sake, why do I bother?" He scrubbed his hands over his face, sighing heavily, as Vesper gaped at him for the second time in the past few minutes. This was becoming a distressing habit. She couldn't *imagine* what her face looked like while she was doing it, but it didn't bear contemplation.

"I ran into him at the National Gallery, of all places," he said. "Or, rather—I expect he planned it all, but made it look as though it were a coincidence." There was a note of such sharp-edged bitterness to his voice as he spoke that it made something in Vesper's chest ache a bit. "It was the end of the day, and the room was nearly empty, so once he'd acknowledged me, it would've felt rude to turn my back." He rubbed his neck. "In retrospect, I'd have been better off doing so."

"What happened?"

"He told me he had something he very particularly wished to speak to me about and invited me to dinner. I wanted to refuse, naturally—I don't think I'd spoken to him since I was at Cambridge and was happy enough to keep it that way—but he must've known, because before I could say anything, he offered to drop by my parents' house one evening." A pause. "Needless to say, I don't want him anywhere near my mum—or my dad and my siblings."

Vesper was revising her feelings about Augustus Grimme-Nox.

"Anyway, he took me to some hole-in-the-wall on Dean Street and started asking all sorts of questions about my work at the Passport Office and whether I'd ever considered doing anything else, et cetera. I tolerated this until we'd finished the starters, and then I told him to get to the point, which he did. His wife was leaving him—number three, I believe."

"Was she the one who had an affair with a shepherd and ran off to live in one of the magical Welsh villages with him?" Vesper asked, recalling having heard the gossip at a party a few months earlier.

"Indeed."

"Wherever did she meet a shepherd in Marylebone?" Vesper asked, intrigued despite herself.

"I believe she went on some sort of restorative walking holiday."

"Rather *too* restorative."

"Vesper."

"Sorry, sorry," she said, holding her hands up in apology, pleased to see the slightest twitch of his mouth. "You were saying?"

"Well, as this was the third of his marriages to end without offspring—his first wife died of complications from pregnancy after a series of miscarriages when I was a boy; the second realized she preferred women and divorced him—he seems to have come face-to-face with his own mortality and decided that I'll have to do."

"You'll have to do . . . what?" Vesper asked slowly. Ashbridge looked grimly back at her, waiting. "Not—not run the Grimoire?" She was genuinely incredulous.

"He seems to be of the mind that beggars can't be choosers; after his slip-up with my mum, he was evidently a bit more careful in the bedroom. So I'm apparently his only option."

"He can't seriously think you'd do it," Vesper said, still reeling.

The passing down of a family's Word to an out-of-wedlock child was hardly unheard of; magical ability was transferred in bloodlines, which was why repeated intermarrying with mundanes tended to weaken a magical line over time. It was also why a spouse could not use the Word of the family they'd married into; Vesper's mother, for example, could still use her own family's Word, but not that of the Holloways. Children could only receive a single Word—once they'd used one Word, no other Word would work for them, even if it were from their other parent's family—so parents had to think quite carefully before deciding which one to pass down to their offspring. (This usually ended up being a fairly calculated decision based on which parent's family business the children might one day be expected to run.)

The fact that the magic prized blood over marriage, however, meant that Grimme-Nox would not be the first man to resort to passing on his magic to an illegitimate child—but only if he *chose* to do so. A child born of a magical family (in or out of wedlock) possessed the latent ability to perform their family's magic, but it could only be activated by their parents teaching them the proper Word.

And yet, Vesper could hardly think of someone less likely to be interested in any of this than Max Ashbridge.

"I don't know what he thought," Ashbridge said, still looking exceedingly grim. "But he dangled what he evidently believed was an irresistible carrot before me—an enormous salary. Told me he'd pay for Jamie—my brother—to go to university, if he wanted. Even offered to buy the building my mum uses for her ballet school, so she'd no longer have to pay rent."

"He tried to weaponize your family," Vesper said, quietly indignant.

Ashbridge looked surprised. "Yes. I don't think I'd thought of it in quite those terms, but—yes. Fortunately, Jamie has never had the slightest interest in going to university. And my mum's school . . . well, she made it rather a point, when my father refused to marry her, not to take a single penny from him. She'd let him take me out to lunch occasionally—it was rare that the fancy struck him; he still envisioned, back then, having his own, proper children to pass the club down to—but she'd never let him pay her for anything else. So I can only imagine her reaction if I let him anywhere near anything to do with her business."

"So you told him to go to hell?"

"In precisely as many words. It got a bit uglier from there."

"Did you start brawling over the dessert course?" Vesper asked hopefully.

"You're alarmingly bloodthirsty, aren't you? No, it was more civilized. He was oh-so-kind as to inform me that the scholarship I thought I'd earned to go to Cambridge had been funded *by him.* He'd been pulling the strings all along—everything I thought I'd earned with my own hard work had his fingerprints all over it."

Vesper decided, quite suddenly, that she hated Augustus Grimme-Nox, despite the fact that she'd barely exchanged more than a few polite words with him in her entire life.

"After that little revelation, I was—well, I was half out of my mind with fury by that point. I informed him how much of a favor he'd done my mother by abandoning her because it led her to my dad, who was ten times the father he would ever have been. This landed about as well as you'd imagine."

Vesper was actually rather impressed. "Max Ashbridge. I truly didn't think you had it in you."

He looked her straight in the eye. "There's a lot you don't know about me, Vesper."

And . . . was it meant to be flirtatious? Had her brain grown addled over the years? Had her many romantic entanglements led her to start hallucinating flirtation where none existed?

"But," he added, before she could grow too muddled as she attempted to contemplate this, "by that point, all that was left was to tell him that I looked forward to watching his club cease to exist the second he died, and that I would not lift a finger to save it. I stormed out of the restaurant and handed in my notice the next day. I knew the F.L.E.A. was looking for new recruits. Everyone at the Passport Office thought I was mad, naturally, as did my entire family, but I didn't give a damn—I was so furious that the wave of anger saw me through the next month or so, as I served out my notice and started the new job. It was only once I'd cooled off a bit that I realized that I . . . might have miscalculated."

"For Merlin's sake," Vesper said, torn between being exasperated and reluctantly impressed. She reached for her forgotten mug of cocoa, which had cooled a bit but was still delicious, of course, because it was cocoa. "And so then the people in the Flea see the Cambridge education and the well-heeled friends and think, *Ah, a toff, we can use him to our own ends*?"

Ashbridge winced. "I wouldn't phrase it quite like that."

Vesper shook her head. "This is really a bit of a mess you've got yourself into."

To her surprise, he didn't argue. "Getting sent to Holloway's wasn't the first assignment I've taken issue with. The pubs that cater to lower-class clientele are the ones we tend to go after first—collecting sizable fines that they can ill afford, just to allow them to stay in business. The ones that can't pay are shut down by the police." He shook his head. "So at least, I thought, going after one of the powerful clubs would even the score, and make me feel as if we weren't solely targeting the working-class element of the magical world. I tried to convince myself of the fact until I walked through the doors of the club, but as soon as I was there—as soon as I saw you . . ."

Vesper held her breath, not even slightly able to predict what the next words out of his mouth might be.

"I got a sinking feeling in the pit of my stomach."

Vesper frowned.

"So," he concluded, "when you floated in with your offer of working together, in exchange for saving the club . . . it was a relief. And here we are."

"And, to be clear," Vesper said, her mind quite full with the revelations of the past quarter hour, " 'here' is 'considering breaking and entering at the Grimoire.' "

"Correct." Sheep chirped at him, probably in protest at him having ceased his behind-the-ear scratches, and he obediently commenced scratching the animal once again.

"Ashbridge, this is ridiculous—if we're caught, the police will be summoned, and we'll have an awful lot of explaining to do. It will expose our entire investigation."

"I can't be seen there, though," he said. "If my father spotted me, he'd know at once that I was up to something."

"Well," Vesper said, realizing at once what the solution was. "I don't wish to state the obvious, but . . ."

"What?" he asked, wary now.

"They run an entire club, and pharmacy, specializing in changing one's appearance. If we wish to pay the club a visit without being recognized, there's an easy solution."

She met his eyes, and saw, from the resigned look in them, that he knew where she was going with this.

"Vesper . . ."

"You, dear Ashbridge," she said, leaning forward and poking him in the chest, "are going to have to use some magic."

Chapter Nineteen

Magic or not, Max didn't want to show up at the Grimoire without doing some reconnaissance.

Over the course of the week, he made a habit of "bumping into" old friends—from his school days, from Cambridge, from his years in France during the war—and joining them for a drink. It was easy enough to gain their confidence, and, with it, all sorts of small details about his father's club slipped out—the name of the doorman. The back alley where male clubgoers often went to take a piss. The balcony leading onto a small, walled garden, which was particularly popular with liaising couples. And the night watchman, who stayed at the club overnight but was often to be seen at last call, indulging in a cheeky drink or potion with stragglers.

And with these details came the beginnings of a plan.

"Ashbridge," came Raffles's bark at work on Wednesday, interrupting a bout of thoughtful contemplation of the logistics involved. There was an intrigued murmur among the other F.L.E.A.s present—Poppington, in particular, looked delighted at the prospect that Max might be about to receive a tongue-lashing.

Max eyed Raffles a bit warily as he took a seat. Her silvery blond hair—always immaculately styled in careful waves, but now a bit mussed—betrayed a state of mental turmoil.

"You rang?" he asked mildly, and Raffles narrowed those unnerving icy blue eyes at him. Any attempts at humor on his part would not be appreciated, then. Noted.

"I wanted an update on any progress you've made in this little scheme of yours with the Holloway girl."

Max crossed one ankle over his knee. He'd known some sort of conversation like this was coming—was surprised Raffles had given him as long a leash as she had, in fact. He felt oddly hesitant to confide in her, however; at some point, this investigation had stopped feeling like work, and more like some sort of private quest.

"We've made some . . . interesting progress," he said, and was rewarded by Raffles shifting forward in her seat slightly. "We're operating under the theory that one of the club owners is deliberately using their own magic to contaminate their rivals' supply of spell powders and potions."

Raffles frowned, considering him with a sharp eye. "To what end?"

"Competitive advantage. If there are accidents at all the clubs except theirs, people will flock to them, perceiving them as the safest option, with the most reliable product. Their rivals will go out of business."

"It seems awfully dangerous," Raffles said, tapping a pen against a blotter on her desk. "Don't they run the risk of people simply abandoning all magical clubs entirely?"

"They do," Max conceded. "I think it's why they've taken pains to keep the effects of the contaminated potions relatively harmless—ensure that it's not enough to frighten people off, but allow them to eventually come to their own conclusions about where it's safest to procure anything magical."

"And do you know which owner is doing this?" There was an edge to her voice as she no doubt considered just how enormous a coup this could be for her.

"Not yet," Max said. What he and Vesper really needed was *time*, and this conversation with Raffles was his chance to buy them some. "We're narrowing it down, but I need another week or two."

Raffles was silent for a moment, scrutinizing him. It was discomfiting, to be fixed beneath that frigid stare for a prolonged period, but he met her gaze, and counted it a small victory when she looked away first.

"I'm sticking my neck out for you here, Ashbridge."

"I know."

"If the powers that be found out that I'd approved this without taking it farther up the line—"

"I know. And I appreciate your trust."

"You came highly recommended, as you are well aware, and heaven knows I could use someone competent in this office." She jerked her chin at the closed door leading out into the open office where the F.L.E.A. desks were, and Max bit back a smile at the thought of Poppington's reaction to hearing this assessment of his abilities. She jabbed her pen against the blotter again, more decisively this time, and said abruptly, "You have until the end of next week. My patience has its limits."

◆

Max met Will at their favorite Bloomsbury pub after work that evening, one of their semiweekly meetings for drinks. Will was looking somewhat disheveled, but this was nothing out of the ordinary; he was prone to ink-stained fingers, mismatched socks, and hair that looked as if he'd been caught in a windstorm on his way to the pub. How he had ever convinced elegant, polished Vera to marry him was a mystery to Max, but the human heart worked in strange, unknowable ways, he supposed. (He refused to examine this truism in any detail when it came to the current state of his own heart.)

"You look tired," Will observed, setting down a pint glass before Max on the worn wood of the table with a faint *thunk*. "Too many evenings spent donning your glad rags and rubbing elbows with the potion-pushers?"

"Something like that," Max said, not rising to the bait.

"Have you bought a new suit? Taken to wearing a monocle? Started calling people 'old bean'?"

Max took a sip of his beer, his mind turning back to the ludicrous secret code at Plenus Venter that Vesper had taught him. He nearly smiled at the memory, but instead flicked a bit of the foam at the rim of his glass at Will. "Are you done trying to annoy me?"

"It is my professional obligation to be as annoying as possible," Will said, making a show of looking wounded. "It's why I still have a job."

"Your job is actually what I wanted to speak to you about," Max said, leaning forward slightly.

Will straightened in his seat, suddenly alert, the teasing gleam in his eye vanishing. "Have you got a scoop for me about your investigation? They're coming thick and fast from the magical world at the moment."

Max frowned. "What do you mean?"

Will glanced around, as if checking they weren't overheard. "One of my colleagues at *The Times* received a tip about whatever's going on at the Marylebone clubs—he says the source is irreproachable."

"Someone from one of the clubs?" Max asked.

"Someone at the Home Office. Seems to think their information is reliable."

Max stared at the foam on the surface of his beer, his mind working. No one at the Home Office was meant to know—no one other than Max.

And Raffles.

"When did he get the tip-off?"

Will was silent a moment, thinking. "Would've been . . . weekend before last, sometime?"

The weekend of the accident at Holloway's—before Max had even told Raffles of his plan.

Who, then, at the Home Office knew? And how? Even if gossip had spread since then, this would have been very early for it to leak.

Max took a long sip from his pint, Will watching him carefully all the while.

"I don't know how deep you're mixed up in this," Will said, "but this seems like a bit of a mess."

"I'm well aware." Max rubbed the bridge of his nose, feeling exhausted, as if the past two weeks had caught up with him all at once. "I need to speak to Ves—Miss Holloway."

"Vesper, is it?" Will waggled his eyebrows.

"I would pay you to never do that again."

"I don't think you've enough money to make that a tempting offer," Will said. "Unless you anticipate a sudden change in your circumstances? Marriage into a family with healthy bank accounts, perhaps?"

Max didn't even bother trying to protest.

"It's been a while since Caro, hasn't it?" Will said, more serious now. "I think this could do you good."

"Don't compare her to Caro," Max said sharply.

He still felt a slight pang of regret when he reflected on the year he'd spent with Caroline. She'd been perfect on paper: smart, educated, beautiful. She was from a mundane family who were wealthy but not aristocratic; her father worked as a banker. He'd begun to assume that they would marry; instead, she had left him. It had been painful, but the ache had soon faded—as she had informed him it would, in their final conversation. "In a month, you'll barely think about me at all," she told him. "And that's why this will never work. I want to be with someone who would miss me for the rest of his life."

The words had stuck with Max, even as he'd argued against them at the time. Because he had caught himself thinking, with increasing dread, of the time—rapidly approaching—when he would not have a professionally sanctioned excuse to see Vesper Holloway most days of the week. And he already knew, without the slightest doubt, that he was going to find that nearly unbearable.

Will watched him for a long moment, reading whatever it was that was written on Max's face. Max was usually quite good at ensuring his expression was inscrutable, but he couldn't bring himself to bother, just now.

Will let out a low whistle. "It's like that, is it?"

"I don't know what you're talking about," he retorted, and Will didn't even attempt to dispute this.

Because he and Max both knew perfectly well that it was a lie.

Chapter Twenty

The useful thing about Vesper's family owning a private club in the middle of Marylebone was that it made it easy to find her.

Or, at least, it should have.

Max worked late Friday evening; Raffles had sent him a stack of licensing permits to look through, which he couldn't help but think was some sort of punishment. The sun set at some point, Max too absorbed in his work to take notice, and when at last he looked up, the sky outside was a dark, velvety blue, illuminated by motorcar headlights and by the warm glow coming from pubs and restaurants on the street below.

He stood and reached for his coat, his thoughts occupied by the licenses he had spent the past countless hours sorting through. And he felt . . . troubled. He was perfectly well aware that some of the clubs and pubs applying to renew their licenses were operating illegal backroom magical bars on the sly—had even been inside a couple of them himself. But he was struck, suddenly, by the simple fact that these were people's livelihoods—not just those of the owners, who could probably stand to lose the money, but those of every person employed. The thought of putting that many people out of work, all for peddling some potions that, honestly, didn't seem *that* dangerous to Max . . .

Well, he felt less certain about his job than he had at any point in the past few months.

Occupied by these somewhat disquieting thoughts, he hopped on an Underground train and emerged at Baker Street, allowing his feet to lead him, almost without his realizing it, to the door of Holloway's. The doorman recognized him and nodded him through. Max's eyes searched for a familiar golden bob. It was nearly eight, but as it was midweek, the atmosphere was a bit more subdued than it would have been on a Friday or a Saturday. In one of the reading rooms—situated at the front of the club and overlooking the street through its bow windows—were a number of men and women, some alone in armchairs with books and cups of tea or glasses of brandy, others in pairs or groups of three, chatting in hushed tones over open bottles of wine. There was a fire burning in the large marble fireplace, and the velvet curtains were half drawn, lending a cheerful, cozy feeling to the room.

Max moved on, still seeking Vesper, taking the time to look around more carefully as he did. He realized that on his previous visits to Holloway's, he'd been so distracted either by searching for the signs of illegal magic or by some maddening conversation with Vesper that he had failed to properly take in his surroundings. There was a dining room with white tablecloths, but relaxed conversation, loosened ties, jackets nowhere in sight, and plenty of tables occupied by women—nothing at all like the stodgy dining rooms of the expensive restaurants his father had taken him to as a boy, when he'd been attempting to be some sort of civilizing influence on him. He wandered on, past another room—one that had a small brass plaque above the arched doorway labeling it THE SNUG, and which contained several overstuffed armchairs and a velvet sofa, a bookshelf absolutely creaking beneath the weight of well-loved books, and a bar cart with a handwritten sign reading HONESTY BAR over a coin box. The rugs on the floor were mismatched and overlapping. The resulting impression was extremely pleasant, and Max suddenly felt every hour of his day weighing down upon him. The velvet sofa, in particular, looked very inviting. He was so preoccupied by fantasies of taking a nap that it took a moment for him to register who, precisely, was currently *in* the snug, heads bent together, deep in conversation.

It was Vesper—and her siblings.

Cecily spotted him first.

"Ashbridge," she called, and Freddie and Vesper glanced up, startled. Max took a few steps into the room toward them, nodded at Freddie, and flicked his eyes to Vesper.

"Hello," he said quietly.

"Did we plan to meet this evening?" Her brow puckered. "If I've forgotten—"

"No," he assured her. "I popped by on the spur of the moment—I hoped to have a word."

"Ashbridge, why don't you join us?" Cecily asked. It was phrased politely, but also as if it might be a challenge—as if she wanted to see if he would say no.

Against his will, he looked back to Freddie, who was watching him curiously. It was strange to feel so uncertain with someone who had once been such a close friend. He'd seen Freddie in every situation—drunk or bespelled, his cheeks flushed and his voice too loud; serious and focused, hard at work on an essay for some class or other; asleep on Max's settee in his rooms at Magdalene, his face oddly younger in slumber; haunted, solemn, on the rare occasion that talk turned to the war. Back then, he would have been able to tell, from a single glance at Freddie's face, whether he was welcome or not. Now, six years on, he found his expression more difficult to read.

Max raised an eyebrow at him. He wouldn't join them if Freddie didn't want him there—but, too, he wasn't going to be the one to walk away.

"What're you waiting for, then?" Freddie said lightly. It was a bit forced, the jovial tone, but Max saw—and appreciated—the effort.

Vesper moved to the side, freeing up room on the small love seat beside her, and Max sat, suddenly conscious of every single inch of her body that was pressed against his—and conscious, too, of the presence of *both of her siblings*, one of whom was his former best friend.

Christ almighty.

"You're looking more tortured than usual, Ashbridge," Cecily said. "Is it my sister? She does have that effect on people."

"A miracle you've not fled from this scheme in horror," Freddie agreed, and Vesper stuck her tongue out at each of her siblings in turn.

Max glanced down at her; she was dressed conservatively

this evening, in a black satin dress that hung past her knees, with a single sparkling clip in her hair. From this angle, he could see the unruly, frizzy curl by her ear—the one he'd often noticed her attempting to smooth, despite its stubborn refusal to behave.

"I think my natural facial expression is tortured," he informed Cecily, who cackled.

Vesper glanced up at him, smiling, the dimples in her cheeks putting in an appearance, and he realized, in a sudden moment of clarity, that he was extremely fucked.

"I hope I'm not interrupting anything," he added, looking away from Vesper with some difficulty and instead meeting Freddie's gaze. He was watching Max and Vesper with an inscrutable expression.

"Top secret plans to infiltrate the government, murder all the Fleas, and install a magical police state, you mean?" Cecily asked.

"Something like that," Max agreed. "Or, you know, plans for the Holloway family Christmas."

"It's only October," Cecily said. "You're liable to send Vesper into some sort of fit if you mention Christmas this early."

"Oh?" He looked down at her. "More of a solstice devotee?"

The magical families celebrated Christmas, along with most of Britain, but they also hosted elaborate, drunken feasts on the winter solstice, something a teacher of Max's had once described as "shockingly pagan" but which Max's mother had always told him was really quite a good party.

"I don't mind either," Vesper said. "I just don't like the carols."

"The carols," he repeated.

"The *Christmas* carols," she said, as if he required clarification. "You know. 'God Rest Ye Merry Gentlemen'? 'It Came Upon a Midnight Clear'?"

"Thank you, yes, I've heard Christmas carols before, you heathen. What's the problem with them?"

"They drive me mad."

"This seems like an incredibly specific and odd prejudice."

"There are people *singing them on street corners*, Ashbridge! Did I ask to be sung to? We don't do it at any other time of year; why am I meant to enjoy it when it's freezing outside and I'm simply trying to get home, or to the tea shop, or to the club? It's unnatural."

"*You* are unnatural. Do you despise joy?"

"I find that extremely rich coming from you, of all people. Please tell me, in great detail, the last time you felt joyful. Was it while sharpening a pencil? Giving someone an assignment at work?"

No, he realized in a rush: It was now—and sitting in a chippy with her the other night, and drinking cocoa in her flat, even as they were quarreling. At some point in the past two weeks, being around *her* had begun to make him feel that way.

"Well," Cecily said, startling Max a bit; he'd almost forgotten she and Freddie were there. "This is *fascinating*."

Vesper immediately frowned. "No, it's not."

"Oh, it is," Cecily said.

"Ashbridge, what is it you wanted Vesper for?" Freddie asked, focusing the conversation.

"I talked to Raffles," he informed Vesper, and her expression puckered. Cecily, meanwhile, leaned forward eagerly.

"Is that Effie Raffles?" she asked.

"It is," he confirmed warily; she didn't have a notebook out, but he was suddenly conscious of the fact that he was in the presence of a journalist.

"This is off the record," he said as a precautionary measure, and Cecily rolled her eyes.

"Do you see a pencil in my hand?" she asked peevishly, but he continued to fix her with an unrelenting stare until she said, "Yes, yes, off the record."

"Yes, it's Effie Raffles," he said then.

"You know," she said, thoughtful, "I obviously disagree with her politics, but she's a *fascinating* woman. I don't suppose you'd be able to convince her to do an interview with *The Spark*?"

"I guarantee you that I cannot."

"He's probably right," Freddie said. "Ashbridge never mastered the art of charming a woman."

"I don't know," Cecily replied, before Max could object to this slander. "He's clearly done something that has worked on Vesper."

Vesper spared an exasperated look for her elder siblings. "Will the two of you please *go away* and let me have a word with Ashbridge? We've a clandestine operation sneaking around the back rooms at the Grimoire to plan."

Cecily and Freddie were twin images of alarm. "Vesper, doesn't that seem a bit risky?" Cecily asked, sounding extremely elder sister–ish.

"Yes," Vesper said; Max could *hear* the irritation in her voice that she was trying to suppress. "Which is why we're *planning it carefully.*"

"You think this is a good idea?" Freddie demanded of Max, who shrugged.

"It was my idea, so I'm hardly going to say it's not a good one."

Freddie and Cecily exchanged eloquent glances but rose to their feet.

"Try not to get yourself arrested, Vesper, or Daddy will never let you hear the end of it," Cecily said, making for the door.

Freddie followed more slowly, giving Max an appraising sort of look. Max met his gaze evenly, recalling his argument with Vesper of a few evenings earlier. Whatever genuine anger he'd once felt toward Freddie Holloway had long since faded, he realized. He gave Freddie a cordial nod, and a quirk of the mouth that passed for a half smile, coming from him.

"It was good to see you, Ashbridge," Freddie said, and extended his hand.

Max glanced at it, and after only a moment's hesitation rose to his feet and shook it. "And you, Holloway."

And with that, Freddie and Cecily were gone. Max lowered himself back into his seat next to Vesper—conscious anew of how closely they were pressed together—and looked at her. She was watching him with an unreadable expression on her face; his eyes met hers, and he didn't look away. The moment stretched between them, the silence growing a bit taut as it lengthened, and at last she said softly, "Thank you."

He gave her a small smile by way of reply.

And then, without another word, he turned to business. "Raffles is growing impatient. She's given us another week to make serious progress, but that's it—we'll need to have something to report."

Vesper nodded, unfazed by the sudden turn from matters personal to matters criminal. "I'm still prepared to go to the Grimoire tomorrow night—if you are?"

He nodded. "However, we've another problem—I spoke to my friend Will, who works for *The Times*. He says another reporter at the paper has been tipped off about the incidents with the contaminated potions and has been sniffing around."

Vesper exhaled a soft expletive. "That makes things a bit more pressing, then. We need to wrap this up before they write something damning—Simon's bill is due for its first reading in less than two weeks." She stilled, seeming to realize what she'd said. And to whom. "I know that we don't agree on this, Ashbridge, but—"

"I don't want your brother-in-law's bill to fail solely because some lunatic is going around trying to poison people using magic," Max said. "It ought—well, it ought to be a fair fight. This doesn't seem fair. And," he added, "there's more. Will is certain that this reporter was tipped off by someone at the Home Office—but *how*? He says the tip came in the same weekend of the accident at Holloway's—before I'd even told Raffles about our investigation. Who in government would have known this was going on so early?"

Vesper frowned. "That doesn't make sense."

"I know. Except . . ." He paused, weighing his words. He didn't fancy himself a conspiracy theorist, but something had been niggling at him, ever since his discussion with Will yesterday.

"I keep thinking about Jacob Finlay—the fact that he went to dinner with Anthony Grenoble, and that he was seen at the

Duke and Earl. And it makes me think . . . who would benefit from this? Not just the owners of rival clubs."

"Someone who wanted to keep Forbiddance in place," Vesper said slowly. "Someone who *wants* people to think poorly of magic."

"Precisely." Max was feeling quite grim, the more he considered it. "We've been lucky, really, that Raffles has wanted to keep our work quiet—if this had become a big Home Office investigation, or if Scotland Yard had got involved, the press surely would have taken notice, and word would have spread even faster."

"But Finlay can't be behind this alone," Vesper said. "Since it *has* to be someone magical who's doing the tampering."

"Right. But Finlay was at the Duke and Earl on the same night as—"

"Your father." Vesper's eyes were wide.

"Precisely."

"Well," she said, "then let's pay him a visit tomorrow night, and prove it."

Chapter Twenty-One

"I wonder what the odds are that this ends with us being arrested," Ashbridge said the following evening, as Vesper climbed into the cab waiting at the end of the mews and scooted across the seat to make room for him to slide in behind her. He slammed the door shut, and gave the address to the driver, who eased the cab away from the curb and into evening traffic.

"It's not as if we're breaking and entering," she pointed out. "Which is a shame, really; this is going to be tricky to manage, *and* it lacks the titillation of picking locks."

"Your plan for the evening should be titillating enough without the added frisson of lockpicking."

"Are you nervous?" she asked, glancing at him. He was looking very handsome this evening, his hair a bit unrulier than usual but the rest of him impeccably groomed: clean-shaven, wearing a nicely tailored suit and tie, his cheeks a bit flushed from the chilly night air. It was the coldest night of the autumn so far, and it had taken her a considerable amount of will to drag herself away from the comforts of a mug of cocoa with Sheep on her lap before a crackling wood fire to bathe and pour herself into one of her slinkier dresses (midnight-blue silk with elaborate beading on the bodice). She had donned her most luxurious velvet cape to go with it, along with a matching hat that was perched at a jaunty angle atop her head.

"No." She raised a skeptical brow at him. "All right—a little. There's an awful lot that could go wrong with this plan, and—" He cast a wary glance at the cab driver and lowered his voice so that Vesper had to lean closer to hear him. "—using magic isn't precisely in my normal line of work."

"Well." Vesper settled back into her seat and grinned at him. "Fortunately, it's in mine."

He looked at her in that steady way of his for a second, and then—miracle of miracles!—gave her a flash of a smile, gone after merely an instant. Vesper was so disconcerted that she was silent for much of the ride to the Grimoire.

By the time they arrived, Vesper had had enough time to grow a bit nervous herself; rather than making for the front door, where there was a short queue awaiting entrance, they wandered casually around the corner and then, with a quick glance over their shoulders, ducked into a narrow alley that ran along the side of the building.

Ashbridge glanced at his watch. "We're a few minutes early."

"Lovely," Vesper said, stamping her feet; her gold satin pumps were beautiful but did little to keep her toes warm. "I've always wanted to lurk in a damp alleyway for several minutes."

"Ought we to look more . . . er." Ashbridge tugged at his collar.

"Yes?" Vesper asked, suddenly intrigued to hear what he was going to suggest.

"Well, if someone happens to glance down a dark alley and sees two people dressed to the nines just skulking about, it's going to look odd."

"Ah." Vesper now understood the reason for the collar-tugging. "You want us to look like we're trying to find somewhere for a quick shag against a wall."

"I don't think I would have phrased it *quite* like that—" He broke off abruptly as Vesper seized him by the lapels and pushed him against the wall in question.

"Christ," he muttered, staring down at her.

"It was *your* idea," she reminded him with a grin. "Now, put your hands somewhere interesting so we look convincing."

Obediently, he placed one hand on her waist—or what he could find of it, given the velvet cape—and brought the other, to her slight surprise, up to cup her cheek. The gesture was unexpectedly tender, and Vesper tilted her head back to look into his eyes, which were dark and serious as he gazed down at her. His face was cast in shadows. His palm was warm against her cheek. And she realized, for all that they were currently in an insalubrious alley, leaning against a wall that had probably borne witness to all manner of troubling things over the years, that she felt oddly safe, pressed against Ashbridge's chest with his skin warm against hers.

Ten feet away, a door opened, startling them both.

There was a clearing of the throat. "Sorry to interrupt, but—"

"Oh, good," Vesper said, too brightly, pushing herself away from Ashbridge as he allowed his hands to drop back to his sides. Delacqua's head was poking out around the edge of the door, and he looked slightly uncomfortable as Vesper and Ashbridge approached. Once she drew near, Vesper could see Hazel hovering anxiously behind him in whatever stairwell led to this back door.

Wordlessly, Hazel and Delacqua extended their hands, which contained a highball glass each for Vesper and Ashbridge.

"The Fresh Faced?" she asked, and Delacqua nodded in confirmation. He and Hazel each had a second glass for themselves, in case anyone noticed what they'd ordered and thought it odd that their appearances had not changed.

"Cheers," she said, lifting her glass, and downing it in three large gulps. Next to her, Ashbridge was contemplating his as if it was poison.

"It's not going to kill you, you know," she said softly, and he glanced up at her. The expression on his face was a bit pained, and she reached out a hand to his elbow. "But you don't have to, if—if you really can't."

"It's not that." His voice was quiet. "It's just—if I'm going to drink a potion for the first time, I wish I'd thought to have one of yours. At Holloway's. I would've liked one of those to be the first."

And Vesper suddenly, ridiculously, had a bit of a lump in her throat. She swallowed past it, but before she could speak, he raised his glass to his lips and drank.

"Thank you," Vesper said, glancing back at Hazel and Delacqua, who were watching all of this with interest. She and Ashbridge handed off their glasses, and with a wave of farewell, the other two vanished back into the club. Vesper and Ashbridge settled in to wait, in the cozy confines of a damp alley, their shoulders pressed together; Vesper was just about to suggest they resume their previous ruse of a liaising couple, when a glance at Ashbridge's face stopped her short.

Witnessing the face-changing never failed to give Vesper a slightly uneasy feeling; Ashbridge looked, for about twenty seconds, as though he were melting, and she could imagine, based on the slightly horrified expression on his face, that she must look similar. After less than half a minute, however, his features resolved into his new face, and standing before her was a man—still tall, still dark-haired, but with piercing blue eyes and cheekbones sharp enough to use as a knife.

"Oh, hello," she murmured.

He raised an inquiring brow.

"You're *very* handsome."

"You're—" He broke off, and suddenly looked as though he were trying not to laugh.

"What?" she demanded.

"You have a sunburn."

"A sunburn!" Vesper felt slightly put out; why should Ashbridge get to look like a catalogue model and she be saddled with a sunburn? "In October?"

"It's not too bad, you're just . . . a bit rosy. And your eyes are blue now."

"So are yours. It's very . . . well." She sighed, a bit wistfully, and he looked at her inquiringly. "It's just, you're *so* handsome. It's distracting."

"You," he said, very thoughtfully, "look a bit like a milkmaid."

"Merlin," she muttered.

"It's the pink cheeks! And the blue eyes, it's all very Alpine and wholesome. And you weren't joking about that cowlick, were you?" Now he *definitely* sounded as though he were trying not to laugh, and Vesper raised a hand to her head, feeling the telltale wrinkle in her hair, despite the fact that everything else about her coiffure remained unchanged, given the limits of this potion.

"I don't know why I wasted time styling it tonight," she said morosely.

The Fresh Faced merely changed a face's appearance for a few hours, having no impact on hair or anything else about the body. After considering the menu options ahead of time, Vesper and Ashbridge had decided that new faces should suffice for them, without any of the more dramatic full-body transformations that some of the stronger potions induced. However, now that the potion had gone into effect, they were operating with limited time; it was half nine, and the club closed at midnight. This meant that their potions shouldn't wear off until after the rest of the clubgoers—and staff—had left; now there was nothing for it but to go inside and begin their performance.

Ashbridge extended an arm to her. "Shall we?"

Delacqua met them at the front door, as arranged, to gain them entry as his guest, since Vesper couldn't precisely announce herself to be Vesper Holloway, given her current disguise. The doorman barely cast a glance at them, not finding anything suspicious in the telltale shimmer of magic around their hairlines. Once they were inside, Delacqua murmured farewell and set off to find Hazel so they could make their departure; given Hazel and Vesper's friendship, they thought it wise not to be seen together, lest anyone somehow guess who they were.

Left to their own devices, Vesper and Ashbridge made a beeline for the bar.

"A glass of champagne and a glass of whisky, please," she informed the bartender.

"Make it a double," Ashbridge put in over her shoulder, close enough behind her that she caught the clean scent of his skin. He still smelled like himself, even with someone else's face.

They downed their drinks in a hurry and ordered another round; Vesper didn't want to risk any further spell powder or potions tonight, not when she needed to keep her wits about her, so it was important that they make a show of knocking back the drinks, so as not to draw any suspicion.

All around them, people were consuming potions; next to them, a woman tipped a packet of spell powder into her mouth, washing it down with champagne. A moment later, she was a redhead with curly hair. Another moment, and she was a pretty blonde. Another few seconds, and she was a man with a neatly trimmed beard. Her companions laughed uproariously at the rapid-fire transformations; Ashbridge's brow furrowed at the sight, making him look suddenly like himself, despite not *actually* looking anything like himself.

Vesper watched the bartender pour a shimmering splash of syrup into a glass, preparing a potion that promised a fetching sprinkle of freckles across the bridge of the nose, before Ashbridge tugged on her arm. "You don't need freckles," he told her.

"But I would look *adorable*," she said mournfully, before regretfully allowing him to lead her away from the bar.

Drinks in hand, they made for a table in the most secluded corner they could find—one that was, conveniently, partially obscured by a potted palm. Useful things, potted palms; Vesper had once had a thoroughly enjoyable ten minutes behind one with one of Freddie's actor friends, without anyone the wiser. Just to be safe, however, as soon as they were seated, she inched closer to Ashbridge.

"In case anyone's looking, it needs to seem as though you're sort of . . . leering at me," she explained, plastering herself to his side. He snaked his arm around her waist, drawing her even closer, and she glanced up at him through her lashes. "Any sign of him?" she asked in an undertone, reaching for her champagne coupe.

An infinitesimal shake of his head. "Doesn't mean he's not here, though—he might be tucked away in a dark corner somewhere."

"So what do we do for the next two and a half hours, until the club closes?"

"Look increasingly lusty and foxed?" he suggested.

"Hard to imagine you looking either way, even with a different face," she said lightly, joking, but she felt his arm stiffen around her, and his hand's grip on her hip grew a bit steely. Had she . . . offended him?

"You seem to have an awfully fixed impression of me," he said in an undertone. The club was noisy, but they were pressed close together, here in their semiprivate alcove, and she could hear him easily, the noise of the music and crowd in the room fading in the background.

She met his eyes, and decided to answer him honestly. "You're not very easy to read, you know. And you've never seemed very impressed by my general . . ." She gestured at herself helplessly.

He laughed, low and dark. "Vesper, I think anyone with a pulse is impressed by your general . . ." He mimicked her gesture. His gaze was warm on her.

"Well." She lifted her chin. "You hide it well. From my perspective, at least."

"Then let me tell you something from *my* perspective," he said, leaning closer to her again, his voice dropping an octave. "There has not been a single evening in the past two weeks that your face hasn't been the thing I've seen when I close my eyes at night."

He reached out a hand and ran his fingers down her cheek. She closed her eyes at the feel of them, relishing the warmth that lingered in their wake. "If you're acting right now, you're very good at it," she managed after a moment, allowing her eyes to flutter open. "Freddie would be impressed."

"Please don't mention your brother right now," he said with a faint grimace, and Vesper laughed—and then, because she couldn't help herself, she leaned up and kissed him. His mouth tasted like whisky, and she cupped her hand around his neck, drawing him closer to her. The hand at her hip slid lower, squeezing her arse, and she shifted in her seat, feeling her pulse pounding between her thighs. She sank her hand into his hair, feeling the locks—usually ruthlessly cowed into order by pomade—curling around her fingers at the nape of his neck. His free hand cupped her chin, angling her head just so, and she reveled in the wet heat of his mouth and the tangling of their tongues.

Drawing back after several moments, she gazed up into his face, unfamiliar in its current form. "I want to kiss you with your real face," she said, hearing the breathless edge to her voice. "The last time—at Grenoble's, I mean—didn't count. We didn't really mean it."

"Then let's make sure we're not arrested tonight, and we'll get the chance," he said, his own voice sounding gratifyingly ragged, and Vesper laughed. "And Vesper? I meant it last time, too."

And his smile, even on someone else's face, felt like the warmth of the sun.

◆

A couple of hours later, Max was beginning to think that this evening might actually kill him. There was the literal concern for his life, given the possible consequences of them being caught trespassing in a private club after-hours. But more imminently pressing was the fact that *he had kissed Vesper Holloway*—he had kissed her, and danced with her, and felt that frankly magnificent bum with his own hands. He'd stared moodily into her eyes (feeling like a bit of an idiot all the while—soulful staring was not precisely his forte), and touched her cheek, and kept a proprietary hand on her hip, and it was all, of course, *entirely professional* in nature, but God help him, he felt like he was losing his mind.

They were in their alcove nook now, Vesper having just returned from a reconnaissance mission to visit the ladies' toilets and fetch another round of drinks, all while plotting their next move; she was sitting next to him with her head slumped against his shoulder, taking—Max could not help but be impressed—

incredibly small sips of champagne, so that it looked as though she were constantly imbibing, even if, in truth, he judged her to be slightly tipsy at worst.

"Is it time for us to commence our cunning plan?" he asked, trying to sound dryly amused, and *not* as though he was incredibly (*incredibly*) aware of the fact that her hand was resting on his upper thigh.

"I believe so." She batted her eyelashes coquettishly at him; the gesture was incongruous on her current face, that of a rosy-cheeked girl from the countryside, and yet still somehow looked so quintessentially *Vesper* that he briefly worried about someone realizing who she was. She knocked back the rest of her champagne, then stood and extended a hand to him.

Together, they stumbled a bit around the edge of the room; Max was careful not to overdo it. This meant, in practice, that he clutched Vesper's hand, leaned forward to murmur in her ear, and tried to look like he had every intention of finding a convenient coat closet to get up to no good in at the next possible moment. He was so focused on this act that he only nearly avoided walking directly into someone.

"Apologies," he said, and then looked up into the face of his father.

Max froze; Vesper's grip on his hand tightened, and he held on just as tightly. There was no reason his father should recognize him wearing someone else's face, but it was unnerving to look into those icy eyes all the same.

"Of course," Grimme-Nox said smoothly, smiling the practiced smile that Max had seen him direct, often enough, at anyone he deemed important. His glance flicked to Vesper—then slipped away again, disinterested: He didn't recognize her. "If you're looking for a dark corner, the garden has some nice options." He jerked his chin in the direction of a set of French doors, smirking a bit. "It's chilly tonight, but I expect she'll keep you warm," he said, with another cursory glance at Vesper.

"Thank you ever so much," Vesper said, her voice syrupy, and Grimme-Nox looked back at her briefly, startled, as if he hadn't expected that she'd be able to speak. Without another word, Max and Vesper were off, ducking through the doors in question, which led onto a terrace overlooking a small garden below; both the garden and the terrace itself were—just as his father had informed him—full of liaising couples, and they wove their way among them, murmuring apologies, before slipping in through a smaller door at the opposite end of the terrace that led to a narrow hallway.

Vesper's manner immediately became more businesslike. "This way," she murmured. Max was beginning to worry that he found competence attractive—and Vesper was significantly more competent than she wanted anyone to realize.

In a trice, they were down one corridor, through a door leading to a stairwell; it was narrow and a bit worn-looking, in contrast with the glossy sheen of everything else about the club—and then Vesper led him down a flight of stairs to a landing, where . . .

"Surely you're not serious."

She frowned. "Of course I am—it's perfect. No one will look for us here."

"It's a cupboard."

"Precisely!"

"A cupboard built for a *child*," he clarified, looking at the door—which came up to somewhere around his abdomen—with great skepticism.

Vesper rolled her eyes, which was all very well for her, he thought sourly; she was easily six inches shorter than him. This would be considerably more comfortable for her.

"Get in, and stop whingeing," she said, her tone brooking no refusals, and he was alarmed to learn the degree to which he (or, more accurately, his cock) liked that tone of voice coming from her. Rather than pondering that, he clambered into the cupboard, and was grudgingly forced to admit that it was roomier than it looked from outside—the doorway was low, but there was more headspace than had been implied. Vesper climbed in behind him and shut the door, plunging them into darkness.

"This is cozy," Max said, settling onto the floor, stretching his legs out before him and leaning his back against the wall. He had to keep his knees slightly bent, but it was considerably more comfortable than he'd been expecting thirty seconds ago.

He heard the rustling of fabric, then Vesper settled herself next to him. She was pressed up against him, the softness of her breast pushing against his arm; he inhaled deeply, which was a mistake. In these close confines, her scent filled his nose—bluebells, even in October. It was an oddly innocent scent for someone who seemed determined to be perceived as anything but. He didn't think he'd ever be able to smell it again without thinking of her.

"How long until they close?" he asked quietly, after the silence had stretched between them for several seconds.

"Another half hour, I think," she said. "And then we'll need to give it another half hour after that, probably, to give the staff time to leave." She sighed, and there was the sound of rustling fabric as she settled herself more comfortably against him. Here, in the dark, unable to see her, he immediately forgot the disguise of her temporary face; it was just her voice, her scent, the press of her body next to him.

It was just . . . Vesper. As simple, and as complicated, as that. He tilted his head back against the wall, staring unseeingly up into the darkness.

After another several seconds, she said conversationally, "Your father's quite an ass, isn't he?"

Max huffed out a laugh, surprised, and rubbed a hand along his jaw. "Quite," he agreed.

She was silent for another few moments, and he could practically hear her thinking. He didn't speak, curious to see what she was puzzling over. "It makes more sense to me—the way you feel about magic," she said at last. Her voice was quiet, serious. "If a man like that had been my first exposure to magic, I expect I'd have a prejudice against it, too."

He frowned into the dark, thinking about it. "Perhaps," he said finally. "But perhaps . . ." He trailed off, still trying to work out what it was he wanted to say—how he felt. It was uncomfortable, questioning an assumption that had underpinned so much of his life for so long.

Vesper, however, was not as patient as he was. "Perhaps . . . ?" she prompted after only a few seconds of silence had elapsed.

"Perhaps I was simply determined to be pigheaded about it. And I wonder if it's been blinding me to the truth of the world."

"Meaning?"

He sighed. "I still don't love the amount of money and power that's concentrated in the old magical families, but I suppose they're no different in that regard than any of the mundane aristocrats. And I'm not out there campaigning to abolish the monarchy and throw the toffs in prison, am I?"

"I don't know, are you?" she asked, and he could hear the smile in her voice. "How on earth am I to know what you get up to in your free time? You might have all manner of strange hobbies."

"Vesper." It was meant to sound stern, but even he could hear that he hadn't come anywhere close to managing it. It was difficult to sound stern when he was fighting against the urge to smile.

"Ashbridge." She made a decent attempt at mimicking his tone, and now he was smiling in earnest.

"Another impression to add to your repertoire. Should I worry you're going to fetch a brown wig and start impersonating me next?"

"Every time you make a joke, I feel as if I'm having a stroke. Or perhaps as if *you* are."

He felt her shift against him again, and then the coolness of her hand against his forehead. "Are you feverish?"

"Possibly," he said, and then caught her hand in his, and—without pausing for even the briefest of moments to ponder what he was doing—pressed it to his mouth.

He heard her breath catch in her throat.

"Ashbridge." Her voice was low.

He drew back to inhale a deep, shuddering breath. "I wish you'd say my name."

A pause. "Why?"

This was the moment at which he could still stop this. He could laugh it off, make a joke or a flip remark, or come over stern, anything to make the space between them feel less loaded with promise.

Another pause, longer this time, and then—instead of doing any of those things—he said quietly, "You know why."

She didn't respond for a moment, the silence stretching between them, growing heavy, and then, finally, she said, so softly, "Max."

And then, in a single, smooth moment, as if he'd been planning it all along, he turned and took her in his arms, and kissed her again.

Chapter Twenty-Two

Vesper hadn't known quite what to expect from this evening's itinerary, but to the best of her recollection, "shagging in a cupboard" had not been anywhere on the agenda.

And yet, that seemed to be the route they were on. Ashbridge's kiss was like a flame to kindling; she felt as though her body had come alive beneath his touch, the press of his hand at her waist, on her arm, cupping her breast, leaving sparks in its wake each time it moved. She made short work of shifting onto her knees, then flinging a leg over him so that she was straddling his lap, and he laughed against her throat, the sound low and a bit ragged.

"Very lucky you didn't accidentally knee me in the bollocks," he said, pressing a kiss to the hollow of her throat. "I can't see a goddamn thing in here."

"It's muscle memory at this point," Vesper said. Her fingers found the hair at the nape of his neck that she feared she was becoming perversely obsessed with. She pressed down into his lap, causing a groan to work its way up from his chest, and his hands were suddenly at her hips, stilling her.

"Keep that up, and this isn't going to last long," he warned, and it was Vesper's turn to laugh, a bit breathlessly. Another moment—occupied, quite pleasantly, by Ashbridge's mouth on hers, and one of his hands sliding from its spot anchoring her hips, up to her bare arm, dragging down the strap of her dress—and then Ashbridge added, sounding impressively coherent, given their current circumstances, "I wish this cupboard had a lock."

"Don't . . . think . . . that they're going to come looking for us," Vesper said; Ashbridge's mouth was now occupied with the bare skin exposed by her gown's sagging neckline, and she felt the wet heat of his tongue through the silk of her brassiere. She hadn't *precisely* selected her underthings with the goal of getting Max Ashbridge to remove them, but it would be a lie to deny that the thought had occurred to her.

She drew back, just enough to fumble for the buttons on his shirt. Her eyes were adjusting to the darkness; she still couldn't make him out in any great detail, but she could at least perceive the outlines of his shadowy figure beneath her. Somehow, the darkness made the experience feel more intimate, not less so; Vesper had always been a make-love-with-the-lights-on sort of girl—after all, she looked *spectacular* when she was naked. Furthermore, she'd always found that it heightened her pleasure, being able to see exactly what she was doing (and what was being done to her). But here, in the quiet of this closet, with Ashbridge's breaths heavy in her ears, able to feel him but not see him . . . it felt private. Special.

She suddenly, in a moment of blinding clarity, realized what it could be like to do this with someone who only wanted to be doing it with *her*, specifically.

She only had a second to dwell on those thoughts, however, because Ashbridge didn't allow her much chance to think. He was sliding down the other strap of her dress, and she was—after a brief struggle—able to free her arms, exposing her entire chest and stomach to the cool air. She banged one elbow against the door, and laughed against Ashbridge's neck, the skin of his stomach warm against her palm.

"I'll have a bruise there tomorrow," she gasped, still suppressing giggles, but she was distracted by the feeling of Ashbridge's fingers on the complicated buttons and laces of her brassiere; removing it would have been a somewhat challenging task under the best of circumstances, but the darkness slowed his progress considerably, and he exhaled a frustrated breath.

"You *would* make this as difficult as possible," he muttered, the only acknowledgment of his struggle.

"Watch it, I paid an awful lot of money for that lingerie set." She shifted on his lap, and he stifled another groan against the bare skin of her breast. She could feel him, hard beneath her thigh, and she slipped an exploratory hand down to the buttons of his trousers, which prompted yet another groan. This was growing quite satisfying—she thought she could listen to those groans all day.

He, however, had other ideas, and clearly decided that turnabout was fair play, because he slipped a hand beneath her skirts, and up her stockinged legs; he traced a finger along the ribbons of one of her garters, up the bare skin of her thigh, and—with little warning—pushed aside the damp fabric of her knickers to give her a stroke.

"Nugh," she said eloquently, and dropped her head to his shoulder as he slid a finger inside her. His thumb began working in small, tight circles, and Vesper's eyes actually rolled back in her head. He kept his movements agonizingly slow—enough to drive her wild, but not enough to send her over the edge. She shifted her hips restlessly, trying to force his hand into a faster pace; instead, he merely added a second finger, prompting another sound from Vesper that, had she been capable of coherent thought, she would probably have felt embarrassed by.

There was a muffled thump as his elbow hit the wall. "For fuck's sake."

"It . . . lacks a bit . . . in romantic atmosphere," Vesper said, the words coming out as gasps. "But it . . . is sort of charming . . . in its own way."

"I don't think you should be able to speak right now," he said, his tone stern in a way that her body liked very much; her thighs tightened around his hand. At that precise moment, they heard the sound of footsteps, and he clamped a hand over her mouth. "Quiet," he murmured against her temple. They stilled for a moment, but the footsteps grew more distant; his fingers increased their pace, and Vesper whimpered against his palm.

"You're so wet," he said, his voice ragged in her ear, his breath hot against her cheek. "Do you hear yourself?" He did something with his fingers that prompted Vesper to cry out, muffling the sound against his neck, and she felt him twitch against her thigh. Vesper would not, in any universe, have taken Max Ashbridge to be a filthy talker in bed.

"I'd be even wetter if you'd speed the hell up," she said, breathless, and he laughed, the sound low and throaty. Vesper hadn't thought it possible to be more aroused than she had been a second before, which just went to show that Ashbridge liked to surprise her. The tight circles his thumb was rubbing grew smaller, quicker, and Vesper ground her hips against him helplessly, small whimpers falling uncontrolled from her mouth. Another minute or so, and she was almost . . . almost . . . there. She leaned back, her head falling back to allow her to gaze, unseeingly, up at the shadowy ceiling, and he leaned forward to place a kiss on the hollow between her breasts, and then seal his mouth over one of her nipples. A slight graze of his teeth, and she was gone, shuddering around him, her thighs clenching so tight around his fingers that she thought dimly, with faint amusement, that he might be trapped there for some time.

A minute, or perhaps an hour, passed.

"I'm going to get a wrist cramp," he said, and she laughed against his neck. It felt so odd to have a man's hand between her legs but to be laughing with him at the same time. She'd never thought anything was missing from her bedroom life, but she realized in a flash that laughter was rare.

"Is this how you normally conduct your investigations?" she asked, and she could imagine his frown at her, even though the darkness prevented her from actually seeing it.

"Vesper. For Christ's sake."

"Just wondering. You're really quite skilled at maneuvering in tight spaces."

"You're going to be the death of me." The way he phrased

it made it sound like a compliment, Vesper thought, growing warm all over.

She drew back so that his hand could slip free from between her thighs and wasted no time in fumbling with the buttons on his trousers, reaching to take him, hot and heavy, in her hand. She gave him a slow stroke, and his breath grew unsteady, but then his hand was on hers, stilling the motion.

"No?" she asked, and gave him another stroke.

"I—Christ," he said, his grip on her wrist tightening. His hand was slippery on her skin—still wet with *her*. Merlin. Surely fumbles in a cupboard weren't meant to be *this* good? She stroked him again, and rose up on her knees.

"I don't suppose you've got a condom in that scrap of fabric masquerading as a dress?" he asked, and she froze. Despite her flighty reputation, there were some things Vesper was *very* careful about. There were potions that allegedly helped prevent pregnancy, but she'd never entirely trusted them, especially as they were somewhat time-sensitive (like all magic these days), and so she always employed secondary measures to be safe. She was fond of George, but had no desire to give him a cousin just yet.

"It's only . . . I know there are potions"—his voice was apologetic—"but, given what happened with my mother and . . . and *him*, I like to be careful." She wished it was light enough to get a proper look at his face, because he sounded almost embarrassed, when there was nothing at all embarrassing about anything he was saying.

"Of course," she said, fumbling to press a reassuring hand to his cheek. "It makes perfect sense . . . and I like to be careful, too. I wasn't thinking." *She* was feeling embarrassed now, truthfully; it wasn't as though she was some naive virgin. She couldn't believe she had forgotten herself, even for a minute. "But," she added, deciding—in a fit of philosophizing—that she might as well make lemonade out of lemons, "you're in luck. I have a very talented mouth."

Ashbridge's reply to that was nonverbal—or, if it *was* verbal, then it was not any language Vesper recognized. But she was too busy pushing herself backward, giving herself just enough space to crouch between his spread thighs, lean down, and lick him from hilt to tip, before taking him into her mouth.

And Ashbridge's contributions to the conversation, for the next few minutes, continued to be entirely incomprehensible.

◆

"Do you think an hour's passed yet?" Vesper asked, stirring against his chest.

"Hmm?" Max murmured, feeling vaguely stupefied. He'd managed to tuck himself back into his trousers, but had made no other move to make himself more presentable, and instead had been leaning against the wall with Vesper slumped against the bare skin of his chest for some indeterminate amount of time. Her skin was impossibly warm, and she smelled like bluebells, but also like sweat and female pleasure and *herself*, and it was the best thing he'd ever smelled in his life. He shook his head, trying to clear it enough to take stock of his current situation: half naked, having just had one of the best orgasms of his entire life with *Vesper Holloway*, who was also, currently, half naked and pressing an open-mouthed kiss to his neck that was making his cock—which he'd thought would be out of commission for at least another hour—perk up and take notice. And he was meant to be *conducting a professional investigation*. It was a good thing he didn't actually like his job that much, because he was fairly certain that if Raffles caught wind of even half of what had occurred so far tonight, she'd have his head.

It would have been entirely worth it.

"The time," Vesper said, enunciating clearly, as if concerned that he wasn't entirely fluent in English, or was perhaps just very stupid. Both descriptions felt somewhat true at the moment. "Do you think the coast is clear?"

Ah, right. Because they were meant to be *working*, not shagging in a cupboard.

"I can hear you mentally scolding yourself for taking your eye off the mission," she said, a bit unnervingly. She sat up and, judging by the rustling sounds, was shifting her dress back into place. "Don't suppose you have a handkerchief, do you?" she asked after a moment, and he reached into his jacket pocket, produced one, and, after fumbling for a moment, found her hand to press it into.

He made quick work of the buttons on his shirt and trousers. They likely looked a state, but on the off chance their gauging of time was off and there was still staff about, at least they'd lend credibility to their cover story.

There was more rustling as Vesper rose into a crouch and opened the cupboard door; the sudden light pouring in from the hall was a bit blinding, even though it was fairly dim and muted, coming from a couple of lamps burning low in sconces farther along the corridor, and Max squinted. Vesper's face, he saw, was her own again, so they must have passed the three-hour mark since drinking the batches of Fresh Faced. Vesper poked her head out and did a brief bit of reconnaissance, then glanced over her shoulder at him. "Looks safe."

Max rose to a crouch, wincing slightly at a twinge in his knees—he was getting too old for shagging in cupboards—and crept out of the tight space, joining her in the deserted corridor. She looked . . . well, she looked as though she'd been doing precisely what she'd been doing: Her golden curls were disheveled (by *his* hands) and her lipstick was smudged (by *his* mouth) and the strap on her dress was a bit off-kilter. Her cheeks were rosy and her eyes were shining. She looked younger than usual, and as beautiful as ever. The sight of her made his chest ache.

He reached out and laced his fingers through hers. "Shall we?"

They crept cautiously down the corridor, their ears alert to the sound of anyone approaching, but the club did seem to be empty; the overnight guard was nowhere in sight, and they were able to make their way unmolested around a couple of corners, up a flight of stairs, and into a narrow upstairs hallway that was clearly not meant for members. They tried the doors, which were unlocked, for the most part, and revealed nothing more interesting than storage closets, a couple of bedrooms (Max wondered with a shudder of distaste what purpose his father might put those bedrooms to), a loo, a small lounge.

At last, however, they reached a doorknob that would not turn beneath their hands, and Vesper said, quietly victorious, "Aha." She leaned close, scrutinizing the doorknob itself, the sheen of the paint on the door; her nose was about six inches away from its surface, which again made Max vaguely nervous, though he couldn't have offered any sort of logical explanation, if pressed, for what he thought would happen if she came into too-close proximity with a magically enchanted door.

"Stop fretting," Vesper said without pausing her inspection.

"I'm not fretting."

"You are," she insisted, still not looking at him. "I can hear it from here."

Max felt that further protests along these lines would not serve him well, and so he instead contented himself with watching her carefully, reassuring himself that he would spring into action at a moment's notice, should . . . er . . . some unknown and mysterious magical reaction emanating from a slab of wood occur.

Reassuring.

At last, Vesper straightened. "I don't *think* it's enchanted," she said, with slightly less certainty than Max would have preferred.

"Think?" he repeated. "You don't *think*?"

"It's quite old," she said defensively. "And with old magic, it can sometimes be difficult to tell. With age, the signs of lingering spells become a bit less obvious—it's the same reason no one notices the magic still lingering around St. Paul's, or the Tower of London, for example."

Max didn't wish to be sidetracked, but this was simply too much to ignore. "I'm sorry—are you implying that there are magical hazards lurking round every corner at our nation's greatest architectural treasures?"

"I hadn't realized you were so patriotic," she said waspishly, and he gave her a repressive sort of look. "Yes, Ashbridge, there's magic lingering around all those piles of stone you hold so dear. Magical education in this country really is shocking," she added in a disgusted mutter. "The fact that this is news to you—"

"All right," he said. "So, you don't think this door is enchanted—shall we pick the lock?"

Vesper stepped back, and reached into her hair, presumably searching for a hairpin.

"Don't bother," Max said, reaching into his jacket pocket and retrieving a small, pocket-size lockpicking kit.

Vesper was delighted. "This is very attractive," she said, watching as he got to work. "I've never seen a man pick a lock before; men are so terribly dull, usually."

"I'm beginning to think *those* men have the right of it," he muttered, his gaze focused on the lock before him. It was old, of good quality, but not terribly complicated. "I don't see any of them engaging in criminal activities in the dead of night. I expect *they're* all safe in their beds." But even as he said it, he felt the strangest desire to smile. He realized, disconcertingly, that he would not wish to have spent tonight peacefully in bed. This had all been rather fun, in fact. He'd not realized that was something his life was missing.

In a matter of minutes, he had the lock picked, the doorknob turning in his hand. He held his breath, waiting for—well, he didn't know what.

"It probably would have just triggered some sort of magical alarm, if it were enchanted," Vesper said.

"So it must not be, then?" Max asked, relieved, given that the corridor was still quiet around them.

"Unless it's a silent one that merely alerts the security for the building, or the owner," she said blithely, then did a double take at the undoubtedly horrified look on his face. "Which is why it might be wise to *hop to it*, Ashbridge." She pushed past him into the room, and he rose to his feet and followed her, his ears attuned to the sound of approaching footsteps. For the moment, at least, he heard nothing.

Behind the locked door was an office, as he might have expected. A quick glance at the diary on the desk showed the handwriting that Max recalled from stiffly worded missives that he'd received over the years. He began to thumb through the diary, not certain what he was looking for; at first, he didn't see anything interesting—dinners with an exhausting-sounding rotation of women with names like Fleurette; weekends away at so-and-so's country pile (eurgh); meetings with various names that he recognized, power players in the world of business and several politicians who Max knew to be pro-magic advocates. So far, so expected.

He paused, however, on one entry from a few days earlier. *Meet with M.K.R.* He flipped through another several pages to confirm—but yes, this was the only meeting solely noted with initials, rather than a full name, or at least a surname. He began to look more carefully through the pages of the diary, until he spotted, a fortnight before the entry he'd noted, an identical one. And there, earlier in the year, another. And another. Each time, initials were used.

"Vesper," he said, eyes still on the page before him. "Do the initials M.K.R. mean anything to you?"

"What?" She crossed to stand next to him.

Max pointed at his father's diary. "He's arranged a series of meetings with someone called *M.K.R.*"

She shook her head. "I've no idea. Do you think it's a . . . coconspirator?"

"Perhaps. If we could work out who it was—"

"But even then, we wouldn't be able to prove anything," Vesper said, frustration creeping into her voice. "All we have now is a series of guesses and half-pieced-together clues. But we haven't any *proof*. We need to keep looking." She moved past him and began to rifle through the desk drawers, her movements quick and efficient. She found a stack of correspondence, which she thrust at Max. "Look through this, and see if there's anything of interest."

Max complied, but found nothing titillating (in regards to their investigation). Vesper, meanwhile, was emptying the desk drawers of their contents in haphazard fashion.

"Hmm," she said thoughtfully a few minutes later, having paused to flip through a thick leather-bound ledger. "Business at the Grimoire seems to have been bad lately."

Max set the stack of correspondence aside, then rounded the desk to stand next to Vesper, peering over her shoulder at the minute scribbles. He was not as experienced as she was at deciphering a business's books, and it took a few beats for him to spot what she had: several months that the club had ended in the red.

"Not surprising, honestly," she murmured, considering the numbers with an expert eye. "He's spending far too much on food—I'd heard that he'd lured a famous chef from a Parisian hotel, but these figures are absolutely ruinous." She shook her head in disapproval; Max watched her for a moment, and she blinked. "What?"

"I find it very attractive that you're such a competent businesswoman," he informed her, and she blinked again—and then, astonishingly, blushed. A smile played at the corners of her mouth.

"Don't distract me with compliments," she said, her voice brisk, and she set the ledger aside, continuing her search through Grimme-Nox's drawers. She had just made it to the bottommost of these, her movements growing hastier, when she suddenly stopped. "Did you hear something?"

"Yes." Max was still for a moment, listening intently—but he definitely heard the sound of footsteps, at a distance but growing louder. He sprang into action, reaching for the piles Vesper had lifted from the drawers and returning them to their homes. His movements were swift and economical. He shut the last drawer with a decisive *click* and seized Vesper by the hand, turning to assess the room for a hiding spot. Beneath the desk? Too small—and too easily discovered. The cabinet? Again, too small. There was a closet in one corner, and Vesper reached for it; the knob didn't turn, and she tugged on it, frustrated. Max reached past her, seized it, and, miraculously, the knob turned and the door opened, revealing a small storage space—there were several wooden crates, still sealed shut, and a few stacks of books that seemed to be overflow from the packed shelves in the office.

"Come on." Max dragged Vesper in with him, and eased the door shut behind them. They held their breath and waited; fifteen seconds later, they heard the door to the office open.

Max was conscious, in the close confines of the closet, of the sound of Vesper's breathing, and his. He tried to steady his breath, inhaling slowly, even as his heart thundered in his chest. He listened to the owner of the footsteps—presumably the night watchman—walk around the room slowly, clearly listening carefully. There was the sound of the cabinet doors opening, then shutting again. And then, suddenly, Max's heart was in his mouth at the sound of a hand on the doorknob for the closet. He reached for Vesper's hand, clammy with nerves—and then, the knob rattled, but it wouldn't turn. The footsteps crossed to the door, and there was the sound of the door opening and shutting again.

Next to Max, Vesper exhaled shakily. "I—"

Max reached over in a single motion and clamped a hand over her mouth. She made a slight noise of surprised disgruntlement against his palm, but to her credit swallowed it almost immediately, and went very still against him. Her back was now pressed to his chest; he took a shallow breath, and inhaled the scent of her hair.

They stood like that for at least a minute—perhaps two—before Max heard the sound he'd been waiting for: a resigned sigh; the door opening; and, this time, the sound of footsteps actually leaving the room before it was shut again.

Dimly, in the corridor, they heard the footsteps retreating, and the sound of another door being opened, some sort of similar inspection being performed. Max at last allowed his hand to drop from Vesper's mouth.

"I'm sorry," she said quietly. "That was stupid of me—I should've been listening more carefully. I didn't realize—"

"Don't be silly—anyone would've thought the same," he told her.

"*You* didn't," she pointed out.

"Well—I like to be cautious," he said, shifting his weight slightly to put a bit more space between them.

"It's not always such a bad thing," she said thoughtfully, before falling silent once more.

They waited, quiet, for several long minutes more, as the footsteps left one room, entered another, the process repeating itself. At last, they grew distant, and there was the faint, rhythmic sound of someone rapidly descending a set of stairs. Max, nearly limp with relief, reached out to open the closet door.

"It was a ridiculous spot of luck that this doorknob is so tricky." He stepped out, turning for Vesper to follow him, but she remained where she was, looking around at the contents of the closet.

"Is it?" she asked.

"What?"

"Is it so tricky?" She followed him out of the closet now, then pushed the door shut. She reached for the knob, tried to turn it. It wouldn't budge in her hand, not even an inch. "Now you try."

Max reached out, and again the knob turned easily for him—not as if it were being unstuck, but smoothly, without the slightest resistance.

"This door is bespelled," Vesper said, a note of eagerness creeping into her voice.

"How?" Max asked. "If I was able to open it—"

"Magic recognizes bloodlines—you know this more than most. It must be bespelled to respond to the hand of a member of the Grimme-Nox family. Not," she added hastily, catching sight of whatever was written on his face, "that you would consider yourself to be one, for obvious reasons. But the magic doesn't understand that. That's why you could open the door, but the guard and I couldn't." She wrinkled her nose. "Ancient magic like this is really quite primitive, I don't think it's a very clever sort of spell at all—it's not as if your father would *want* you to have access to this closet, whatever it is. I think some sort of strong mundane lock would really work much better in a situation like this."

"Don't tell me you've finally come to see things from my point of view, now that I've finally started to come round to yours," he said dryly, and she grinned at him. The grin faded after a moment, however, and a thoughtful expression replaced it.

"There must be something in here worth hiding—you wouldn't use a closet with that sort of spellwork on the door for just anything." She stepped forward, pulled the lid off one of the crates, and peered inside. "What on . . ."

Max was next to her in a trice. The crate contained campaign flyers from the last election. The Tories had triumphed; he recalled his father being seen at numerous events for the Alliance Party, which was campaigning fiercely against the Tories and Forbiddance, and had reflected with some satisfaction, once the results were announced, that his father, at least, would be disappointed.

However—these campaign flyers were *for* the Tories.

Vesper moved to the next crate, and opened it—broadsheets, relaying the text of a speech given by a Tory MP who'd been up for reelection.

One Michael Knight Raffles.

M.K.R.

Vesper looked up and met his gaze, her eyes wide.

"I think," he said quietly, "we ought to phone your sister, because I suspect we've got the scoop of the century for her."

Chapter Twenty-Three

In the end, it wasn't as difficult to unravel a cunning plan involving government officials, members of Parliament, and the scion of an ancient magical family as Max would have expected.

All one really needed was a couple of journalists.

Cecily and Will arrived at Vesper's flat the next day looking puzzled to have been summoned so urgently on a weekend morning, though rather *not* puzzled to find Max already there, wearing the previous evening's clothes.

"This is fascinating information that I shall be returning to when we have less important matters at hand," Cecily informed her sister as she accepted a cup of tea from her.

Will was somewhat less diplomatic about it. "I knew you needed a shag," he said to Max bluntly, the instant the two of them were alone in the sitting room for half a second while Vesper and her sister argued over jam preferences in the kitchen. "Look at you—you're *grinning*."

"I'm basking in what is hopefully soon to be a professional success."

"No—you've just had a good shag," Will said definitively. "This means I won my bet with Vera; you were a week sooner than she expected."

"I don't suppose you'd consider refraining from betting on my love life in the future?"

"So long as Vesper sticks around, I won't say another word," Will said with a grin, but his face softened after a moment. "I quite like her, you know; she keeps things interesting."

This was, Max thought, one of his favorite things about Vesper, too. It was becoming quite a long list.

Will and Cecily were briefed on the situation as it currently stood while pastries were consumed; Max had darted out to collect them from the bakery around the corner that morning while Vesper slept next to him. They'd been too exhausted and exhilarated when they arrived home in the wee hours of the morning to do anything other than tumble into bed and fall asleep a moment later, but Max had awoken in the soft morning light to find Vesper curled up next to him, a soft frown curving the edges of her mouth in her sleep. He'd felt warm and tender at the sight, and instead of lingering to contemplate this, he'd crept out in search of baked goods. When he'd returned, he'd awoken her with a kiss; she had mumbled sleepily, made a variety of incoherent protests about the early hour, and then twined her arms around his neck, pulling him back down into the warmth of her body.

It had been quite a while before he'd got up again.

Once he had, though, they'd both sprung into action.

Cecily and Will looked increasingly awake as the magnitude of the potential story they were being handed dawned on them.

"Do we need some sort of proof?" Vesper asked, sounding uncharacteristically anxious as she and Max finished their summarization of their findings so far. Will had fished a notebook out of his pocket and was scribbling away; he glanced over at Cecily, and then they shook their heads in unison.

"No," Cecily said, thoughtful. "Or, at least, I don't think so—this is plenty to get us started. We really just need *one* person who's willing to talk." She looked at Max, assessing. "I take it you don't want to approach your father with this?"

"He and I do not have a history of calm and reasoned conversations," Max said dryly. "I doubt that would end well. Besides, I can't imagine he'd have any motive to admit it—this could destroy his business."

"True," Will said. "Ditto for Raffles, I'll bet—if he and Grimme-Nox orchestrated this together, it'll be the end of his entire political career."

"What about Finlay?" Vesper asked suddenly, leaning forward. "We think he's mixed up in all this somehow, but if he didn't directly plan it, I wonder if we can convince him to talk? Offer to keep his name out of the papers in exchange?"

Max grimaced in distaste at this, but was forced to concede it was a decent plan.

"I doubt he'll speak to me," Cecily said ruefully. "He's, er, not a particular fan of *The Spark*." She looked at Will inquiringly. "Perhaps *The Times* would be more to his taste?"

"Or," Vesper said, eyes flicking to Max, "*perhaps* the perfect person to approach him initially wouldn't be a journalist at all—but an eminently trustworthy and upstanding government employee?"

Which is how Max found himself calling out from work sick on Monday, and instead standing, at the respectable hour of eleven o'clock, outside Jacob Finlay's office door in the Palace of Westminster.

Feeling a bit as if he were inhabiting a different universe, he gave his name—and, crucially, his professional title—to the secretary who opened the door of the antechamber, and he was, in short order, shown into Finlay's office, where the man in question awaited him behind an imposing oak desk. The entire situation felt like a strange historical artifact; nothing about the twentieth century was evident, barring a discreet wireless tucked onto a bookshelf.

"Mr. Ashbridge, is it?" Finlay asked, lifting his gaze from the thick stack of correspondence on his desk. "It's only out of my affection for Mrs. Raffles that I'm seeing you: My schedule is quite busy today."

"Of course," Max said, with a respectful nod. He'd been sure to mention Raffles's name to the secretary at the door—if this conversation went as planned, then he didn't need to worry about word getting back to her. "I appreciate your time." He took a seat without being invited in one of the uncomfortable wooden chairs opposite Finlay's desk, and he said, without preamble, "I'd like to discuss your involvement in a series of poisonings at the Marylebone clubs."

Finlay, ever the politician, had a pretty good poker face, but even he was unable to keep any hint of emotion from his expression, and for a moment he looked genuinely startled. "I'm sorry?"

"Well," Max said, leaning back in his seat, "it's come to my attention, courtesy of a couple of reliable sources, that there is plenty of evidence to suggest that you are somehow wrapped up in a scheme involving Michael Raffles and Augustus Grimme-Nox, and that the magic at various clubs has been tampered with."

"Magic is a dangerous forbidden substance—something I presume you're aware of, given your line of work." Finlay gave Max a thin smile. "I'm sorry to hear there's been some trouble, but this is quite a wild accusation."

He was very good, Max thought in a detached sort of way. Unfortunately, he wasn't *quite* good enough: His hands were gripping the arms of his chair just a bit too tight.

"Ah." Max smiled faintly. "My mistake. That's unfortunate—I have a couple of friends at *The Spark* and *The Times* who are quite interested in this story and were hoping to cut some sort of deal with you to keep your name out of the proceedings, but I'll simply tell them you're not interested, and let them write whatever story they will."

With that, Max rose to his feet, turned, and walked to the door.

He only made it halfway across the room before Finlay said sharply, "Wait."

Careful to keep any trace of smugness or triumph off his face, Max turned. Finlay was regarding him with a coldly appraising eye—he had the air of a man who was rapidly reassessing an opponent.

He was silent a long moment, then said, "I'd want assurances."

Max inclined his head. "I think they can provide them."

Finlay considered him for another few seconds. "I fail to see where you come into this, Mr. Ashbridge."

"Call it a . . . personal interest."

Finlay looked unimpressed. "Lots of men have blown up their entire careers for personal interests. It would seem you're merely the latest in that noble line."

"Let me worry about my career—and I'll let *you* worry about preserving what's left of yours."

"I wonder if Effie Raffles knew who she was hiring," Finlay said, sounding genuinely curious.

Max couldn't prevent the small smile that crossed his face at this. "Well, I think she's about to find out."

◆

That evening, he arrived at Holloway's to be greeted by a smug-looking Cecily. She was sitting in the snug, nursing a cup of tea and typing furiously on a typewriter, consulting a tattered notebook filled with shorthand scribbles.

"Ashbridge!" she said brightly, beckoning him when he poked his head into the room. "Brilliant work this morning."

"I take it you and Will had success in your interview with Finlay?"

Cecily nodded happily. "Chamberlain's still with him, going over the finer details. I wanted to get a head start on drafting the copy—Chamberlain will join me later." She sounded extremely pleased with herself, in a particular way that Max was beginning to suspect was a Holloway family trait, before adding, very sharply, "George, do not even think of putting that in your mouth."

Max blinked, then leaned forward, craning his neck; tucked between the edge of the armchair Cecily occupied and the wall was a small, dark-haired boy who appeared to have pried up a loose floorboard to reveal some sort of bounty hidden in a pillowcase. He was currently holding an old coin up to his eye to scrutinize. This must be the nephew that both Vesper and Freddie had discussed in such haunted tones.

The boy looked up and deigned to take notice of Max. "Who are you?"

"Mr. Ashbridge," Cecily said. "He's a friend of Auntie Vesper's."

"I thought you didn't like Auntie Vesper's friends," George informed his mother, his chubby face creasing into a frown. "You said she always chooses the wrong men to be friends with."

"Well," Cecily said, laughter in her voice, "Mr. Ashbridge is an exception. For that reason, I'm hoping he and Auntie Vesper will be friends for quite a while."

"Do *you* want to be friends with Auntie Vesper for quite a while?" George demanded of Max, a fierce scowl on his face.

"I do," Max said gravely, and, thus mollified, George returned his attention to the coin.

"Cecily, I—oh, hello, Max," Vesper said, poking her head around the door. "Cecily, do you know how long Simon and his cronies plan to occupy half of the downstairs dining room? It's only, the Gentrys have two tables booked at eight for some sort of family do, but I didn't want to interrupt Simon's meeting—"

"I'll go let him know," Cecily said, closing her notebook and rising to her feet. "The bill is due to be read next Monday, which is perfect, if Chamberlain and I can run our stories this week." Cecily and Will had agreed to work in partnership and publish their planned scoops in tandem, sharing the byline in each of their respective papers. Will, too, was in discussions with the reporter at *The Times* whom Effie Raffles had been leaking to—a fact that was happily confirmed by the reporter, once Will had explained the situation.

"Is the information from Finlay going to be enough to go on?" Vesper asked.

"Plenty," Cecily said. "He was only too happy to tell us, in considerable detail, about Michael Raffles's scheme. Apparently Raffles had originally had the idea of *actually* poisoning some of the drinks at various clubs, but Finlay was old school chums with Grimme-Nox—strange bedfellows—and it was Grimme-Nox who suggested tampering with the magic instead. Figured Scotland Yard would be less likely to investigate if it was just bad magic, rather than something deadly."

"And Grimme-Nox's goal was simply to damage the reputation of the other clubs?" Max asked.

Cecily nodded. "He was having financial troubles and hoped to drive business away from the other clubs and toward the Grimoire. Evidently, he's on the hunt for a wealthy heiress to make wife number four, both to prop up his finances and hopefully give him an heir to leave the club to, so this was intended as a sort of . . . stopgap measure." She grimaced. "It's appallingly calculated, and I look forward to no one in the magical community speaking to him for the rest of his life, once this news gets out."

"I can't decide whether to be pleased we figured it out correctly or horrified that someone would attempt this."

"I'd stick with pleased," Cecily advised. "Particularly when you consider that he may have done us an enormous favor, given how bad this will make Raffles and the entire Forbiddance movement look by association. I think Finlay's hoping that, by speaking anonymously and pinning it all on Raffles, it'll look like a single bad apple, but Simon's optimistic that this will be the last nudge some of the MPs need to come round to his way of seeing things."

Vesper met Max's eyes as Cecily left the room, George trailing in her wake. "Nicely done," she said, offering him a tentative smile, and he matched it.

"I've never got to threaten someone with the destruction of their entire political career before," he said. "It made for an interesting Monday, at least."

"And what of tomorrow?" Vesper asked; there was something a bit dark and uncertain in her gaze, something Max didn't understand. He, at the moment, had never felt lighter.

"Tomorrow, I have something else in mind entirely."

◆

The next day, Max quit his job.

He'd thought about it the entire evening; Will had shown up at Holloway's soon after Max had, and he and Cecily had worked, heads bent together, late into the night. Max had sat with them, poring over their notes from Finlay, marveling at the details of the plan. Vesper had vanished at some point to see to the running of the club; the evening had only been interrupted when Hazel Thomas had shown up, Delacqua in tow, shortly before midnight, to breathlessly report that there had been an accident at Mauve's that night—a young lady had taken a packet of spell powder and been gripped by a sudden, terrifying fever, one so high that she rapidly became delirious.

Cecily and Will had exchanged grim looks. "We can run this on Wednesday," Cecily said confidently. "My editor already has a fact-checker at work verifying as many details as possible—and he agrees that we can't afford to delay."

And Max decided that he couldn't, either. So on Tuesday afternoon, just after lunch, he walked into Raffles's office and handed in his resignation, effective immediately.

"You cannot be serious," she said, gaping at him as he stood before her, having declined the seat she'd offered him.

"I am, actually," he said, feeling downright cheerful; some of this must have shown on his face, because Raffles narrowed her eyes at him.

"Ashbridge, you're in the *middle of an investigation*," she said, and Max shrugged.

"Work it out without me," he said.

"If you think I'll be providing a reference for you after this behavior—"

"A reference from you is the least of my concerns, actually," he said.

And then he walked out the door.

And straight to Holloway's.

"Ashbridge, don't you have a job?"

Freddie was behind the bar today, mixing cocktails alongside Amir, looking entirely at ease.

Max walked to the bar. "A glass of champagne, please. I'm feeling celebratory."

"I find this frightening." Nevertheless, Freddie reached for a bottle.

"I've just quit my job," Max announced, and Freddie's hand slipped, the bottle nearly sliding from his grasp.

"I know men are drawn to my sister," Freddie said, recovering his grip and reaching for a glass, "but I've never known her to have quite *this* effect on one before."

Max accepted the glass of champagne. Freddie poured one for himself, then hesitated. Max reached across the bar and tapped their glasses together. "Cheers." He waited for Freddie to take a sip, and then said, "I'm sorry, you know. About—"

"I know," Freddie interrupted. He paused, then added, "I'm sorry, too. I thought about it for a long time afterward, and always regretted that I didn't . . . I don't know. Try to see things from your perspective, I suppose. It felt like too much time had passed, though—I figured you wouldn't be interested in hearing from me."

"I had my head up my arse," Max said, and Freddie choked out a laugh around a mouthful of champagne.

"Is my sister to credit for removing it?" Freddie asked slyly.

"Ignoring that horrifying imagery, I expect she is." Max offered Freddie a small smile, and Freddie gave him that blinding Holloway grin in return.

"What's this?" Vesper asked, sliding onto the barstool next to Max's.

"Ashbridge has quit his job," Freddie announced, and Max got to enjoy the novel sensation of watching her gape at him.

"You can't seriously think that, after what we've learned, I'd want to keep working there?" he asked her, tilting his glass at her. She reached over, plucked it from his grasp, and took a sip.

"Of course not. I just thought you might *warn* me first." She handed his glass back to him. "What's next, then? Back to the Passport Office? Or something else for the Foreign Office—you could work for an embassy, perhaps?" The words were uttered casually, almost carelessly, and she didn't meet his eyes as she spoke.

Max stared at her, frowning. "Why would I do that?"

Vesper shrugged. "It's still government work, but it's something different—very interesting, I'd imagine. And it would allow you to travel—weren't you saying you'd never been able to travel as a boy? You deserve to see the world beyond whatever you saw in the war: That's hardly the same as the canals of Venice that you saw in all those paintings."

Max felt as though he were holding a conversation in a language in which he wasn't fluent. "I have an entire life here in London—I'm not planning to move abroad."

Vesper shrugged again, giving a careless flip of her hair. "It was just a thought—you've nothing to tie you down, after all, I thought you might like to explore something new." She glanced at him now, lightning-fast, out of the corner of her eye.

Nothing to tie him down.

Was this her way of informing him that she didn't consider this—whatever it was, between them—to be serious?

If so, it felt like a piss-poor way for her to let him know, particularly with Freddie standing five feet away, making rather a show out of peeling a lemon for garnish while sneaking surreptitious glances at them. Farther down the bar, Amir was muddling basil, and Max saw him roll his eyes at Freddie.

"If you're going to eavesdrop, you may as well just do it openly," Amir said, leaning toward Freddie, and Max watched Freddie blush.

Max turned to Vesper, who had snuck another sip of his champagne. "Well," he said, reeling from the past three minutes, "I suppose I'll consider all of that. Thank you for the . . . er . . . suggestion."

"Of course," she said brightly, her smile blinding and cheerful, even as she still couldn't quite meet his eyes. "I'm going to go see if Anna needs any help in the back—and Freddie, have you made any more spell powder this afternoon, or do I need to handle it?"

In a whirl, she was off, leaving Max reeling in her wake.

Freddie leaned toward him, his expression thoughtful.

"That," he said, with the air of a naturalist having observed fascinating animal behavior in the wild, "was Vesper taking preventative action."

"Well," Max said, his voice sounding bitter even to his own ears, "she's quite ruthless about it. Ensured I didn't get any funny ideas."

"Oh." Freddie laughed. "No. Sorry—you misunderstand. She's taking preventative action for *herself*. She's worried you're not going to be interested any longer, now that you're done playing detectives, and so she's setting you free."

Max stared at him. "She can't possibly think that."

Freddie shrugged. "Vesper's used to people wanting her for a night—she's spent the past few years ensuring that she never spent time with a man who would demand anything more. It's been quite a while since she really cared for anyone, and I think she's afraid."

"I can't imagine your sister afraid of anything," Max said, even as his thoughts snagged on the memory of the conversation he and Vesper had had at Grenoble's, the forced lightness of her voice as she'd told him of the married man who had led her on, and the unmarried one who had fallen in love with someone else. He'd been able to tell, even then, that the memories still bothered her—but only now did he realize how much. She had a good mask—one of the best he'd ever seen. And he'd fallen for it.

"I don't think she knows what to do," Freddie said wisely, "now that she wants someone for . . ."

Forever, supplied Max's mind.

He didn't say it aloud—not to Freddie.

But it whispered to him for the rest of the afternoon, and for a night of fitful sleep.

In the morning, when the papers landed on his doorstep with the scoop of the decade, it was still whispering.

Chapter Twenty-Four

The buzzer to Max's flat sounded at seven Wednesday morning, and he was less surprised than he should have been to find Augustus Grimme-Nox waiting on his front steps.

"Oh," he said.

"Oh," his father agreed. "I won't take too much of your time—I expect a visit from Scotland Yard sometime this morning—but I wonder if I might bother you for a cup of tea."

Max could think of few things he'd like to do less than have a cup of tea with his father, but the longer he had this conversation on the front stoop, the more likely it was that one of his neighbors would take notice, so with a jerk of his head, he led Grimme-Nox upstairs.

"I expect you're feeling very pleased with yourself," Grimme-Nox said, the second the door had closed behind him.

Max turned to face him, crossing his arms over his chest. "I am, actually."

Grimme-Nox nodded. It was interesting, Max thought

dispassionately, how genetics worked. He and Grimme-Nox shared many of the same features—the broad shoulders, the dark hair—and yet he didn't think they looked the slightest bit alike; it was no wonder that no one had ever guessed at the link between them.

"You know, when I first heard you were working for the Fleas, I'll confess it . . . irked me." Grimme-Nox's voice was mild, almost disinterested, and he began a slow circuit of the room as he spoke, his keen eyes taking in every detail of the space. "You are my only son, much as you and I might both wish it otherwise. I find you a disappointment."

Once, this would have wounded Max. He would have denied it, but deep down, it would have cut. Now, he found himself peculiarly unbothered by it.

"The feeling is mutual," he said.

Grimme-Nox gave the ghost of a half smile. "Eventually, though, I realized this could be useful—to have a son whom I knew perfectly well to be unbribable, working for the Fleas . . . I told Raffles that you would be the perfect person to send in to take down the other clubs, particularly if you saw anything that seemed at all dangerous."

"Raffles knew I was your son?" Max asked, thinking back to his—apparently entirely misguided—conviction that any knowledge of the connection would ruin his career.

"Of course." A small, sour smile played at the corner of Grimme-Nox's mouth. "Once I recovered from my disappointment in your determination to turn your back on your heritage, I saw how useful you might be. The first incident at Plenus Venter was a test; I wanted to make sure my appearance-changing potion would last long enough, and that no one would take notice of me."

"As a handsome man with long eyelashes," Max said, and Grimme-Nox inclined his head.

"I see you did your work thoroughly. Please forgive me if I don't offer my congratulations, given the circumstances." He paused by the fireplace, resting his forearm on the mantel. "At Holloway's, you were meant to make a fuss—shut the club down. Word would spread. People would grow wary. And then we'd repeat the pattern at the next club—and the next one. Until only the Grimoire was left, our potions seen as the only safe way of procuring magic. However, when you failed to take action that first night, I convinced Raffles that this could be to our advantage—keep the Home Office and Scotland Yard out of matters for a while, just to be safe; allow rumors to spread through the magical community, then sweep in and shut down a whole load of the clubs in one fell swoop, once enough time had passed and you'd witnessed enough accidents. I thought it was useful, having you on the case—someone whom I knew would not be swayed by any of the magical temptations of the Marylebone clubs. However"—and here, his voice hardened—"I see I underestimated your weakness for pretty blondes who are free with their favors."

Max met his father's eyes. "I won't even bother telling you not to speak about Miss Holloway that way, because I've come to realize something recently."

"Oh?"

Max took two steps forward. "Nothing you say matters to me anymore. I took the job with the F.L.E.A.s to make you angry—to show you that I rejected you, and your world, and everything you stand for. But when I started working with Vesper, it had nothing to do with you; I wasn't thinking of destroying your business, or sending you to prison—knowing how well-connected you are, I doubt you'll end up there anyway. The longer we investigated, the more I cared about solving the case, about making sure no one got hurt—and the less I thought about you at all. You're . . ." He paused, searching for the correct word. The one that felt most true. "You're irrelevant to me."

That caused a spark of anger to appear in his father's eyes at last—the first time Max could ever remember seeing Augustus Grimme-Nox looking truly angry.

It should have been satisfying—but once again, Max found that he simply didn't care anymore. This realization *was* satisfying.

"I'm your father. Like it or not, I'll never be irrelevant."

Max looked at him for a moment, considering this man who believed his blood, and the magic that coursed within it, his family name, all of it, to be of such importance—and, for the first time in his life, he pitied him.

"I have a father already—a much better one than you'll ever be. And he's the only one I need. Enjoy your meeting with the police—I'm guessing they're *very* eager to speak to you."

He opened the door and stepped back. His father gazed at him for several seconds before slowly making his way toward the doorway.

"I know she's pretty, but she's still one of us—she's part of *my* world." A hint of a satisfied smile crept across Grimme-Nox's face as he paused a few inches from Max.

Max looked back at him steadily. "I know," he said simply. "But it's not your world anymore—not to me. It's *hers*."

And then, he took no small amount of satisfaction in shutting the door in Grimme-Nox's nonplussed face.

◆

Vesper awoke to the sound of a knock on her door.

She'd been at the club late the night before, yet when she'd arrived home, sleep had taken a while to find her. She kept replaying the words of her conversation with Ashbridge over in her mind, wondering what on earth had possessed her. The second he'd told her that he'd quit his job, it was as if a glass of cold water had been dumped over her; despite the fact that she'd known their professionally sanctioned excuse to spend time together was coming to an end, she still hadn't been prepared for the news.

So, she'd started speaking—and before she knew what had happened, she was mixing potions in the backdoor bar and trying to put the memory of Ashbridge's hurt, bewildered face from her mind.

It felt fitting, somehow, that after fuming about her family's lack of faith in her ability to manage the club, it should be her own personal life that she'd prove incapable of managing.

"*Meow*?" inquired Sheep sleepily from her spot tucked up near Vesper's feet, and Vesper dropped a kiss on her soft head as she pulled on a dressing gown and made her way to the front door, shivering in the morning chill. There was sun streaming in through the windows, and she could catch a glimpse of blue sky out the sitting room window, but the quality of the light indicated that it was still quite early.

She opened the door and found Ashbridge standing on her doorstep.

Vesper gaped at him; then, horrified, raised a hand to her hair, which was no doubt standing up in all directions. She was wearing an absolutely appalling pair of pajamas, one she had made a personal policy to never allow a member of the opposite sex to ever lay eyes on. She had not so much as glanced at herself in the mirror—there was no telling what she looked like. She undoubtedly appeared considerably less than a vision of seductive perfection.

Ashbridge—*Max*, she thought helplessly, remembering the intimate feeling of his name on her tongue—was looking at her as though she were the loveliest thing he'd ever seen.

"What are you doing here?" she asked. "What time is it, even?" She'd been so sleepy and confused upon awakening to his knock she'd not even glanced at a clock.

"Quarter to eight," he said, looking far too cheerful about this fact. His cheeks were rosy with cold. His hair was curling—that one stubborn lock was falling onto his forehead. He was wearing a cozy jumper. He looked absolutely delicious.

"Quarter to eight," she repeated faintly. "Do you realize that that is essentially the middle of the night to me? Why are you here?"

"Because I wanted to speak to you." He sounded quite sure about the matter. "I'd like to come in. I'll make you tea, since I suspect you'll need fortification for this conversation."

"How reassuring," she muttered, and yet somehow, instead of sending him on his way, she found herself stepping back and letting him walk through the door into the flat, his presence, as always, seeming to shrink its size.

She allowed him to lead her into the kitchen, where she staggered her way to the table and watched in mute astonishment as, without awaiting an invitation, he set about making tea. A kettle was filled and set to boil, tea leaves were spooned into a pot, milk was fetched from the icebox. He paused, glancing at a jar of spell powder labeled simply FOR A MORNING BOOST—another of Mackleworth's creations. He glanced over his shoulder at her, lifting the jar. "Would you like some?" he asked, and she gaped at him before nodding.

"Just half a teaspoon should be plenty."

He nodded and spooned it into the pot along with the tea leaves.

Vesper wondered if she was still asleep.

In no time at all, he'd placed a steaming cup of tea before her, then set the milk jug and sugar bowl alongside it.

"Am I drunk?" she wondered aloud, taking a sip of her tea. "Bespelled?"

"I suppose only you can answer that question," he said, taking a seat opposite her, "though I would expect that if you'd taken anything last night, it would have worn off by now."

"Max Ashbridge, please explain to me what you are doing in my kitchen."

He glanced up at her, a teacup looking delicate in his strong hands. He had a callus on his middle finger from years of holding a pen and pencil; she remembered the feel of it against her fingers.

"I'm here to show you that I'm not going anywhere." She frowned, and opened her mouth to reply, but he raised a hand to forestall her. "I'm not going to Paris. I'm not going to Rome. I don't want to work at an embassy. I don't know *what* I want to do next, but I can do it here in London, where my life is."

She found her voice. "I suppose you don't want to leave your family." She should have expected that, considering how his voice tended to warm every time he spoke of them.

"No," he agreed. "But also, I don't want to leave you."

The words felt loud in the quiet of the kitchen. Vesper felt her heart kicking up a perilously quick beat in her chest, and something rising in her throat. She feared that it was hope.

"Ashbridge—Max—I don't think—"

"No." He cut her off with a shake of his head. "I don't think you're *thinking* properly at all. You're just . . . reacting. You're used to enjoying a man for a night or two. You don't mind leaving them, because it ensures that you're never left." He leaned forward. "But I've no intention of leaving you. Not now, not—" He broke off, watching her warily. "Not until you ask me to. *If* you ask me to."

Vesper's throat felt tight as she watched him sitting there in her kitchen, drinking a cup of tea that contained a substance that he'd spent his life despising, saying the sorts of things she hadn't thought she cared if a man ever said to her, until now. She was frightened by the feeling of fierce joy that she could feel rising within her.

"Why?" she asked simply.

"Because I'm falling in love with you," he replied, equally simply, and she stared at him, lost for words. "I'm fairly certain you're doing the same with me, but you don't need to say it," he added, and she frowned at him.

"I can say whatever I want," she informed him, crossing her arms, and amusement flashed across his face. It felt like a privilege to see it there, with him making no effort to hide it from her. "And I don't know why you would assume *that* when I tried to send you to Geneva last night."

"Don't think I would enjoy Switzerland," he said thoughtfully. "Too cold."

"That's hardly the—"

"I know. Your brother was quite helpful in this regard, actually."

"My *brother*?" She could only imagine, with faint horror, what Freddie might have said to Max.

"He seemed to think that you were attempting to set me loose, before I could be the one to do the leaving. Intelligent man, Freddie."

"Last week he got caught shagging a producer behind a pile of kilts backstage," she informed him.

"In some ways," he amended, then paused. "Is his new show set in Scotland?" he hazarded, a bit uncertain.

"It is not," she said gloomily, and then he laughed.

It felt as though the sun had come out in the cozy confines of Vesper's kitchen with that laugh.

"My point is," he said, recovering, "if you . . . if you truly don't want me here, I'll leave, and you'll never hear from me again. But *I* don't want that. And I don't think you do either."

Vesper's hand, as if of its own volition, stole across the table, so that she could lace her fingers through his.

"I don't," she said, her voice quiet, too. "I just didn't want—I didn't want you to feel tied to me, just because we—"

"Shagged in a cupboard?" he suggested dryly.

"Well, yes. I didn't want you to think that I expected you to stick around."

His hand tightened on hers. "I *want* to stick around. And I want you to know that you deserve that."

Vesper felt a helpless smile creeping over her face. "I can't believe I'm falling in love with a civil servant with an enormous stick up his arse."

He smiled then—a true, proper smile. It lit up his face, making his gray eyes bright. He looked years younger. "Not a civil servant anymore." His smile turned a bit smug, which should have been annoying but only made him seem handsomer to her, in the moment. She needed professional help, clearly. "And I think you like that I am . . . er—" He broke off, clearly grasping for a more flattering way to phrase it.

"Constitutionally incapable of enjoying yourself?" she suggested, but she didn't mean it, and the way his eyes crinkled at her told her that he knew it, too.

"Take me to your bedroom, and we'll see how much I like to enjoy myself," he suggested, with a casual sip of tea, grinning at her when she gaped.

And then, of course, she took him up on the suggestion.

◆

That evening, the Holloways broke with tradition and had a family dinner on a *Wednesday*.

Vesper knew she was going to enjoy the evening the moment

she walked into the drawing room, her fingers laced with Max's, and watched her mother drop an entire bottle of champagne.

"Vesper, you might have warned us!" Amelia chided, though she looked exceedingly pleased as she said it.

"If I'd known you would treat champagne so cavalierly, I would have," Vesper said; the bottle had mercifully landed on a rug, which softened the blow, and so was unharmed.

"Hullo, Ashbridge," said her father, reaching out his hand, which Max shook. Vesper had briefed him thoroughly all afternoon—during the portions of the afternoon she'd been capable of intelligent speech, that is; they'd spent much of the day in bed—and had, in a bit of a panic at the last minute, tried to talk him out of joining her at all.

"It might be best for me to prepare them," she'd said, borderline hysterical, with one earring in.

"It'll be fine," he'd said, handing her the other earring. "They might as well get used to having a former Flea in their midst."

"F.L.E.A.," she corrected, and the grin that spread over his face was so distracting that it was some time before they finished getting ready, and many of their clothes needed setting to rights.

"I see you took my advice," Freddie said to Max, sounding maddeningly smug from his position at the piano, picking out a tune.

Vesper rolled her eyes. "You needn't sound so pleased with yourself."

"Simon's the one who ought to sound pleased at the moment," Cecily said. "After the meetings he had today he thinks he has enough votes for the bill to pass." She and Simon were on the sofa, George sprawled across both of their laps, fast asleep.

"Isn't it a bit early for bedtime?" Vesper asked, nodding at her nephew.

Cecily waved an unconcerned hand. "He got into some of my sleep potion from Mackleworth's. Took an adult-sized dose, but since he's still breathing normally, we've decided not to fret."

"How long has he been asleep?" Max asked, looking alarmed.

Cecily thought for a moment. "Nine hours." She shrugged. "If he's not awake by tomorrow morning, I suppose we ought to start worrying."

"*Start*—"

Before Max could work himself into a tizzy, he was interrupted by the cheerful *pop* of a champagne bottle being uncorked; in short order, glasses were passed around the room. Amelia tapped hers.

"I thought we might have a toast?" she suggested.

"Hmm," Freddie said, "whatever might we toast?" He smirked at his sisters in turn.

"Cecily's reporting?"

"Or . . . hmm. Perhaps Simon's hard work?" Cecily proposed, touching her chin thoughtfully.

"Very good points," Amelia agreed gravely. "Or perhaps—did you have another idea, my love?" She looked at Lucian inquiringly. But her husband wasn't looking at her—he was looking directly at Vesper.

And a moment later, Vesper realized the rest of the room was doing the same.

"I think," her father said, a bit more quietly, "that we might have underestimated you, Vesper."

"And Ashbridge," Amelia chimed in.

"And Ashbridge," Lucian agreed.

"Fortunately, the Fleas did, too," Freddie said, and his father quirked a half smile at him.

"Quite." He looked back at Vesper, who was standing next to Max, champagne glass in hand. "I'm proud of you, Vesper. Of the work you and Ashbridge have done, and of the work you've done running Holloway's the past few years. And I'm sorry if we made you feel that we didn't trust you."

Vesper felt a smile slowly spreading across her face, and slid a glance sideways to Max, who was smiling down into his own champagne.

She lifted her chin. "Thank you," she said, nodding. "And thank you, of course, to my capable government ally." She inclined her head courteously toward Max, who nodded somberly. "Now, does this mean that you'll call off the nannies?"

Next to Cecily, Simon snorted in a poor attempt to conceal a laugh; Vesper's mother, too, seemed to be suppressing a smile. Her father merely smiled at her, inclined his head, and said, "The club is yours to run as you see fit, without interference from the rest of the family—unless you ask for it. You're more than capable of managing things yourself—probably better than I could."

"Hear, hear," Max said firmly, and lifted his glass. "To Vesper."

"To Vesper," echoed the rest of the family—except for George, who uttered a particularly loud snore instead.

"We're proud of you, love," her mother said, a couple of minutes later, when the room had fallen back into conversation, and

Amelia had come to stand next to her daughter. She glanced slyly at Max, who was deep in conversation with Lucian and Simon. "Though I should think it's *obvious* we trust you, if we're happy to welcome a *Flea* into our drawing room."

"Former Flea," Vesper corrected. She looked up at her mother. "You don't mind?"

Her mother was silent for a long moment, her gaze thoughtful. "I don't mind," she said at last. "I've always liked Ashbridge—he was ever so polite when Freddie knew him, and I thought it a shame that politics got in the way of their friendship. I find him even lovelier now, seeing the way he looks at you. But"—and here, she hesitated again, as if searching for the right words—"the fact is, it doesn't matter if I mind. *You* like him, and I think it's about time the rest of us started trusting your judgment a bit more."

Vesper, for a moment, couldn't speak; her lower lip was suddenly not feeling at all sure of itself. However, she had never been one to allow an opportunity to pass her by, and so she said, quite cheerfully, "I'm glad to hear it. Because I've been thinking I'd like to paint the office at Holloway's bright pink."

Her father still had excellent hearing, it turned out; a pity, Vesper thought idly, as she listened to the eruption from that quarter. In the end, however, he was easy enough to soothe, once she agreed to settle for a pretty jewel-toned wallpaper instead.

It had, of course, been what she'd had in mind all along, but there was no need for him to know that. Men really were dreadfully easy to manipulate.

Max caught her eye, a look of suspicion on his face that only deepened when she smiled angelically at him.

Most men, she amended. Of course Max would be an exception, as he was to so many things.

It was, she feared, why she liked him so much.

◆

The next morning, the sun was high in the sky by the time either of them mustered the energy to leave the bed, and it was Vesper, not Max, who retrieved the morning newspapers from her front step. She brought them back to bed, crawling in beside Max, who had drifted off into a light doze in the wake of their recent exertions, stretched out on his stomach, the muscled expanse of his back on display. She paused to appreciate the sight, and the way his face looked younger in slumber. Then she dropped a copy of *The Spark* on his head.

"Mmph," he muttered, which Vesper found satisfying. She was used to being the one difficult to rouse, but she tended to find sex energizing, whereas Max, she was learning, lapsed into something approaching a coma afterward. She decided to take it as a compliment.

Today, the front page of *The Spark* read *RAFFLES RESIGNS FROM PARLIAMENT; GRIMME-NOX QUESTIONED BY METROPOLITAN POLICE.*

"I expect your father—Grimme-Nox, I mean—has had an absolutely *awful* twenty-four hours," she said happily, and then watched as a thoughtful expression crossed his face. "What is it?" she asked, curious, and he glanced at her.

"He came to see me yesterday morning," he said, his voice low and still rough from sleep. "Before I came to see you. I think he was trying to—I don't know. Unnerve me? Get the last word?"

"And did he?"

"No," he said, "because after a few minutes, I got tired of listening to him, and simply told him goodbye and shut the door in his face."

Vesper let out a hoot of delighted laughter. "I wish I could have seen that—he must be *furious.*"

"Probably," he agreed, but he didn't sound as though he cared much one way or the other. "It's just that I realized, as we were talking, that I don't care. After all this time, this ridiculous *fixation* on trying to best him—I simply don't care what he thinks about any of it."

"Good," she said softly, and leaned over to kiss him. It was meant to be a quick peck on the lips, but he dropped the paper and curved his hand around her neck, pulling her closer. She felt herself smiling against his mouth.

"If Simon's repeal bill passes, I expect things will change at Holloway's," she said, a while later once he'd released her and she'd caught her breath. She was leaning against him, her head on his shoulder. His arm was round her shoulders, his fingers tracing a pattern along the bare skin of her arm. "It will be nice to think about other ideas for running the club, rather than just focusing on how to work around Forbiddance. I was thinking . . ." She trailed off, wondering how he would react. She felt his head move as he glanced down at her.

"What?"

"I was wondering about speaking to my parents about expanding our membership—or having a certain number of memberships available at reduced cost." She chanced a glance up at him, and his gaze was warm. "I kept thinking about the things you've said, and the way you viewed magic as something for the privileged elite. I'd like . . . well, I'd like to change that. I love magic, and I want more people to experience it. I know there are some pubs for the working classes, but I'd like to make Holloway's a more welcoming place." She toyed with the bedspread. "I was hoping that you'd be willing to help me with that . . . if—"

"If?"

"If you wouldn't find it too much, to be involved at a magical club." She sat up, allowing his arm to slide from her shoulders. "I don't expect you to change your mind about magic overnight but, well, the club is a big part of my life. We can keep our work separate. But I was hoping, if you were willing . . . you might want to help me make it something better, instead."

He leaned down and kissed her. "There's still a lot about magic that I don't like," he said frankly, and he pressed a hand to her lips to still her when she opened her mouth to reply. "But I've come to realize that the magical world that my father and those tossers at the Duke and Earl represent—it's not all of it. *You've* shown me that." He paused, then added, "I'd like you to show me the rest of it, too. If you wanted."

"I do." She smiled at him, then, so wide that her cheeks ached. She wrapped her arms around his neck, and said, very solemnly as she pulled his face down to hers, "Of course, magic is still illegal, pending legislation in Parliament, so as a law-abiding citizen, I suppose I'll simply have to wait—"

He stopped her words with his mouth; she felt his smile against her own. And when he laughed as he kissed her, it felt like its own kind of magic.

Acknowledgments

Fantasy was my first love as a reader, and I've dreamed of writing my own novel full of magic for as long as I've dreamed of being a writer. My career has felt like a series of dreams coming true, but this one is extra-special to me. A million thanks to:

Kaitlin Olson and Taylor Haggerty, who continue to understand the sort of books I want to write, and who are so incredibly smart and hardworking as they help me make those books a reality.

Megan Rudloff, Zakiya Jamal, Ife Anyoku, Jasmine Brown, Gab Greenstein, Holly Root, and everyone else at both Atria Books and Root Literary who works so hard to bring my books into the world. It truly takes a village, and I feel fortunate beyond belief to get to share one with all of you.

My author friends, near and far. You know who you are. Sarah: I dedicated this book to you because it wouldn't exist without your friendship and your feedback.

And, as always, my family and friends, more than ever. The insane, frantic summer in which I finished writing this book was both wonderful and terrible, full of joy and grief all at once. Thank you for Maine bus station welcoming committees and Austrian train station pick-ups; for rib-cracking kid hugs and baby snuggles; for long walks and delicious meals; for road trips and hikes; most of all, perhaps, for sympathetic ears. I love you.

About the Author

Martha Waters is the author of *And Then There Was The One*, *Christmas Is All Around*, and the Regency Vows series, which includes *To Have and to Hoax*, *To Love and to Loathe*, *To Marry and to Meddle*, *To Swoon and to Spar*, and *To Woo and to Wed*. Originally from South Florida, she is a graduate of the University of North Carolina at Chapel Hill and currently lives in London.